Bridget van der Zijpp is the author of two previous novels: *Misconduct* and *In the Neighbourhood of Fame*. *Misconduct* was shortlisted for the 2009 Commonwealth Writers' Best First Book Prize, South East Asia and the Pacific region, and for the 2009 Montana New Zealand Book Awards Best First Book of Fiction.

I laugh me broken

Bridget van der Zijp

I
laugh
me
broken

Bridget van der Zijpp

Gallic Books

London

A Gallic Book
First published by Te Herenga Waka University Press
New Zealand in 2021
vup.wgtn.ac.nz

First published in Great Britain in 2023 by
Gallic Books, 12 Eccleston Street, London, SW1W 9LT

A CIP record for this book is available from the British Library

ISBN 978-1-913547-50-9

Typeset in Adobe Garamond Pro by Gallic Books
Printed in the UK by CPI (CR0 4YY)

2 4 6 8 10 9 7 5 3 1

MIX
Paper | Supporting
responsible forestry
FSC® C171272

… A gigantic, violent hand seemed to grasp the ship. The wave swung her on high and threw her forward. It flung us crashing on the coral reef. Our masts and rigging went over, broken like matchsticks. The shattering impact of the ship smashed the coral, and pieces flew in all directions like shrapnel from an exploding shell… The *Seeadler* had heeled over until her deck was almost perpendicular. The water swept over the deck, and the swirling eddies bombarded us with chunks of coral. I clung to an iron post near the lower rail… In a moment, the wave had ebbed away, leaving us high and dry. It had passed over the circling reef and the lagoon, though not over the main part of the island. And on its way it had swept hundreds of thousands of birds' nests into the lagoon.

I arose, scarcely knowing whether I was alive or dead, and stood alone with one foot on my slanting deck and the other on the rail. For a moment, I thought I was the only one saved.

'Boys, where are you?' I shouted weakly.

'Here,' came the reply, 'still standing like an oak.'

—*Count Luckner, The Sea Devil*, Lowell Thomas, 1927

1.

When I first saw the small balcony overlooking an urban park, it perfectly matched my ideas about living in this city, spending time out there, writing. Having arrived in autumn, though, this was probably more romantic than practical.

My new housemate, Frankie, had left coffee and bread on the bench in the kitchen. Last night she'd shown me to my room, mentioning something about her job at a co-working studio where she wrote content for start-ups including one, she'd said, rolling her eyes, that made luggage suitable for taking into space.

It was already past noon, and my ears were still ringing from the plane. I took a kitchen chair out through the double doors and sat inhaling deeply, replacing the stagnancy of twenty-four hours of filtered cabin air. The trees were only just beginning their seasonal turn, and from the playground nearby I could hear the screeches of kids having fun. Also the odd phrase: 'Spinnst du?' Down below was a sheltered courtyard, its surrounding walls covered in tags and graffiti. Somebody had taken the time to spray the word *Hundstage* in large letters. Dog days. A band? A movement?

Soon a group of young teenage boys assembled there, as if it was a regular thing, to play hardcore rap and shit-talk, and the paving created an amphitheatre effect that threw their voices right up to the second storey. My school-level German was not enough to understand what they were saying, but the tone of it was posturing and raucous. They sniffed something off the blade of one boy's knife and then took off their jackets and started wrestling with each other, jumping off low walls, practising something that looked like a mix of capoeira and parkour.

I retreated back inside, but while a person can sit at the table in their new apartment, in a city that's unknown to them, telling themselves they are well, that doesn't mean they are. I let uncomfortable thoughts seep in like a pernicious gas. Ordinary tiredness? My fingers tingling? Overthinking? I had actually done something on the plane that I was having trouble explaining to myself. I'd stolen an expensive pen from the man with a gurgling stomach who had sat next to me on the last leg. He'd been marking some business papers with it and I'd caught occasional glimpses of flow charts, lists of names and numbered paragraphs. Without really knowing anything, I decided his work was sinister, so when he eased out of his seat to go to the toilet I slipped his fat silver pen into my bag, quickly and stealthily, like an operative whose job it is to unsettle. When he came back he looked around, and under his seat, and asked in a starkly confronting manner if I'd seen it. I shrugged and he didn't press further, but for the rest of the journey I was made so uncomfortable by his heavy aura of suspicion that I half wanted him to go to the toilet again so I could put the pen back. So, is this how it starts? Minor oddness. If a person dares to search symptoms, their eyes will swim in and out of focus, and something awful will prickle at the back of their neck... *usually begins in the extremities of the body... involuntary twitches in fingers, toes, and face... in the early years a subtle loss of coordination... cognitive problems become noticeable... difficulty thinking through complicated tasks...*

Oh God. Quickly, quickly I deleted the search off my phone, not yet ready to line up any hard facts. Yes, of course I was tired. Just ordinary tiredness. Who wouldn't be after a flight all the way from New Zealand to Berlin? And that man, well…

There wasn't anything that resembled butter in the fridge, and not a single piece of matching crockery in the cupboard. Such relaxed disorder made me think of its exact opposite, when Jay had first moved into my place, bringing with him a whole line-up of identical jars neatly labelled with the names of spices and dried pulses.

I happened to glance out through the window above the sink as an older, tougher-looking group arrived down below, more fully formed, genuinely gangster. The loud talking stopped and all the boys jumped to their feet. The two groups scuffled with each other for a while. There was some violent shoving – one boy was knocked to the ground and bounced up again. There seemed to be dangerous insults being muttered into faces. Would it escalate to the point I needed to ring the police? What even was the number to ring? Eventually the leader of the invaders snatched up the rucksack of one of the others, took something out of it, nodded to his mates, and they all turned around as one and sloped off. The remaining boys suddenly didn't have much to say to each other. They just sat back down on their bench seats, hunched and humiliated, and turned their speaker up extra-loud.

Too loud. Peak intrusiveness. I wanted them to go away now, and I moved back out to the balcony to observe them more conspicuously from two storeys up, hoping my inconvenient presence would be enough to move them on, but it wasn't.

So, we all sat there, me and some local boys, listening to

their rap, right in the heart of Mitte, in the former East, in an area once on the confined side of the wall – I knew that much at least. 'Is any of that wall still up?' my stepmother had asked before I left. I hadn't known for sure, but had looked it up and found the dotted line on a map that denoted where it had once been.

These boys were too young to have lived with the divided city, but I guessed some of their parents might have. Did they ever sit down with their fathers and mothers, I wondered, and try to find out what it had been like for them? Or were they just too busy skanking their way towards their own history?

Some sparrows – were they called that here? – were pecking away at croissant crumbs on the outside tables at the café across the road. The birds scattered when I sat down with my Americano but only a few seconds later they brazenly hopped back. Vital work: the coldest season would soon be on its way. I shooed them away with my hand, brushing the crumbs to the ground, and the man seated at the next table, rolling a cigarette, looked up. He leaned over and asked in heavily accented English if I had a light. I shook my head but asked in return if he minded if I bludged a cigarette off him. Only an occasional smoker, something about watching those boys scuffle made me want to access the dissolute side of myself.

'Bludge?' he said. 'Where are you from?'

'New Zealand,' I told him.

'Ahh, far.' He pointed to himself and said, 'Bozorgmehr. But people call me Boz mostly.'

'Ginny,' I responded.

After he had finished rolling the second cigarette he

pulled a lighter out of his pocket and lit up for both of us.

'You have a lighter,' I commented.

He exhaled, and said, 'Yes.' He took two more long, slow drags on his cigarette, then added, 'Did you know there is a linguist called Roman Jakobson who outlined six reasons for conversation. Imparting information and so forth, and the fifth is something called *phatic*, and that's when you start a conversation for reason of human interaction. Like when you have a watch but at the bus stop you ask somebody the time just to open the dialogue. Or when you say it's a lovely day. Everybody knows it's a lovely day, but you do it to begin something perhaps.' With the hand that wasn't holding his cigarette he lifted a small espresso cup to his lips and took a refined sip. He seemed very aware of the kind of impression he wanted to make. 'So yes, I have a lighter.' He smiled with what was the opposite of diffidence. 'My small fraud has been exposed.'

He had succeeded, if his intention was to charm me a little.

'So that's your thing? Linguistics?' He was wearing the kind of clothes that might be described as professorial – a brown suede jacket over a black shirt, academic-style round glasses.

'And philosophy. I've been living for a while in London completing my PhD but recently I decided I want to write a book, so I came here. It's more affordable.' As he brought the cigarette to his lips for a last draw, I noticed his immaculate fingernails. One eye was half shut in a squint against the smoke from the shortened stub, and he added, 'Also there is another reason.'

He extinguished the cigarette, took out his wallet and handed over a photo of an angelic-looking girl. 'Seven,' he said. 'Light of my life. Do you think she looks like me?'

I studied the photo closely. There was no absolute resemblance that I could see. Perhaps the girl had his olive skin, his dark eyes, but while hers were round receptacles of innocence, his had an amused, calculating quality that also seemed mixed with a little world-weariness.

'Yes, a bit,' I said, but only to be polite.

As he slid the photo back into his wallet, he said, 'Her mother got posted on a job here, so I decided to follow.'

'You're not together?'

He shook his head and, gazing in the direction of the designer-chair shop across the road, said wistfully, 'Just a brief glamorous affair while I was on a research trip in France.' Turning back, he added, 'I only found out about my daughter a few months ago. But she's very special, so I'd like to get to know her a bit. And I needed some fresher fields. Gives me a chance to research some new ideas.'

Afterwards I'd think a lot about his use of the word glamorous. Did he mean his lover was glamorous, or was he, or were they glamorous together? Did they do glamorous things, or was the affair in a glamorous place? He was obviously the kind of man who was practised in the art of creating immediate intimacy with strangers, but I detected an odour of untruth in his words, so I also spent quite a lot of time thinking about how it comes to be that a woman doesn't tell a man that she's had his child.

'What do you think makes her so special?' I asked.

'Who? My daughter?'

'Yes. Just now you said she's very special.'

'Good genes.' He smiled, and then added with too-late modesty, 'Mostly from her mother, obviously.'

He had no reason to know that I was a person with fresh and uncomfortable thoughts about genes sitting just below the surface. 'And the ideas?' I asked.

'They are coming, I think, on their way in, but they haven't exactly arrived in my head.' He grinned. 'So why are you here?'

'On a kind of research project,' I told him.

'Who with?'

'I'm a writer,' I said, with the same sense of fraudulence that always arose when I dared to define myself like that on such a thin record of achievement.

'Ahh. How great. We two writers meet by chance. If we are to be friends, then we will have to negotiate our separate territories. And so…?' he asked. 'Your project?'

'Well, it's complicated, but essentially it's about a German Count. A real Count, a sort of buccaneer from the First World War.'

'Aha. There should be no overlap there then. And? Why that?' He glanced at his watch and said, 'Actually, no, hold it. I have to rush. You nearly made me forget I have an important appointment I need to get to.' As he gathered up his things he said, 'See you again? I'm here most days around this time.'

I finished my coffee and cigarette, thinking this felt like a small accomplishment, to have already met another writer on my first day here.

When I returned to the apartment, Frankie was waiting for me in the kitchen with a pot of jasmine tea, a lit joint and a mood to chat. She was from Australia, had a nice open face and spoke with a sly loquaciousness that bordered on manic. She instructed me not to answer the bell unless I knew who was coming, and to be on the lookout for a certain person. She picked up her phone and showed me the picture of his face. Interesting sharp features. High cheekbones, wide eyes. I wasn't sure if I was meant to say he was handsome or frightening. 'I met him at Mauerpark a few years ago,' Frankie said. 'I was having one of those days when things were just all a bit too foreign and a bit too much, so I just wanted somebody to hold me very close for a while, if you get what I mean. I was sitting there in front of a busker feeling a bit tearful when he and his friend came along on bikes. I did that thing, you know, when you just stare a bit too long into somebody's face and then look away again, then look back.'

'Is that a thing?'

She occupied herself pouring us each some tea from a pot in the shape of a money cat, a large chip on the end of the spout making the flow haphazard. The kitchen smelled faintly of burnt dust and stored potatoes and a general lack of attention to detail. 'I was doing it to a lot of men that day, actually, but he was the one who couldn't take his eyes away from me. He was shy though. He biked off into the park, but I saw him stop and look back at me. Then about twenty minutes later he came back, I knew he would, and was standing by a tree, alone, near me. I indicated the seat next to me, and he came and sat down. He had hardly any English, and back then my Deutsch was pretty shit and so was his. At first we could only communicate by gestures and the little common words we both had. We walked together in the park and within minutes we were kissing.'

'Really? That was quick.'

Frankie's laugh was careless enough to indicate that she was aware of how she might be coming across and that she was unbothered. 'Anyway, we did a bit of rolling around in the grass for a while and then I invited him back to my bed. It was good. He was very tender. And I liked the lack of communication between us. All gestures. No words.'

'Oh. Um… so it went sour?'

'Okay. We got together a few more times and then we started using Translator to communicate when we were lying in bed. It turned out he was living in a refugee compound with his wife and two children, one was a new baby. He started saying, Ich liebe dich, and that he wanted to come back to Australia with me. But you hardly know me, I'd type. I was so lonely, he wrote, and then you looked into my eyes and I fell in love. And what about your wife and kids, I'd ask. They will be all right, he'd reply. They can go back to Kosovo. I'm better off with you. I can send them money. But I don't love you, I'd say, and he would shrug and say it doesn't matter because he loves me. He wouldn't be deterred. So, I told him I was too old for him. Didn't even blink.'

'How old was he?'

'Hard to tell, but probably somewhere in his twenties maybe,' Frankie said, passing over the joint.

I had been trying to measure Frankie's age against my own thirty-six years, but it was difficult to guess, partly because I was finding her confidence intimidating. She was wearing a faded green sweatshirt with an image of Joni Mitchell on it that had been washed so many times it was raggy with a lot of little holes that only served its aesthetic. Her black hair was tied up into a high animated ponytail that also contained some flecks of grey, and this made her style seem not so much about seeking to camouflage anything but more to draw attention to her vitality. On each eyelid she had a perfect trail of eyeliner that ended in an upward flick, and I didn't know it yet but I would begin to think of it as being placed there with indelible ink because I never once saw her without it for as long as I knew her. When Frankie told me that she had flashed all of her fingers twice to emphasise the age difference between them, I said, 'Twenty years older than him? Surely not.'

'Let's just say I may have passed my fortieth birthday and never speak of it again,' Frankie said, laughing, and I was surprised, had thought she was younger. 'Anyway, after that he sent me a barrage of messages. Help, the authorities are coming to the compound! They are kicking us out! I need to come and live with you! It's my last chance! I looked it up and that was actually happening. They'd declared there was no further chance of asylum for the Kosovans and were sending them home. They'd sometimes only give them twenty-four hours to pack their things. He started sending me texts that his friend had taken him in, his wife and kids had gone back, he had a job on a painting gang, and he needed me. We can live together now, he wrote. He sent me millions of messages. He sent me music clips with lyrics I couldn't understand, but you could tell by the images that they were cheesily romantic. He sent me friend requests. He had sixteen friends. They were all women. Some of them looked like sex workers but maybe they were just girls that liked that kind of look. The others were either social workers or had occupations like yoga teacher. In the end I told him that I'd gone to live in Amsterdam, and I shifted flats. I felt really bad, though. It was all so desperate. And it taught me a lesson.'

'And that was a few years ago? He's still around?' I glanced towards the balcony as if I now had to be alert to him scrambling up over the rail.

'It's been a while. But I learned he's not the kind of guy who gives anything up.'

'Not dangerous though?'

'I hope not.'

The joint had gone out in my fingers. Frankie took it back, and in quick competent movements she re-lit, took a fresh drag.

'What lesson?' I asked. 'Exactly?'

'Well, you know. He was in a bad situation. He would've done anything, and all I wanted…' Frankie exhaled and waved a hand in front of her face to dissolve the smoke. 'Shit, I'd almost forgotten what a complete fuck-up I am. At least on the apps it's a simpler transaction. Everybody knows what to expect, more or less.'

I nodded, as if I'd had experience of such things myself. It was good to know that while I was a churning mess inside, I had at least landed in the company of someone who had a natural draw towards mess.

Frankie stood up and started rummaging in a cupboard. She came back to the table with a half-eaten packet of biscuits. 'So, you have a sister living here?' she asked.

'Stepsister,' I clarified, taking a biscuit and biting down. It wasn't fresh but I didn't care. 'Mel. But she's down in Spain at the moment.'

'I heard,' Frankie said. 'She's a complicated one, I guess.'

I just shrugged, not too clear on how well Frankie actually knew my stepsister.

I've found you a place in a WG, Mel had written on Messenger just a few days ago, taking me by surprise. I'd thought I would be staying in her apartment while she was away. Several months ago she'd said it would be empty and had offered it up, not just for me. For both of us, me and Jay. Fresh horizons, she'd suggested, before mentioning she had a costume job coming up in Seville that meant she was going to be away for quite a while. If we could pay a bit we'd be doing her a favour, she added. But then I decided to come earlier, and without Jay, and for some reason Mel's contract wasn't going to last as long as she thought, so she'd be back in Berlin soon.

A WG? I wrote back.

A shared apartment, Mel replied, adding: *The room that belongs to my friend Elle. She's got some seasonal job on a bike-touring company in the Dolomites and is hoping to go on to do the Iceland season when the winter's over but wants to hang on to her place for a while just in case it falls through. So, kind of an indefinite sub-let situation.*

OK, cool, I responded.

Mel could probably sense my hesitation, a boring sort of self-protection formed after years of being let down.

It's all furnished, Mel wrote. *You don't know how lucky you are. The apartment situation is dire in Berlin. And her housemates are really nice. Or one of them at least.*

There was a tacit agreement between the two of us that we'd always get along better if we weren't living in the same space. It's not that we don't like each other, but when our parents got together Mel was eight and I was seven, and we'd been forced to share a bedroom. It brought us face to face, earlier than most, with the testing reality that people can exasperate each other with their different styles of living. I knew that I was the one who came out ploddy and regular, compared to Mel.

'Who else lives here?' I asked Frankie, looking around the kitchen. It was the only common space in the apartment, and was fitted out with the kind of junky furniture that looked like it'd been picked up off the street – the pockmarked table, the mismatched chairs, the sunken old sofa with a blanket thrown over it to cover its worst flaws. It signalled a kind of scruffy coolness, a blithe lack of attachment, even after some years of being here.

'Just Florian,' Frankie said. 'I call him Junior Bear. You won't see him much.'

2.

'Going on your own? But why would you suddenly decide a thing like that?' Jay had said.

'But I'm ready to go, I've cleared out my building contracts,' Jay had said.

'And the wedding?' Jay had said. 'You can't just pull it all out from underneath us like that.'

'Is it… are you unhappy? I thought we were good,' Jay had said.

Later when he started to get petulant, he protested that writing about the Count was his idea.

And my reply, so thin: 'But darling, you're not the one actually doing it, are you? And it's because I care so much about you it would be a distraction. I just think I might get more done on my own. I feel a kind of urgency over it. Let me go first and maybe you can join me later?' And then I'd tried to reason: 'And at least this way we won't have to give away the cat.'

When Mel had offered up her apartment, I'd said to Jay one evening, 'If we're going to base ourselves in Berlin for a while, it would be good to find something I could work on that connected the two countries.'

Jay told me that when he was a kid his dad used to love telling him stories about this audacious German folk hero who came down to the Pacific during the First World War. There was an immediate spark: it had daring, it had adventure, it had a messy historical back-view.

'I have a particular fascination,' I wrote speculatively

to a publisher, 'with the incident in December 1917, when Count von Luckner was a prisoner of war on Motuihe Island after his cruiser, the *Seeadler*, was shipwrecked. Whilst at the camp, he faked setting up a play for Christmas and requested props which were later used in his escape attempt. Stealing first a fast motorboat, and then a scow, he took off for the Kermadec Islands with a sextant made from things found in a barn, a sail sewn from a stage curtain, and a map he copied from a school atlas.'

Daredevil seemed good enough for a working title. 'I hope, while in Germany, to visit the city of Halle where he lived.'

I'd done scant research before I sent off the proposal, having quickly read the 1927 biography that once belonged to Jay's Kiwi dad. That book had such a tally-ho tone – *Take a windjammer out as a cruiser? Sneak through the blockade and go buccaneering on the high seas? 'By Joe!' I thought, 'that's something'* – I could see why young boys of a certain era might've loved it. The publisher wrote back cautiously that it was an interesting idea but perhaps I would need to include some material about the Count's controversial return to New Zealand in 1938 on a speaking tour that was funded by the Nazi Party. 'Of course he attempted to disavow it but I've always thought the murkiness of this added a further layer of fascination to the tale,' he wrote, nicely avoiding judging too harshly my terrible ignorance of the available history. But by that time the subject matter had me in its grip, and I couldn't say exactly why. There was the obvious and immediate appeal – the bragging raconteur with a love of the sea and all the irresistibility of a fun uncle. And I was somehow charmed by the idea that chasing down the escaped Count had once been an amusing cause célèbre for a whole generation – keeping people glued to their daily papers and inciting small-boat owners to set sail in random pursuits – but was now simply forgotten history. And it was also that the suggestion had come from Jay, whose close family on his mother's side had lived through some of her home country's terrors and disappearances, and the layers of breached trust and counter-breaches, and institutionalised racial insults, historical resentments, complex religious reformations and calls for separatism. Sri Lanka's political history was so dense and overheated and opaque that Jay had never tried to explain it to me with any expectation that I would fully understand. And yet he had wanted bedtime stories of mad imperialist ambition on the South Seas, warning shots across the bow, and gentlemanly rules of engagement.

The publisher had supplied the letter that supported my grant proposal, and I'd successfully received the money which was both an endorsement of the idea and the motivation to go ahead and write.

When I broke the news that I wanted to go on my own, using the need to really establish myself by writing a second book as an excuse to postpone the wedding, Jay's immediate response was to feel robbed of an adventure. But then everything was quickly subsumed by his rising feelings of betrayal and desertion. I was always on the dark side of the argument, the hidden side, and it was hard for me to maintain my secret as he railed against me and suggested that if I left without him, if I postponed the wedding, he might not want to be the fool who waited around.

'Just give me some time to get my head around it,' I pleaded, not really believing his words even though his expression had turned sour. And not really meaning the count's story either.

*

'Maybe now would be a good time to connect with your mother's family?' Jay had suggested when we'd begun to plan our wedding. We'd decided to get married mostly as a matter of gentle convenience, or so I thought, liking the idea of travelling to Berlin together within the superstructure of a legal union. But Jay, more than me, got caught up in it all and before I knew it we were booking venues and discussing invitations. His mother was planning to fly in some of her relatives from Sri Lanka, and he didn't say it but there was an implication that it might shame him if I didn't somehow try to equal the effort.

I'd never had any contact with my maternal side before. The only thing I'd ever known about my mother was that she was so overcome with melancholy she ended her own life. I had no memory of her, had been only a toddler, and immediately afterwards my father took me from Canada to New Zealand, where some years later he married Lorelei, who had an almost pathologically sunny disposition and a daughter, Mel.

Jay had occasionally tried to probe about my mother's suicide. 'Does anyone know why she did it?' he asked once. 'Was she unwell?'

'When you're little,' I'd told him, 'it's hard not to think it had something to do with her not wanting to love you, and as you grow up you begin to wonder how she could've been so selfish.'

Jay's eyes that usually gleamed with a lovable brand of positivity became saddened, and he said, 'People who are thinking straight don't do what she did. If you knew more, you might be able to find a way to forgive her.'

It wasn't that I had never tried to ask my father, but

every time I brought it up his face closed over and an evasive curtain of misery came down. He seemed to regard his grief as a private, personal thing, but as he continued to turn away I began to resent it as a profoundly self-absorbed thing. He was in the last-chance saloon, dying of liver cancer and doped to the eyeballs on morphine, when I tried to press him one last time. I had been processing everything with a hysterical optimism, refusing to accept that, imperfect as he was, he too could be taken from me. He wasn't uttering much that made any sense by then, and only said, 'Her whole family was tormented,' before turning his head away, once again, from the effort of remembering.

I didn't know if there was any truth to this when, prompted by Jay, I began the search. It turned out it wasn't all that hard to find my relatives. I located the death notice for my mother, wondering why I'd never thought to do that before. *Died suddenly*, no mention of how, but it did provide a glint of information about siblings. From there I followed leads until I found a cousin, Zelda, on Facebook and sent a private message.

Zelda wrote back almost immediately:

Gosh Ginny (of course we've been thinking of you as Virginia all these years!) How amazing to hear from you. I'm very sorry to hear that your father died. We didn't know. Are you well? It sounds like you are thriving now. Getting married! Congratulations. I wish we could be there but unfortunately it's quite short notice and commitments mean we are unable to make it. We wish you all the best and send our love, and hope you will stay in touch.
Love, Zelda
PS Are you planning to have a family together?

Perhaps we were, I replied, if it happened, but we were also planning some adventures and had been given an opportunity to base ourselves in Berlin for a while.

Zelda wrote again a couple of weeks later, saying she was coming to New Zealand and hoped we could catch up.

The Auckland hotel that Zelda had booked herself into had uniformed staff greeting visitors at the front entrance and a small round water feature between the door and the check-in. My cousin was immediately noticeable as the bundle of nerves waiting on a wide sofa in the foyer. I already knew from her Facebook photos that she looked quite a lot like me. The same lightly curly hair, the same dark down-sloping eyes, and I guessed we both must look like our mothers. Zelda stood as I neared, we hugged, and I could feel her heart thumping strongly against mine. The weirdly familiar smell of her made me feel like a lost and disoriented stray that had finally located its herd.

'Gosh, I would've known you anywhere,' she said.

We moved down to one of the groupings of chairs in the sunken hotel bar. 'A brochure in my room said they do a sort of high tea here, shall we order that?' she asked with a lopsided smile that felt recognisable.

After I had heard what Zelda had to say, I would cling to the notion that I was much more like my father, that his genes had been the more dominant, that internally he had passed everything he had on to me. Even though as a teenager I had staunchly rejected any commonality in his taciturn nature, in his greater interest in the daily paper than the activities of his daughter, in his belief that attending long hours at his workplace to earn the household income meant that he was acquitting his duties as a father and husband, and in his determined and uncelebrated consumption of whisky in the evenings. Before I would start to grasp so desperately at all the qualities I might not have appreciated in him, I took a small pleasure in looking for obvious similarities in this woman I had just met. The nerviness of her actions as she motioned the waiter over. The air of repressed impulsiveness. The timidity and apologetic shine in her eyes. And the physical – her long-fingered hands, her foot twisted around the other ankle, just like my own. There was also Zelda's general tone, a sort of warm, maternally available quality that I knew was absent in me.

After the waiter had accepted our order and gone off again, I said, 'So what brings you down here?'

'Well, you, of course.'

Zelda had made it sound so incidental in her email that I had let myself think, even though it made no sense, that she must have been coming for business or a holiday. Not entirely for me. But this aroused a surge of wariness. The absence of my mother's family in my life had been too profound and too lengthy for me now to embrace them with any instant turnabout affection. While I had never felt wholly related to my stepmother Lorelei, she had always been present in my life in every way my own mother had not been. Now here was this stranger with whom I had a link so strong it was throbbing between us, I couldn't fully deny it, and I was thrown into a wash of interest and reluctance as Zelda was saying, 'I have something I need to talk about with you and it can really only be done face to face, otherwise…'

'Otherwise?'

'I don't know. It's just quite big.'

My heart seemed to stop beating normally. 'About my mother?'

'Yes, in a way.'

'Why she did it?' For some reason my father's face flashed before me. Was this the moment I would find out about his terrible culpability? Had I always suspected it?

'In a way.'

Zelda opened her handbag and looked inside, and then shut it again without taking anything out. She looked back up at me with eyes that were burning with a temporary lack of resolve.

'I'm not quite sure how to begin,' Zelda said, and looked around uncertainly as if somebody might be available to step on in. 'How annoying. I've been on that plane for what seems like a lifetime thinking about nothing else but what I would say, and now when I'm here in front of you I feel like I've forgotten everything.'

There was a long, thoughtful pause and then she sighed and made her start. 'See, your mother might have been upset because her mother, our grandmother, had become very unwell. It's this thing... how can I describe it? It starts out as an unsteadiness which over the years grows into a full-on twitchy sort of body tremor and progresses to eventually... well... a pretty terrible cognitive decline. And it was in the family before that – our great-grandfather died quite young, but his two brothers and some of their children... and our grandmother had one sister but she died in a car accident. And then Caspar, that's our mothers' older brother, our uncle, well, he started to get it. In the early generations the family didn't really know what it was. They used to refer to it as a kind of curse, and it is, but now we know it has a name.'

The blood in my veins really didn't seem to be moving anymore. 'A name?'

'Huntington's disease.' She looked searchingly into my face. 'Have you heard of it?'

'Not really,' I managed.

'Gosh, I've made a mess of this,' Zelda said. 'I could've explained it better. I'm so sorry to drop it on you like that. It's just... so hard to put it in words.'

'Is that why she did it? Did she have it?'

'We don't know. But probably not at that time. See, it is usually fairly late onset. Mostly in our family people were in their forties when they developed symptoms. So, we don't know if she had the gene.'

'The gene?'

The waiter brought over a three-tiered cake stand loaded with many over-iced tiny cakes, chocolates and evenly cut sandwiches, announcing cheerfully and slightly flirtily, 'Here we are, ladies.' An assistant followed him with silverware and crockery. We both stared palely at what seemed, at that precise moment, the very symbol of redundancy. The waiter, mistaking our expressions for sheer astonishment, said, 'Yes, it's a bit on the too-fabulous side isn't it!'

Once they had moved out of earshot, Zelda said, 'I'm so sorry. This must all be a terrible shock.'

'There's a gene?'

'Yes, they can test for it now.'

'So?'

'So, if a parent has it there's a fifty–fifty chance of inheriting it. But if your mother didn't have the gene mutation there is nil chance.'

'But we don't know if she had it?'

'That's true.'

'And your mother?'

'Doesn't have it.'

'How many in their family?'

'Three. My mother, your mother and Uncle Caspar.'

'So, if your mother doesn't have it, does that increase the chances that mine did?'

'No, I don't think it works like that.'

We sat there for a while, not speaking, just looking at the cakes, the sandwiches, the chocolates, all sitting like obstacles before us.

'And the other. Our uncle? He has it?'

'Caspar? Yes. He was much older than his two sisters. He started to show obvious signs when he was in his early forties.'

There were simple sums to do. Only four years left until I was also in my forties. 'Why are you telling me this now? I'm planning to get married soon. I don't hear anything at all from the family all these years... you knew all this... why now?'

She grimaced a little. 'I know, it must seem odd. I talked to my mother a lot about it. I think when your father took you away there was a feeling in the family that it might be better for you to grow up away from the... difficulty of it all. If it happened, it happened, but you didn't have to live with the fear written so evocatively in your future. See, with our uncle Caspar, it's been truly hard watching him. He became very... aggressive. And our mother had already been through the whole progression with our grandmother too. And it affected us all. And even though my mother doesn't have it, and I don't have it, there's that sense that we are lucky and our uncle isn't, and so we try to do what we can for him, and he had children of course and, well, that's not a good story either... and I think we all thought, and it's inaccurate, I know, maybe even irresponsible, but we let ourselves think that once you were out of the family then that somehow meant you had a chance to escape it, or something.'

The look on her face was apologetic.

'But you've decided to bring all this to me now, just before I get married?' I was feeling a rising tide of rage. Who were these people?

Zelda looked down at her hands before saying, 'Do you remember that I asked if you were planning to have a family?'

Something within me contracted.

'That's what my mother and I have been debating all these days, since we heard from you. We've gone over and over it. See, if there was nothing that could be done, we might've been more likely to just let you live your life without this black cloud over your whole future... does that make sense? But if you're going to have children – well, there is something that can be done now. You can be tested, and if you have the gene mutation there is pre-implantation testing these days. So that even if it turned out you had it, your children could be spared.'

'And you and your mother decided all this? Decided at first that I didn't need to know. And then decided that I did.'

'Flick,' Zelda said. 'I need a drink.'

It didn't matter that the wine list in the hotel bar was ridiculously overpriced. Nothing mattered. We ordered an expensive bottle of Otago pinot noir, and Zelda chatted about her fairly godly life back home, her three sons and their sporting achievements. I found myself barely able to listen. The wider family pitched in, she told me, to pay for her fare because they decided it was important that somebody come over and tell me face to face. When she began saying something about the bureaucracy of trying to get our uncle's family into a new trial, something about new gene silencing therapies, I tried to concentrate. I could acknowledge that taking a short-run trip to New Zealand to tell me this was a stretch for someone who'd barely left her home province before, but I was starting to think I hated her.

'How did she do it?' I asked.

'You never knew?'

'For some reason I always imagined she'd walked into the sea and drowned.' Oh. Only with a retrospective glance could I see now that my debut novel – about a deep-sea diver who restlessly travelled through oceans of the world, taking on lovers, and dying heroically in the cause of saving the migratory path of the blue whale – might have been about the imaginary mother I didn't have. In my mind she must always have been in the sea, somewhere.

'Do you want to keep on thinking that?' Zelda's eyes urged me to say yes.

I had always believed I never thought about my mother. 'No. I'm ready to know now.'

'Okay. I'll tell you the facts.' Zelda's features went blank and unreadable. 'Just before your father got home, she locked you in the bedroom and shot herself in the head. With a hunting rifle. At the kitchen table. She sat in a chair and used her toe on the trigger. It was messy.'

'Oh. She didn't spare anybody.'

A very direct look into my face. 'No,' Zelda said. 'It was very upsetting.'

3.

I had few possessions in Berlin. My clothing, some research books, my laptop. A fat silver pen that I couldn't bring myself to use. The new sheets on my borrowed bed. Elle had left some things. On one wall was a faded Miró poster from Galerie Maeght, 13 rue de Téhéran Paris 8, and my eyes were often drawn towards it. I made it into a kind of subjective Rorschach test. Could I still see playfulness in its forms?

Some men with cherry pickers, chainsaws and high-vis vests had been noisily working on a big tree in the park, but now they had packed up and gone home for the day. I didn't know what kind of tree it was – there were no leaves. I didn't know if the reason there were no leaves was that it had some affliction, or it had lost them earlier than most in this season, or it was dead. Logically, it was dead, or at least had some kind of internal decay – that would be the most likely reason they were cutting down a three-storey-high tree, branch by branch, in an urban environment that craved any leafy greenness. If people were cutting down something that big in my neighbourhood at home, I might've gone outside to find out the reason why. But here there was the language gap, and also the gap in personal attachment – on a new continent I had some licence not to care quite as much.

The sky darkened, and as the night progressed new sounds began to intrude into my room. I'd heard some muted noises from the apartment directly above, although there hadn't been much talking going on up there, but now a phone buzzed twice, and a few minutes later somebody put something on the stereo so loudly I could tell it was the Ramones. Soon there was the chime of a doorbell, and then the sound of the door opening. Muffled voices, some slow steps across the room. Not purposeful steps, more dancing. The pock of a stiletto mixed with the slap of bare feet. The shoes were kicked off, and the dance continued – two shuffling sets of feet. And then came the clunk of something landing on the floor. A belt buckle? Trousers dropping? A flung dress?

Not long after that there was the sound of bodies, elbows, knees and softer areas hitting the wooden floor, and then some cries from a woman, rhythmic half-sighs, half a certain kind of pleasant agony, and a rocking. The volume of her cries rose, and went on. And on. And on. After what felt like an unfeasibly long time, and just when I began thinking there was a false tone coming from the woman, a desperation to continue believing in the game, there was some animal grunting and it all stopped. Before the woman left there was the short unintelligible murmur of a conversation which, I let myself imagine, might have been the discussion about payment. A few minutes later the stilettos were back on and the door was closed behind her.

A person can lie on their bed for hours, unable to make themselves move, thrown and completely incapacitated by the briefest episode of pins and needles in the littlest finger on their left hand, trapped in some tawdry lower mantle, absorbing sex noises coming from above, telling themselves they are sane, but that doesn't mean they are.

I had been prone to random fears as a child. Nobody I knew had ever seen quicksand, unless they were making up fantastic lies, but death by quicksand was an exciting possibility whenever I was out in any kind of wilderness. I was afraid, also, of freezing to death when falling through ice, being stung to death by a cloud of killer bees, and of dogs with rabies. And I tried not to be the tallest thing in any open paddock – death by lightning. If I looked at this clearly, I could see that it wasn't so much wasted energy, more that the high melodrama probably distracted from deeper, darker anxieties that lurked in a place that was too awful to probe. Teenage fears that I had inherited some tendency to decide it was all too much one day, and – well, this was the thought, back then – walk into the sea. Locked away was the even uglier, solidly corked dread that I was so unlovable that a person might decide to end it all instead of living on with me.

Strangely, Zelda's revelation had relieved me of that thought a little, because another completely new logic for my mother's suicide had come to me. Not so much about not loving, but possibly about loving to the point of being driven insane enough to take up a twelve-gauge rifle. For the first time in my life some conditional daylight had reached my abstract notion of mother's love, even if it was complex enough to make me feel both lighter and heavier at the same time.

After the episode of pins and needles subsided, and I was able to convince myself it was only because I had been leaning awkwardly on my arm, I still couldn't stop myself from running the statistics – a ceaseless cycle, like a tape being continuously run through a machine by an operator always hoping to see a positive outcome:

If one parent had Huntington's, risk factor is (only) 50%.

But if the parent didn't have the gene – Good News!! – you may multiply the risk factor by 0%.

If it is unknown if the parent had it at the time of her death, but it is in her family, the risk factor is still 50%. The heir could try to divide this risk factor in half but, in reality, the scary percentage is inescapable.

But if the parent committed suicide the likelihood that she did this because she recognised early symptoms in herself that she had previously seen in a family member means the parental risk factor must be multiplied by a number that is, ah, quite high.

Alternatively, if this wasn't the reason that the parent committed suicide, then the risk factor for the disease stays at 50% and the risk factor for inheriting an additional anxiety disorder is, ah, quite high.

If X = *absolute knowledge* that comes from daring to take the gene test, then this is divisible by Y = *courage*. The courage factor (Y) will need to be adjusted by an as yet undiscovered determinant. Either a positive integer (+) = *prospect of a cure*, or a negative integer (-) = *no prospect of cure*.

So, if M = the hard matter of the disease, then C^2 = the speed in which a cure or at least a treatment could be developed within the healthy lifespan of the descendant (discoverable with a little digging into the health sector?). The resulting outcome, let's call that E then, would be the energy that could be put into the resumption of love. Or something like that. But then there would also have to be some calculation devised for the probability that the lover has become too annoyed to ever take MC² back.

It wasn't a better statistician I needed, it was proper research.

'So, how is it?'

'It's okay. The flatmates are interesting. My room's quite small though. It would've been really cramped for the two of us.'

Silence. Open wound radiating hostility over the internet.

'How are things back there?'

'The cat seems to be missing you. It pissed on your office chair.'

'How did you meet Jay?' Zelda had asked with faux brightness as we started in on our second expensive bottle of pinot noir, drinking it down at kamikaze speed in the sunken hotel bar. Adding, 'It's so wonderful you're going to Europe together. You know, your parents had their honeymoon in Europe too.'

I told the story, the barest details. How I had been biking to a meeting, late, and travelling fast, when my front wheel hit something and flipped me forward, catching one leg on the crossbar and violently contorting the other on the ground. And how the biker behind me, who was Jay, but I didn't know him then, had stopped to help disentangle me. 'Careful,' he kept saying, and I had said, 'I'll be fine. Don't worry about me. You keep going.' And he had replied, 'Did you hit your head? I'm not going anywhere.' And I'd said, 'Really, I'll be fine. I just need a minute,' and when I tried to put my right foot to the ground such terrible pain shot through me that I let out a loud gasp. And he had joked, 'Yep, you're definitely good to go,' and had pulled out his phone and stayed with me until the ambulance arrived.

I had told this often, but I could barely muster the energy to make it entertaining, and Zelda's face had become strained too. She was beginning to understand that what she may have thought of as a good deed, coming all the way to New Zealand to break the news, was now being received with polite but intense anger directed straight at her.

Shortly after that we called it a night. Instead of going home I booked myself a room in the hotel and – with the slightly-below-comfortable temperature of the air conditioning making the room feel like a humming isolation unit – lay alone on the big bed, thinking about the only person who really mattered. Could I tell him this? That suddenly everything he imagined about us growing old together was threatened? That if we got married it might be committing him to look after an invalid who wouldn't be able to walk, or talk, and had a – what did Zelda call it? – a pretty terrible cognitive decline.

I almost knew what he would say. He was definitely a stick-around kind of a guy. After the surgery on my leg, he kept visiting me in hospital, bringing cakes with deliciously subtle flavours that I later found out had come from his mother's kitchen. He'd taken my bike back to his home and fixed it. On about his third visit he mentioned, as he offered yet more treats, that he had grown up in New Zealand but was half Sri Lankan.

I'd said, 'I'm glad you told me. I knew you must be something interesting.'

'You never asked me.'

'I suppose I just assumed you were what you were, and if you wanted to tell me you were something in particular then you would.'

'And now I have,' he said.

He had come and built a temporary ramp at my flat so I could manage more easily with crutches. He often popped in with extra groceries he'd picked up at the store and then suggested that while he was there he might as well cook dinner. He was so doggedly unlike anyone I'd ever been attracted to before – mostly cool-hearted creative types who could tolerate relationships only when they provided some artistic or sensory stimulation – but he completely inveigled his way into my life with his heroic kindness.

Sometimes when we were in bed together and he had his hard-muscled builder's arms around me, and was trying to make me laugh with his slightly off humour, I'd start to think there was a flimsiness to our kind of fate. What if I hadn't hit the rock? What if he'd left home just a few minutes earlier that day? What if my tibia hadn't fractured and I had just said thanks and got back on my bike? It was unlikely I'd have met him in the course of my everyday life. If I'd been introduced to him at a party I probably would've too-quickly decided he wasn't artistic (or difficult) enough for me. But chance brought us together so that his stickability could rub up against my reluctance in a way I couldn't escape. And in the end I became fond of it, and reliant on it, and started to love the big, generous, wanting soul that he is.

But then along comes Queen Fate, back again, this time holding her diabolical 50–50 coin.

Lying on that hotel bed I tried to imagine if I could take the test. My first instinct was to go straight to a clinic, but as I thought about it more I let myself picture what it would really be like to receive a bad result. Terrible physical and mental decline coming your way. And soon, probably. How does a person cope with that? Would it be better, actually, not to have this kind of certainty? I hadn't had an inkling up until now. Maybe I could rise from this bed and just continue on the path. Go ahead! Get married! Pretend you're one of the lucky ones. Ignore this phantom terror poking its morbid finger into you. And what was that gene-therapy thing Zelda mentioned? I hadn't really been able to listen. I needed time to figure all this out. I really needed time.

I once overheard Jay telling someone the story of how we met and he said, '... so bloody-minded that if I hadn't stayed around that morning she probably would've got back on and biked to her appointment on that broken leg.' If I knew anything at all, it was that if I told him then I wouldn't be able to escape his concerned gaze. Did I really want to do this to him? And to me? To be trapped in the sticky mud of his watchfulness and become less than a self-functioning unit? To turn love into solicitude? And also, there was the question of children now. Even if I did the thing that Zelda had talked about, the pre-implantation thing, what kind of parent would I be? As absent as my mother had been for me?

For the first time in my life I believed I was really thinking about self-sacrifice. Wasn't the most noble act, the greater love, not to tell him, not to force his obligation? At least until I knew what I was really dealing with.

4.

'Come on aboard,' I replied. 'We have lots of news.'

We were in our shirt sleeves, and looked like ordinary seamen. On deck he said proudly:

'I am a Frenchman.' As though we couldn't have guessed it.

'A Frenchman? Fine. How is France doing?'

'Ah! France, she is victorious, or will be very soon. *Ravi de vous voir.*'

He fairly bubbled over with delight when we offered him a bottle of champagne. Being homeward bound, he was in a frolicsome mood. A generous taste of the champagne, and he was ready to embrace us. He thought our supposed joke, which certainly would have been somewhat cruel, was the result of our being tipsy. He slapped me on the back, as one cheery skipper to another.

'Captain, what a terrible fellow you are to have fooled me like that. But now I feel as though a stone had dropped from my heart.'

'Beware,' I thought, 'that your stone does not come back twice as heavy.'

He was such a cheery, convivial soul that I hated to break the bad news to him. I left the progress of events to do that. He wanted to have a look over our ship. So I ushered him aft to my cabin, and threw open the door. He took a step forward and recoiled. On the walls were pictures of the Kaiser,

Hindenburg, Ludendorff, and Von Tirpitz, and a large German flag.

'*Des allemands!*' he groaned.

'Yes,' I said, 'we are Germans.'

'Then we are lost, *per Dieu!*'

'Yes, *per Dieu*, you are lost!'

There was a single spot just inside the kitchen window where the morning sun streamed directly onto part of the grungy old sofa which had become my reading place. I put down my book, unable to concentrate on von Luckner's jaunty account of himself, or anything much else, and instead sought distraction by scrolling through a Facebook group called Free Advice Berlin. Somebody had posted a photograph of a weird-looking insect with long nippers. What kind of hell beast is this, they asked. I found it in my clean towels. Somebody suggested they burn all their towels and maybe their house too. Somebody else wrote run, run for your life. Another person put up a gif of Darth Vader. A sensible voice said it was a pseudo-scorpion. It's a good guy, they said. It eats the eggs of moths. Oh, wrote the original poster, what a pity I squashed it already.

A young man with black hair tied up into a topknot came out of Frankie's room. He gave me a quick sheepish wave as he left the apartment. Shortly after, Frankie emerged, wearing only a long T-shirt, and flopped down next to me. 'I don't normally let them stay the night,' she said. 'But that boy just goes at it again and again until we both fall asleep with exhaustion. Hardly talks, just gets down to business. He can find places I didn't know I had. I won't hear from him again for a few months until he wants to do it again.'

It was an odd feeling, sitting that close to a person who was probably not wearing any underwear and who'd just had her every place plundered. Frankie looked at my face and said, 'Oh shit, have I shocked you?'

'No,' I said, rearranging my expression. 'But are you trying to?'

Frankie laughed, got out of her chair and put some coffee into the stovetop espresso-maker. 'Do you know why I came here? I used to be Fiona from Townsend, married, no kids. Tried, it just never happened. Eventually my husband got a co-worker pregnant and left me for her. I couldn't really blame him. By that time his urge had become strong. And all those friends I used to hang out with on the weekends were now spending their Saturdays on the sides of sports fields, or at school galas, and having barbecues in the evenings with other families. They would invite me, but...'

'Yes, I understand what that's like.'

The espresso pot was steaming, and Frankie poured out two cups. We had it black. There was never any milk in the fridge.

'So, one day I was at this flea market and I found one of those fifties-style hand-coloured photos of a Palomino horse standing in the tundra, its mane flowing, its nostrils flaring, free and about to gallop off to who knows where. I hung it in front of my bed, and on Monday morning I woke up as usual with this familiar dowdy sort of feeling I'd been having, as if there was nothing much to get out of bed for, just a job I wasn't enjoying, and friends I was lower-rank priority for, and bugger-all available men to hang out with. But I looked up at the picture and I suddenly thought actually I don't have to live this life. I could live that life. Mane flowing. Nostrils flaring. Free to gallop off to any place in the world. By the end of that day I had booked a ticket out of there.'

'And you became Frankie?'

'Why not? I needed to reframe myself. And do you know what I discovered here?'

'What?'

'Interesting young men who like to fuck older women.'

'And that's what you want?'

'Yes, for now. It's fun. I'd tried to encumber myself with children and a marriage and all that goes with that and it just hadn't worked out, so it's made me rethink the value of that life. Turns out I am so free. Fate has made me free to do what I want. None of my old friends back home can say that. And you know another thing I like about being here? Nobody has ever asked if I have kids.'

'So now you just gallop around instead?' Could life be so easy? Is this the option? Just gallop around, doing whatever, gallop, gallop, mane flowing, right up until that gallop turns into more of a lopsided palsy and the free spirit topples over? And then what? Shoot the thing in the paddock?

'Yeah,' Frankie said. 'Not to take that metaphor too far, but something like that, I guess.'

She took a sip of her coffee and grimaced. 'Feel like going out and getting a decent coffee and a toastie?'

We walked together through the park, past the café that's now a Swiss restaurant that, Frankie told me, was once a community centre where pensioners went to dance on Sunday afternoons in the GDR days. It seemed like the trees had a slightly wistful air. There was that sense of dying days, that a big change was about to come. 'This autumn the weather has been hotter than normal, like an extended summer,' Frankie said. 'The poor trees don't know what to do. They're not turning red like they would normally.'

A café on Weinbergsweg had a row of green chairs out front, and after we'd ordered we joined the line-up of people who were sitting with their faces to the sun as if they were preparing for the coming darkness by taking in the last available stash of vitamin D. Within a few minutes a man came up and asked for money. He was dressed in a suit but wasn't wearing shoes. Frankie shook her head, 'Tut mir leid,' but I felt like the need to ask was bad enough and handed him a euro from my pocket. He moved on to the next group of people.

'I've never seen that one before,' Frankie said. 'They start off like that and the next time you see them they're a drug-fucked wreck. I feel like running after him and saying don't do it. Don't go there.'

'You could.'

'I know, but I won't.'

A young guy was scribbling into his notebook next to me. I sneaked a glance at what he was writing:

Yes, Jac thought.

She has got it.

She doesn't want to talk to you.

'Do you ever think about running after Florian?' I asked Frankie.

Our other housemate always had his door closed. I still had not properly met him, and we never knew if he was in his room or not. Frankie had already mentioned that she had wondered how long she should leave him before she knocked on his door to find out if he was still alive. Instead, she said, she looked for small signs. Were his shoes by the door? Had they moved? Was his towel in the bathroom damp? One night I'd been on the way to the toilet when the front door clicked open at around 5 or 6am. He passed me in the hall, looking nocturnal-creaturely, ghostly and pale, with dark circles under his eyes, like he had been consumed and spat out again. I didn't really know how much responsibility we, the strangers he lived with but tried not to interact with, needed to take for his welfare.

'Oh Florian,' was all Frankie said.

Back at the apartment we dragged a couple of lounge chairs out onto the balcony and sat there for a while, not talking, just listening to the distant voices coming up to us as a general murmur. Somewhere a man was playing a trumpet. 'When the saints go marching in'. I had also seen a group of travellers on the S-Bahn play a rousing version of that same song on their guitars, while their tiny, grubby children went among the commuters with their paper cup out. That song was some kind of money-spinner.

Frankie was leaning back into her chair, eyes closed. 'I went to Turkey once,' she said.

'Did you? And?'

'I went for a few days to visit this friend I'd made in one of the language classes I took when I first got here. It wasn't long after Istanbul airport had been bombed, so I was nervous going through there. Anyway, I got there on Friday night. They lived in this sort of posh seaside area, Bebek, and we immediately went out to dinner. On our way we passed this bar and my friend commented that lots of famous people go there. She said she wouldn't be seen in there without a professional manicure and a pedicure. Anyway, we stopped in after dinner. We were standing outside with our Raki Breezers, watching as this guy pulled up in a classic Aston Martin and threw his keys at one of the staff who then tried to park it prominently in front of the bar in the mad Friday night traffic. All of a sudden everybody's phones went off. My friend's too. When she hung up she said, Something has happened. My mother told me we need to get some milk and bread and go home, she said. Back at their place we turned the television on and saw the images of those army boys lined up on the bridge. I hadn't been there for a single night and already I was in the middle of a coup.'

'Really? How dramatic.'

Frankie opened her eyes and looked across at me. 'Yup, it was pretty dramatic. Of course all the broadcasts were in Turkish so I couldn't really understand, but my friend and her husband told me that all the media were owned by the state so it was not possible to trust what was being said anyway. After a while I went to bed. The mosques that usually broadcast five times a day were going the whole time, and somewhere in the distance I could hear gunfire. Then at about 4am I heard a noise and looked out the window and saw something that looked like a rocket go through the sky. I put up a post online about it and people back home got really excited. Do we need to get you out of there? they wrote. Shall we ring the Embassy for you? I realised I had been attention-seeking, putting it on there. It was quite successful. Anyway, the next morning my friend's husband told me that it wasn't a rocket, it was jets going supersonic to seem like rockets.'

'Supersonic? What? Is there a button?'

'Yeah, imagine that,' Frankie said. 'Right, boys, hold on to your hats. I'm about to push this here supersonic button on the dashboard!'

Down below us in the park some women were screeching. We listened for a moment but then the screams turned to laughter. Somebody was chasing them for fun.

'Later, we walked down to the village to meet some of their friends,' Frankie continued. 'Normally it would be a bustling hub, but this morning there was only one seaside café open. Their friends were saying that it felt like a set-up. That it was some play from Erdoğan to give him more state power over the people. Have you seen the movie *Wag the Dog*? they said. It feels something like that. They told me that the mosques had been broadcasting a message telling people to go out into the streets to defend their democracy. Is that their job? one said. I saw my friend show something on her phone to her friend and she said, Can this be true? They all said how horrible it was and there was a sort of unspoken agreement between them not to show me. Later, when we got back to the house, I asked my friend about it and she told me that one of the soldier boys had been beheaded by the mob. Do you know we have conscription here? she said. I don't think those boys even knew what they were doing, she said. They were probably told by some higher-ups to line up there, like it was some exercise, and then that happened. I feel so sad for their mothers, she said.'

'Beheaded? Really? Fuck.'

'I tried to talk to him last night, that guy, about what was happening there now. He refused. He said he couldn't talk to me about it because it made his heart ache too much. Then he said a curious thing: The heart is bigger than politics.'

'What did he mean?'

'I'm not sure but I think he meant that he was homesick.'

5.

Mel was back and had arranged for us to meet up outside the Reichstag where she had booked into a restaurant on the top floor for lunch. She'd had to give our passport details in advance just to enter the Parliament building. Now, as we stood in the security queue, alongside all the tourists heading up to the glass viewing dome, Mel was attracting glances. She was holding her coat, wearing a low-cut off-shoulder vintage dress that displayed a new wild-flower-style tattoo that extended across her chest and tentacled up her neck. 'At least you'll be relieved you don't have to stay with me the whole time,' she was saying.

'I wouldn't say relieved.'

The queue was moving slowly but we were now inside the door of an entrance hut. 'So, you have a new contract sorted out?' I asked, knowing better than to try to question Mel about why her latest costume job had ended so suddenly. If it had been anything to do with 'artistic differences', my famously impetuous stepsister would just brush it off and it would take months for the truth to come out.

'I've got a couple of months' downtime, then a six-week job in London,' Mel said.

'Great. Those contacts you made on the *Lord of the Rings* set really paid off in the end, huh.'

'Sure did,' Mel said, then, raising her arms and speaking upwards: 'Thanks, Sir Jackson, for working my fingers to the bone on Hobbit-wear.'

'Up? I thought he would be geographically located more down below.'

The two children behind us began whispering together as if they were dangerously thrilled by the loud dropping of the word Hobbit from the tattooed lady in front of them.

'You could've had my apartment while I was away on that next job, I suppose, if you were planning to still be here,' Mel said. 'But I ended up doing a sort of house-swap with this London director I know. It means I can use his place and he can come here to write a treatment for his next film or something.' As an afterthought she added, 'Perhaps I should introduce you, if you're still here. Maybe you would have something in common, both being writers, I mean.' There was a certain tone to this last sentence, as if Mel found having to now refer to me as a writer a little bogus.

'Anyway, it's great to see you. You look amazing. That new tattoo,' I said.

'I know, an artist from Kiev living here in Berlin. She's amazing.' Mel brushed her hand across her neck, then said, 'Isn't the Philharmonie near here? Somewhere across the Tiergarten?'

I took out my phone, like a personal assistant to the rich and famous, located it on the map and pointed vaguely behind us.

'Can we go there after lunch? I'll take a selfie for Jonah.'

'For Jonah?'

'He's second violinist in the… oh, I think it must be the London Philharmonic but actually maybe some other orchestra.' As we took another few steps forward she added, 'Likes to tie my hands and ankles, write words all over my body with a felt-tip pen and then leave me there while he goes out and has an espresso down the road.'

'And you get out of that?'

'You should hear him play.'

Had Mel said this so loudly for the sole purpose of further provoking the gape-mouthed family behind us?

At the security check we placed our bags and phones in the plastic bin, and Mel was asked to also put in the sunglasses which were pushed up on top of her head. As she did so, she sweetly asked the stern-faced security guard if he needed her to take off any more of her things. 'Nein,' the guard said, absolutely unamused.

We were escorted into the main building and directed to wait with a group near a lift shaft. Another security guard walked past, a set of keys clinking on his hip. Mel beamed a wide smile at him to see if she could break the officious look on his face. She couldn't. Around here they received the kind of training that inured them from the actions of any turbo-flirt who entered the building. I could feel the familiar pattern settling in already. Mel radiating her particular brand of flagrant energy, and me alongside made subordinate. But this was part of the thrill too, this jolt out of blandness. I would always remain the shy child forcibly bonded together with the bold one, the teenager who used to observe her stepsister across the dinner table and wonder whether every family had a finite source of extroversion that settled onto only one individual, or whether that person's extroversion sucked the life out of everyone else present.

'That sound always reminds me of your father,' Mel said.

'What sound?'

'Keys. Clinking keys.'

Oh, true. He would come home from work carrying

that big set of keys. Heading directly to the sideboard, he would put them down with a clunk and set to pouring himself a tumbler of whisky as if he couldn't bear to be in the house without a drink on board. As soon as the drink was assembled, he would pick up his keys again, mutter something about going out for a cigarette, and take his glass, and quite often the whole bottle, and go outside to unlock the shed door, staying out until he was called in for dinner. The jangle of keys was both the anticipatory sound of my father's arrival and of him once more rebuffing us all.

'I've never really thought about it before, but he must have had many doors in his life,' Mel said.

'Maybe it was just that in his world a fat bunch of keys was a status symbol.' He was the boss at his furniture factory after all. Maybe keys clinking in his pocket was a way of giving his staff fair warning he was coming up behind them.

In this building, where every person coming in was counted and closely watched, it wasn't permitted to take the elevator alone, presumably in case you get away from the crowd and stumble randomly into the chamber or assail an important politician in the corridors. An escorted ride upwards, and we were all released onto the landing and began walking slowly around the circular dome. Mel and I had a few minutes before our table-booking, so we lingered for a while, absorbing the landscape laid out before us. I'd seen aerial photos of bombed-out Berlin after the Second World War, the whole city devastated and reduced to rubble, but now here it all was – so resolute and squat in the rebuilding.

Mel said, 'So, I have to ask, what's with the alone thing, anyway?'

'You mean Jay?'

'Well, wasn't he coming too? Then suddenly here you are alone. It's finished?'

On one side of us was a big family talking loudly in Italian, and on the other an excited group of teenagers. 'Oh. No,' I said vaguely. 'At least I don't think so. It was just he couldn't get the time off work, and I felt like I could get more done on my own anyway, and the wedding, well...'

Mel didn't look torn up by the idea that we might not be together anymore. She never wanted to settle down, she always said. In the life-view formed at what she considered to be our dull family hearth, there was no credit available for anybody wanting anything other than a spontaneity verging on recklessness and a feline ability to escape shackles. If we were sisters in anything, it was that I was the only person in the world who understood how intensely this came from her not wanting to be like her own talkative, unambitious mother.

'You know, I found out my parents came to Europe on their honeymoon,' I said. 'Now I sometimes find myself wondering if they came here, or near here. I guess it would've been before the fall of the wall.' Had they walked these streets below us? Could I imagine them into being? Animate them, redeem them?

'It's funny,' Mel said. 'I don't think I've ever really pictured him having much of a life before. Your father on a honeymoon.' She was positioning herself for a selfie, but then she said, 'Wait. You've had contact with the family?'

'A little.'

'Did you find out more about your mother?'

Two squealing children ran past us. 'Her suicide, you mean? Not really.' Not here.

Sometimes when we were young we used to speculate together about why my mother might've committed suicide. Mel basically believed it was because she'd had to live with my father, whom she despised. Sometimes Mel would make up an alternative version where my mother hadn't died but had run off with an impresario called Melville who had a troupe of singers called Melville's Martins – neither of us even knew what a Martin was back then, except that it was a bird – and people would hire them to sing songs outside supermarkets with lyrics that rhymed with cheap.

Inside the restaurant the maître d' seated us with restrained but anticipatory courteousness, pulling out our chairs and filling our glasses with mineral water. This place had precisely the air of repressed politeness and required obedience to make Mel break out and do something disconcerting. People who didn't know the history of our stitched-together family used to comment on how different we were as children. Chalk and cheese was the frequent expression. I was the quiet observer in the corner, while Mel was winning the prize for the girl who was definitely too big for this little town. My side of the room was a spick and span apology for existence, while Mel's was a chaotic celebration of life: walls plastered with style icons, pots of make-up spilling off the vanity and grubbying the carpet, abandoned art projects in every corner, and a door slammed shut against any of Lorelei's efforts to make encroachments. Reading by torchlight after lights out was as dangerous as I got. Mel, meanwhile, was climbing out the bedroom window and letting boys finger fuck her in cars.

'Why did we want to come to this boring-ass place again?' Mel asked, after a waiter had ostentatiously placed down exactly the right cutlery for our order. Everybody else in the room seemed to be hushed into submission by the importance of the surroundings.

'You said Lorelei said that her friend said that her cousin said that her neighbour said it was a must-do,' I reminded her.

'Oh yeah. How stupid of me to listen,' Mel said.

'At least the view is nice.'

Mel nodded. 'We're lucky with the weather today,' she said, but mockingly, and in the tone of voice that Lorelei usually used.

I took a sip of the water. 'Did you ever wonder how our parents got together?'

'They were both fucked in their own way. Your dad needed someone, I guess, and my mother liked to be needed.'

'Yeah, maybe she was attracted to profound sadness.'

'Profound sadness? That's what you call it? More likely she knew nothing at all about alcoholics. Probably she thought she could save him.'

And here we both were in Berlin, his blood, her blood, together. Mel couldn't even give him minor credit for running a business so successfully that the royalty payments from his patents still gave all three of us quite a bit of liveable income. Or that he had not discriminated between the two of us when he had created that legacy.

Our first course came. Vichyssoise, very nuanced.

'He was the one who found her, you know,' I ventured. 'My mother. After she did it. With a gun.'

Mel's second spoonful was halfway to her mouth. 'Really? Shit,' she said, putting the spoon down again. She stared out the window. 'I guess that would sure take a lot out of a man.'

I turned my gaze to the window too, wondering: did it? Was he once charming and dashing, with a romantic life so great that after his first wife's death he became numb with old pain? Becoming capable of only two things: maintaining an unquestionable work ethic, and being more or less present for the miraculously dedicated Lorelei who enjoyed looking after his every need inside the house? I wished now that I'd followed him out to the shed, sat there too until he started talking to me. Mel would've been scornful if I had, though. She wanted me to hate him as much as she did.

By the second course, I began to edge towards what I really needed to talk about. I'd chosen the wiener schnitzel from the menu. 'When in Germany...' I'd said. Mel had selected the only vegetarian option, but when she asked the waiter to leave off the Büffelmozzarella he'd struggled to suppress his disappointment.

'Do you ever think about genetic inheritance,' I said. 'Like what you got from your mother, say?'

'Fuck no. Well, maybe. Sometimes I think I'm in a battle against my genetic inheritance. That I do all this crazy stuff just to make sure as shit that I am nothing like my mother.'

'Do you dislike her that much?'

'No, not dislike. I just have no respect for her. The way she ran around after your father.'

'He liked it. I think she did too.'

'Did he? Did he like anything?'

Our eyes met, and I found myself resenting the absoluteness of Mel's loathing. She had it in her to be kinder but she was not in that mood today. The difference between Mel's grief for her father and my grief for my mother was that Mel was still able to think of her father as a lost hero. He had been a policeman who died in a work incident, stabbed in a brawl, when she was only four. She used to keep a photo of him by her bed. Handsome in a puffy brown leather jacket that was at least fashionable at the time, looking like the man to call in any emergency.

A few tables away there was a large man holding forth importantly about something within his group. 'Do you think he's come up from downstairs?' I whispered. Mel shrugged. He could be a famous politician here, the president, for all we knew. We were just a couple of blank interlopers skimming across the surface of real German life.

Maybe something had really happened with Mel's job? Perhaps the collapse of her contract had to do with some disgrace or failure, or perhaps she was trailing some off-set scandal that had set her this much on edge. A degree of guardedness was sometimes the better option with Mel, who had that child-bred aversion to anything she perceived as fragility. And anyway, I suspected I already knew what she would say in this kind of mood. Take the damn test. Don't mouse out of it. If you are going to live your life in some tragic way, better to know that the tragedy is authentic. Anyone who hadn't let that all-engulfing dark cloud float over their imagination would obviously say that. Or maybe that is not what she would say. In her own way she was running from everything too, finding distraction from thinking too hard. Maybe I only let myself think that's what Mel would say because it was the advice I was constantly trying to give myself.

'What words did Jonah write on you?' I asked.

'Oh, he liked a bit of high art,' Mel said, pushing her plate aside.

'Like?'

'A little she strove, and much repented, and whispering, I will ne'er consent – consented.' A small gratified smile. 'Byron, apparently.'

'Wow, that's…' For my last birthday Jay had given me a vacuum-cleaning robot because he'd seen that I didn't like cleaning floors much. And I quite liked the thing, principally because the cat had taken to sitting on it and travelling around the house with a very stupid expression on its face. But also because the fact of his giving me the robot transferred the overall responsibility for the state of the floors to him. If I were to present myself naked and hand him a felt-tip pen, he would be so crippled by panic about what he was supposed to write that he wouldn't be able to think of a single word.

After lunch we crossed the wide boulevard that had the Brandenburg gate at one end and Victoria's column at the other, and entered the Tiergarten. As we wandered further into the park the traffic noise receded and Mel began using Lorelei's voice: 'If your underwear elastic ever gives way when you're walking down the street, the best thing is just to step right out of them and keep going. But that silly fellow.' That silly fellow, our favourite childhood example of ensuing mortification, had picked them up and run after Lorelei saying, Excuse me, you dropped something. After the netball away-game incident, silly fellow solidified into our code for self-inflicted folly. That time one of the kids in the car had announced they needed to go to the toilet, so Lorelei had pulled into a service station and we all trailed in after them, me and Mel and a load of our team mates. The door wouldn't open, and Lorelei called out to us and all the customers in the service station that it was stuck. It was urgent, so Lorelei rattled and wrenched the door until finally it flew open, exposing a man sitting there with his pants around his ankles and an alarmed expression on his face. 'Why didn't the silly fellow just call out?' she said to us all in the car, her cheeks flaming.

I knew what Mel was doing. Even though we might never exactly be on the same plane, we were bound in one thing: we had stood side by side on the platform that had provided a sometimes amusing view of our parents' fallibilities.

'Why do things like that always happen to her?' Mel asked.

'I think it's because she always makes herself available to everything. For anyone. And if something terrible happens she finds a way to tell us so that we all enjoy laughing at her. It's sort of generous.'

'You like her a lot, don't you?'

'The way I see her, warm, giving, big-hearted.'

'Nobody would say that about me.'

'That's a good thing?'

Mel wasn't prepared to admit to accepting this in herself, and she wasn't prepared to admit to not accepting it either. Eventually she said, 'Actually I don't think I give a fuck.'

It became clearer to me now that there might have been some overcompensation in the way Lorelei had parented me. She hadn't wanted me to feel the great loss in my life, so she embraced me with an enthusiasm that could've been a tad manufactured. Probably Mel had sensed that. Her small seed of resentment growing early into active rebellion against all of Lorelei's small kindnesses.

'Listen,' I said, 'there is something I really need to...'

'Vorsicht!' Two women approached us, seeming both excited and scared. We must have looked confused, because one of them switched to English. 'Careful,' she said. 'Don't go that way. There sits a man playing with his penis.'

'I think he is waiting for some mens to come along,' her friend said, more pragmatically. 'It happens often in that part of the Garten, I am thinking.'

We thanked them and veered off onto another path, although I could tell Mel was curious. I began to tell her about the sex I'd heard coming from upstairs, how I thought there might have been some kind of paid exchange at the end.

'Paid exchange?' Mel responded. 'Jeez, Ginny, what are you like? It just sounds like a hook-up. Honestly, where have you been? Oh, that's right, inside that cosy little nest of yours.'

We reached the busy road, and crossed over to the Philharmonie with its fantastic golden façade. Mel was fussing with her phone, positioning for the camera. Not wanting to observe her taking a photo of herself for her lover, I was drawn over to an outdoor exhibition nearby, one of many I'd noticed in this city that doesn't allow its citizens to forget. This one was for the victims of 'euthanasia' killings. *In 1933 the National Socialist regime issued a 'Law for the Prevention of Genetically Diseased Offspring'. It allowed forced sterilisation. It also indirectly called into question the right to life of human beings with psychiatric illnesses and mental or physical disabilities...* There was a photo of poor little Anna Lehnkering, *a sweet mild-mannered child who found learning difficult. As someone with a 'hereditary disease', she was sterilised in 1935 and admitted to Bedburg-Hau hospital in 1936. Here, she was regarded as difficult and 'incapable of work'. In 1940, she was asphyxiated by gas in the Grafeneck killing centre.*

I went down the line of exhibits, unable to pull myself

away and feeling dread rising up in me. *The National Socialist regime used films, magazines, posters and even school education to warn people of the 'uneconomic burden' that the 'idiots' and 'insane' supposedly posed to the population… 'useless eaters' were murdered.*

There wasn't a list displayed there but I knew a list must have existed, and that Huntington's would probably be on it.

On the way home, I began to feel as if I had a cold coming on. The prospect of getting sick seemed a bit like stepping onto an elevator that could make a rapid descent into some scary basement area where life-altering switches might be flicked into the on position. Any remedy, no matter how desperate, seemed necessary – so I dropped into a nearby bar and asked for a Schnaps, expecting to get a glass of clear liquid with a pipe-cleaning effect on my throat. But the grumpy barman looked affronted and nearly shouted, 'Was für Schnaps?' He pointed, gesticulated really, at the entire top shelf.

'Is Schnaps not just Schnaps?' I asked weakly.

With a level of indignation that seemed unwarranted, he slapped a card down in front of me and pointed to a list that, in one quick glance, I could see included vodka, brandy, whisky… ahh, Schnaps was perhaps the German word for liquor?

I slunk out the door, saying, 'Sorry, sorry,' this bar becoming one of the places I would never return to.

In a Späti I bought two bottles of wine and spent the next twenty-four hours, and then the next twenty-four hours, in bed playing Toy Blast on my phone and not thinking about anything. Just trying to get to the next level, to just complete the next level, to just try one more time to accomplish the next level, just one more time, just one more drink, and then when that was done to just try the next level again. Es tut mir leid, that was the expression for sorry. And other words unfamiliar in the mouth, Danke, Dankeschön, Bitte, Vielen Dank, Gerne, Tausend Dank, Herzlichen Dank, Bitteschön, all the variations: line up the word for the right subtlety and boom!, press down. Why had that memorial been so affecting? It would make anybody sad. That horrible accounting that made some people lesser in the world. Useless eaters.

By the end of a couple of days I hated myself. I didn't have a cold, but I was so tired my eyes looked bruised.

When I finally emerged from my room, Frankie took one look at me and asked if I'd been having a problem sleeping. This led to me confessing that I was many, many levels up on Toy Blast. 'The problem is that I'm quite good at it, so they keep on rewarding me with more free hours – and once you've earned them…'

'It's quite meditative probably,' Frankie suggested kindly, as if she was talking to a powder keg that was ready to blow.

'Is it? I think it just makes you braindead. I'm really grumpy now. Maybe because I've wasted so much time.' And while I was doing that there'd been a complicated thought about apathy, which I had seen somewhere – where was it? – was a symptom.

'Maybe you needed to.'

'I think you're just being supportive. Look, I'm getting my phone out right now and deleting it. Maybe I have an actual addiction to this sort of thing. It's more a completist thing than anything else, I guess.'

'Yeah, like millions of people in the world,' Frankie said.

'It's just that it's so rewarding,' I responded, my finger hovering over the tiny X. 'There's a child's voice that says Ammmmmazzzzing and laughs when you've managed to line up a really good explosion. And there are these toy animals, elephants and puppies and what have you, and you have to save them by blowing things up, and when you do, they go Wheeeeeeee!!!'

'Delete it,' Frankie commanded. 'And then just tell yourself the time wasn't completely wasted. Yeah, probably while you were doing that you were working through other things in the back of your mind, ordering stuff around maybe.'

Was I? By lining up coloured cubes on my phone? Like ordering neurons, maybe. And the snorty pigs you had to blast away like some kind of malignancy. And then there was that ice that would render the whole game redundant, square by square, if you didn't keep on top of it. 'You really are supportive,' I said. 'I think I need you to roll your eyes and tell me I'm a complete fuckwit.'

'I can do that too,' Frankie said, placing her warm hands on both sides of my face and pulling it towards hers before whispering the words, 'You absolute fuckwit. Write your book.' It was quite effective.

'Here's an idea,' she added. 'I have two free tickets to an opera tonight. Come with? Not sure what it will be like, but get away from yourself, maybe?'

To see an opera performed in an old church in a city whose informal motto is 'Poor but Sexy' is to expect a challenge to convention. This version of *Die Fledermaus* felt not quite professional and not quite amateur. Almost, I was thinking, like an exceptionally good performance from the Manawatū Opera Society.

The first act was performed in what was essentially a tearoom off the church's main hall, converted into Eisenstein's drawing room in such a way that it required a lot of imaginative effort from everybody there. After a quick glass of wine during the break, we were all herded up some wide concrete steps and in through the main doors of the church, where we sat in pews, staring at an impressive shaft of luminous blue light that landed where the altar had once been, awaiting the start of the palace ball scene. A crack of a whip near the back announced the arrival of Prince Orlofsky, and when we turned we saw that the role was being performed by a woman. She strode ferociously up the aisle, dressed in a tight leather suit with a dangerously plunging neckline, whip in hand, her first aria begun. The rest of the cast were also wearing some form of skimpy leather for this act, and the final two set pieces turned out to be more or less a writhing orgy but with operatic singing.

We stayed seated on the hard benches for the break between the second and third acts, and the young woman sitting next to me said hi with a minor wave of her hand. She looked shy. A lonesome traveller eager to make contact. She was in the next production, she said. Once a year this company brings young people from all over the world to workshop with experienced directors, and they put on four operas. She'd come from Brazil, she said. And was in *Hansel and Gretel*.

'A lead role?'

'No,' the girl said. 'I am one of the biscuit people. But it's fun. Instead of a house in the woods we, the biscuit people, live in the attic and our jumpsuits are made out of polypropylene.'

'Glamorous,' I said, and the girl laughed.

Frankie leaned over and asked who had written the music for *Hansel and Gretel*.

'I think it was, um, somebody called Engelbert Humperdinck,' the girl said, uncertainly.

'No!' Frankie said. 'That can't be right. Engelbert Humperdinck wrote an opera?'

'Yes,' the girl said. 'I'm pretty sure that's right?'

'But do you know who Engelbert Humperdinck is?'

The girl shook her head and Frankie started singing 'Please Release Me' in a low voice. The girl looked blank, so Frankie switched to 'The Last Waltz'. She had a nice voice. Husky but very tuneful. The girl still had no idea, so Frankie pulled out her phone and showed her an image of Engelbert Humperdinck in his seventies heart-throb period, with shoulder-length hair and a big droopy moustache.

'Oh my God,' the girl said. 'He looks exactly like my grandfather back in Brazil.' She took Frankie's phone and looked more closely at the image.

'So, he wrote an opera?' I said, wondering if my stepmother knew this. 'Who knew he had it in him? That's so weird.'

'OMG,' the girl said. 'I can't wait to show the others that photo. They'll die!'

Frankie took her phone back and started scrolling through Engelbert's biography on Wikipedia. 'Oh, hang on,' she said. 'It says here that Engelbert's real name was Arnold George Dorsey and he tried for years to make it without any success. But then he got a new manager, who was Tom Jones's manager, and that guy suggested he take the name of some obscure German composer whose main claim to fame was he wrote the opera for *Hansel and Gretel*.' She did some more searching and showed us the period photo of the gnomish-looking man who had really written *Hansel and Gretel*.

'Oh, thank God,' the girl said. 'Imagine how stupid I would've looked. I'm saying bloody nothing about Engelbert Humperdinck tomorrow.'

Frankie and I were still laughing about it when we got home. Florian was in the kitchen, eating something out of a bowl. Wet noodles and nothing else. It was almost a shock to see him there, like coming home to find the possum that had been living in your ceiling was now sitting up at your table. He was young, perhaps in his early twenties, but he had a fulsome ginger beard and was definitely on the bearish side. Now that we were sitting opposite each other I felt him run his eyes over me quickly, taking in some basic facts – female, thirties, straightish – and went back to concentrating on his noodles, seeming to decide that I was of minus-zero interest. Frankie told him about the Engelbert Humperdinck thing, and he said, quite earnestly, 'I see there was a misunderstanding, but I have never heard of this man. Why are you so much laughing about it?'

'Oh, I don't know, Florian,' Frankie said. 'Maybe it's because Arnold Dorsey and his new manager were sitting around somewhere, probably drinking, I would guess, and his manager said, Hey, I've got an idea for you. Why don't you call yourself Engelbert Humperdinck after this obscure German composer who wrote the opera *Hansel and Gretel*? And Dorsey said, Wow, what a great idea. And he didn't just take Engelbert or Humperdinck but the. Whole. Damn. Thing.'

Frankie looked over at me and rolled her eyes in a way that acknowledged we were from the same hemisphere at least.

'And maybe,' I added, 'because we very nearly set up that girl from Brazil to go into the opera company that had given her the opportunity of a lifetime and tell everybody that *Hansel and Gretel* was written by a seventies middle-of-the-road pop icon.'

That set us off laughing again.

'Ha ha,' Florian said sarcastically. 'Ich lach mich kaputt.' He picked up his bowl and headed towards his bedroom.

'What did he say?' I asked Frankie. 'I something me broken?'

'Laugh. Lach is laugh, meaning like laughing your head off, but, you know, sometimes drily.'

'I get it.'

6.

Somebody on Free Advice Berlin had posted asking whether it was okay to wait for a friend to come back from a trip to help you if you had a tick in a place you couldn't easily reach. No, people wrote. You can get terrible diseases from ticks. You need to get somebody to carefully take it off. You need to take it to a medical centre and get it tested. They carry borreliosis. One person asked where she'd got it from, and she said just sitting in Tempelhof Park. Eww, another said, I am never sitting down on the grass there ever again.

Scrolling around, wasting time, wasn't getting me anywhere. It wasn't research or writing. It wasn't helping me move towards any decisions.

I started following my Canadian cousins, but only in a lurking kind of way, stalking them on every available platform, getting to know them, or their milestones at least. Zelda's pages were mostly focused on the homely achievements of her children. Perhaps that's why I hadn't noticed the Huntington connection when I'd first looked. As I delved further, her pages started to look like exemplars of denial compared to those of her sister Margarethe, who had both a different surname and a completely different look: short-shaven pink hair. She had put up some old family photos. There was one of her grandfather holding her grandmother. They were perhaps in their fifties, somewhere pretty, flowering shrubs in the background. It was possible to see that the grandmother couldn't walk easily, or hold herself steady on her own. She was smiling into the camera, lopsidedly, leaning on the grandfather's arm. He was smiling too, as if this was quite fun, helping her make this small achievement, getting her out of the house for a while, smelling the flowers, posing for somebody with a camera. It was only when I started thinking that Margarethe's grandfather looked nice, like a man who might have natural wisdom, that it came to me that he was my grandfather too. And this was my grandmother.

Margarethe was something like a good-person warrior for the Huntington's cause. Leading up to Huntington's Awareness Day she had rallied a whole lot of people to sew up reusable shopping bags and sell them to help fundraise. She provided patterns and detailed instructions, and put up photos of herself busy at her machine, with her little children in the background cutting up the templates for the bags about to be sewn. One of them, a toddler, looked too young to be allowed to wield scissors, but it was for a good cause at least. Margarethe had made a website where people could go to make their purchase. Help us find a cure! Buy, buy, buy! Plus, you are doing good for the Environment! Reusable bags are eco-friendly! Made of repurposed fabrics!

Later she announced that she had made a $1,256 donation to 'the wonderful care facility that is looking after our uncle'. And she posted a photo of Uncle Caspar, semi-catatonic in a wheelchair, with some friendly-looking nurses waving at the camera.

From Margarethe's page it was possible to identify our other cousins, Uncle Caspar's two sons. One of them, Phillippe, had written a blog about finding out he had the gene. His father had lied and always told him, for some reason, that he had already taken the test and didn't have it. Phillippe, thinking he was home free, had ecstatically embraced life and gone ahead and had children at a young age. And then his father started to show some subtle movement disorder and kept losing jobs. When Phillippe and his brother pushed their father – who by this time was not washing himself and was getting into paranoid arguments with his neighbours about cars parked at the kerb and dog poo on his lawn – to take the test, he angrily resisted. Phillippe began to wonder if the lying had been the earliest of his symptoms. But by this time, their father's diagnosis was clear. Phillippe got tested and found he carried the faulty gene. He was forty-three now and at stage two level, which meant that a neurologist was 50–89 per cent sure that he was now showing signs of motor abnormalities related to HD. The worst part, he wrote, had been worrying about his two daughters, Lena and Angie. The only solace was that in the next ten to fifteen years it seemed likely that a treatment would be developed to at least limit the symptoms. But would it be in time for him?

From Phillippe's site I began following links to other people who were blogging about their 'journey'. One woman wrote about the problem of her designer clothes. She had to wear a bib to eat, but her involuntary movements meant that sometimes food got through at the gap at the top. That morning she had dispensed with her bib and eaten her breakfast standing naked in the kitchen. Her husband thought she should embrace the stains on her expensive clothes as an art-piece and a statement. Another man wrote about a turning point towards separation when his symptomatic wife got irrationally angry at their nine-year-old son and started raining blows down on his head.

One woman wrote about how difficult she found it to express enthusiasm to other people because her face was now a down-turned mask. She also mentioned her growing difficulty in understanding her husband's humour. She decided that she would signal she had understood a joke by saying 'Ha – hahahaha', but when she tried it he thought she was laughing sarcastically, and this created more issues. One said she was struggling with keeping the intellectual show on the road and would feel sad about no longer being able to concentrate enough to read books, but the disease actually blunted her ability to feel anything.

I called Lorelei and we talked for a while about nothing much. Lorelei wanted to know what I was eating for dinner, and if I had seen Mel, and told me about a woman in her retirement village who pushed her little dog around in a pram, and the woman in the unit next door who had finally gone into the full-service dementia-care unit, and how somebody had put a basket of nice lemons out by the community centre and she had taken a few and made a delicious lemon curd, although she was a bit on tension hooks about how it would turn out, but in the end it was nice and she'd given some to the husband of the woman who had been taken into care. I teased her about making a quick move and Lorelei pretended she didn't know what I was talking about.

'Do you still have those old Engelbert Humperdinck cassettes of yours?' I asked.

'No, dear,' Lorelei said. 'I got rid of all those when I moved. I think. Why, dear? Did you want me to keep them for you? Is he having some kind of revival or something? Oh, now that you mention it, I did used to love those songs of his. Remember how we sometimes used to sing along to that cassette when your father wasn't in the house. What was the song again? Oh, that's right. "Last Waltz", wasn't it? Was he the one ladies used to throw their knickers at? Or was that Tom Jones? I went to a Tom Jones concert once, did I ever tell you that? He was already a bit worn out by then, bit of a damp squid, but he was still kind of something...'

It was nice to hear her voice, the simple, chatty inanity that had soothed over my childhood. She had always liked to talk so much that it seemed like she never really minded that her husband barely said a word. Were they different in the privacy of their own room, though? Did she grow quiet enough to draw something out of him? Was he vulnerable with her? I'd like to think he softened in the bedroom and sought warmth and affection and, well, love. Or did he bark his commands at her too? 'Open your legs!' Perhaps she, the humble, loving, giving replacement wife, was titillated by subservience. Maybe when she heard him barking his commands at us it created a reverberating thrill within her. Were there secret glances between them that we had missed?

7.

I had gone into the museum to try to understand more about the late-1800s German world view that had seeded the Count, and was presented with a monarchic empire that was freshly unified and Prussian led, with angry borders and a deep pride in being the champion steel-maker of the Industrial Revolution, where education was exalted but women barely got a look-in, and men knew their place on the ladder of authority. What was there for young boys to do back then? Play war games, obey their fathers and revere the Kaiser?

Soon enough I had wandered on into the Hitler years and found myself standing in front of it.

July 14, 1933 Sterilization Law:

Article I of the 'Law for the Prevention of Genetically Diseased Offspring' defines who was to be examined and then sterilized: (1) Anyone who suffers from an inheritable disease may be surgically sterilized if, in the judgement of medical science, it could be expected that his descendants will suffer from serious inherited mental or physical defects. (2) Anyone who suffers from one of the following is to be regarded as inheritably diseased within the meaning of this law:
1 congenital feeble-mindedness
2 schizophrenia
3 manic-depression

4   congenital epilepsy
5   inheritable St. Vitus dance (Huntington's Chorea)
6   hereditary blindness
7   hereditary deafness
8   serious inheritable malformations

Back at home I was unlocking the apartment's front door when a man came down the stairwell. On seeing me he said, 'Hallo. Ich bin Christoph.' He thrust out his hand.

'Ginny,' I replied, and he said, 'We speak English, yes?' How did he know from one word?

I had decided it must be a single person living above me but had not imagined such a giant of a man. He had an abundant science-society-style moustache and beard, and a shiny baldness at the top of his head that suited him. But most prominent were his narrowed, mischievous eyes.

'I'm just heading for a beer down the road,' he said. 'Want to join? No big deal.'

'A beer,' I said. 'Actually, now that you mention it, I think I might be desperate for a beer. Now?'

'Ja, oder...' he said. 'I mean... do you need some time?'

'No, good to go,' I said. Had I even remembered to brush my hair?

Immediately I felt him to be a jovial sort of person, different from what I had imagined. As we entered the bar, people looked our way. He was so large he must create a change in the atmosphere wherever he went. Christoph ordered for both of us. 'Zwei Pilsner, Bitte,' he said, and I could relax into being with someone who had more than language competency and, it became apparent, was well known here.

'So, Australian?' he asked as we slid onto some barstools.

'Kiwi.'

'Oh, I was close,' he said, and then he apologised. 'That's like saying a Scottish person is English, I guess. Or a Canadian American.'

'Yes, I suppose, but we're separated by a sea. An entire ocean, in fact, the Tasman.' As it came out of my mouth it sounded not quite right, a minor crossing of the line between friendly conversation and something closer to defensive correction. This bar had a sense of worn Berlin cool, not too accessible, not trying too hard. I added more warmly, 'Actually, I was born in Canada.'

'Your parents were Canadian?'

'Not exactly. My mother was born in Canada.'

A man brushed past us on the way back from the toilet. The rubber on the bottom of his shoes made suction noises as he walked across the sticky floor. He was wearing a T-shirt that had *I Like Dope and I Do Dope Things* printed on the front. It appeared purposefully stupid on a sixty-year-old man, but maybe it was a form of advertising. I wondered if he might actually be a dealer, but there were no obvious indications. He did resume a seat near the front door of the bar where, I thought, he might be best positioned for attracting customers, if that was his thing.

I reached for my glass. 'And you? Where are you from?'

'Rhinelander,' Christoph said. 'From the friendly state.'

'But your English is really good.'

'Spent a bit of time in Brighton.'

'Brighton? Why?'

'My mother's sister married an Englishman. I used to go and visit my cousins nearly every summer. I liked the seaside there. And I did some postgrad work in London.'

'Ahh, and so how did they meet?'

Christoph took a draught of his beer and then used his

hand to make a covert swipe of his moustache.

'My aunt and uncle? He was posted here for a while.'

'Posted?'

'Army. Nothing extraordinary. Actually the old fucker had a joke he liked to tell whenever I was around. It went like this: a couple adopted a German baby, but as he grew up he never talked. At first, they were worried and they tried everything they could to get him to talk, but soon enough he was doing well at school and at sports and everything so they agreed not to worry about it and just accepted that he was not a talker. But on his eighth birthday they wanted to create some sort of celebration of his heritage. They decided they'd cook him an apple strudel. When they presented it to him, he took one bite and said, Der Strudel ist tepid. They were amazed. You can talk! Why have you never said anything before? He said, Vell, up until now everyzing has been adequate.'

A laugh erupted out of me like a secret denial coming to the surface. Christoph laughed heartily with me, and I said, 'Sorry.'

'What? You are apologising for laughing? You think we can't enjoy a laugh at our own expense? Have you never seen the comedian Loriot? He made a career out of sending up our German stiffness.'

Christoph took another gulp of his beer and added, 'Actually, the funniest thing about that joke is my uncle stopped telling it after he once told it to a Russian co-worker of his and the guy said that they told a very similar joke in his homeland, but in it the boy was English.'

A thought briefly occurred to me that a man might choose to have sex on the floor of his apartment precisely because of the possibility the person below could hear, and also that he might already suspect I was that person.

'And your postgrad work?' I inquired.

'Film restoration. I work at an archive here,' he said.

The door opened, and two laughing women entered. I saw their eyes flick over the bar, checking out who was there, and land on Christoph. When I looked back at him, I saw that he had noticed he was receiving attention – and that he enjoyed it.

'And your reason for coming here?' Christoph asked.

'Well... I came here to write a book,' I told him. 'A novel.'

He didn't seem at all surprised or impressed. Every expat comes to this city to write something, create something, make something.

'Ahh. And so... ? About?' It was a slightly perfunctory question. His attention was now strongly pulled across the bar. One of the two women was staring at him, and when he turned his gaze back towards me, I saw her nudge her friend. Even though I was sitting right beside him, it seemed he was able to telegraph his theoretical availability across the room. My previous idea about him having paid for sex seemed highly unlikely. I didn't really mind that he sensed his chance and was drawn to these two women, but at the same time I felt oddly diminished by the way his attention was already faltering.

'It's about a German Count,' I said, but it came out flatly, with all my growing doubts also accidentally inferred. 'A real Count, from the First World War.'

'The First? Oh yeah? Why that?' he asked. I thought I saw a flash of scepticism in his question. Distrust about the obvious kind of take a foreigner might apply to any character from the German side of the war. It reminded me of how on the way to the museum I'd absent-mindedly wandered into the bike lane and a rider had come up behind me and shouted 'Achtung!' At first I thought he had meant it comically, like other German words in the common lexicon – Schnell, Verboten, Jawohl, Mein Liebling, Herr Führer – and then it dawned on me how much Germanness had been satirised in the films and comics of my youth.

I found myself stumbling for an answer that might interest Christoph, because really, what use would he have for this? What use would anyone have for this? I excused myself and went to the bathroom, taking my time washing my hands, looking into the mirror at the face of a fraud while I dried them with a paper towel. I hadn't even started writing yet. Mostly I had been spending my days wandering around trying to let some ambience bounce up off the pavement at me, lingering around monuments, noticing how the past was formally acknowledged. The seated Heinrich Heine at the entrance of the park just down the road with the inscription at the base: *We do not seize an idea but the idea seizes us and enslaves us and whips us into the arena like forced gladiators to fight for it.* And robed Goethe in the Tiergarten, holding his scroll and looking out with gentle wisdom to the future with the allegorical figures of Drama, Poetry and Science represented at his feet by women holding lyres and with naked sons. The giant self-important Marx and Engels down near the Spree, all the big men, and in Alexanderplatz, Neptune posing magnificently in his shell atop a fountain, while around the base the four women representing the rivers of Germany sat with their naked breasts gleaming brown after so many hands had rubbed off the green patina.

When I returned, the two women had taken a seat on either side of Christoph, so I waved goodbye from across the room, and he shrugged helplessly, as if to say, What's a man to do? I laughed. I liked the big sexy beast, and at least this way we might be friends, here in this place where I hardly knew anyone.

8.

My morning was Jay's night. Every day I woke to a link from him, funny gifs or videos. Mostly involving cats or dogs, but not always. There had been a run of raccoons doing cute but ridiculous things. I sent him back smiley faces, and sometimes, when I came across something that would amuse him, I sent a link too. But never as often as he sent them to me. I knew what this really was, just a way of saying you are in my thoughts but without the pain of having to talk. This morning he sent a link to pandas trying to climb up a snowman and sliding back down onto their fat bottoms. *So clumsy*, he wrote. *How did they ever survive as a species?*

When we did occasionally talk online he didn't ask about us. Neither of us wanted to raise the discussion of when I might be back. Instead he asked about my project. I felt it as pressure from him. He seemed to think that if I made some progress on my research then I would be able to think about reuniting very soon. And I played the game. I told him that I was gathering some good research, that I was evolving the idea, that the other day I wrote lots in a café, that soon I was going to Halle. I kept anecdotes in store for him.

'I saw some photographs in an old magazine I picked up in a café, these men in a town near Dresden,' I told him. 'Every year they turn the place into a sort of Wild West to celebrate the birthday of Karl May. People come from all over dressed up as cowboys and Indians and they eat buffalo burgers and wear bear-claw necklaces and sell feathered headdresses.'

'Really? Weird, and sort of not cool,' Jay said.

'Yeah, but it kind of rang a bell. I remembered the Count saying he'd been inspired to become an adventurer because of an obsession with Buffalo Bill. He once claimed that he'd walked a thousand miles along a railway line from San Francisco to Denver and knocked on a door and asked for Buffalo Bill but was told he'd wasn't home because he'd taken his Wild West show off to Europe.'

'A thousand miles! He was so full of crap.'

'I know.'

'So are you going to use that somehow?'

'I don't know, probably not, but you know, context-building.'

I could tell he was trying hard to be good-humoured and not needy, but should I really just be distancing myself from him instead? Sometimes I suspected myself of being melodramatic. This running away. But then I'd make myself remember there were reasons, an unexploded grenade of reasons, left to maturate in some dark place, like a tumour I was choosing to ignore for the time being.

Frankie's door was open, and she was sitting in her bed, her knees up under the blankets, looking at her phone. She patted the space next to her as I passed, as if she'd been waiting for an opportunity to do so. I went in and slipped my legs under the duvet, and Frankie took one of her pillows, puffed it up and placed it behind my back. The nearby window was ajar but her room still felt fuggy from recent sleep. In the distance I could hear the sound that was becoming a signature of my time in this apartment

– the steely clang of a tram making its way up the gentle slope towards Pankow.

'I've been sitting here trying to figure an angle on what I'm doing,' Frankie said. 'Look at this one. BODEGABOY. He's been wishing me Buongiorno every morning. Now he's trying to step it up. He wants me to come and kiss him in the park. Lipstick kisses. But he's confessed to me already that he's very short.'

She handed over the phone:

F: Pink or red?
BB: Red, pink is like barbie, I like women.
F: Even in pink I am woman.
BB: And high heels?
F: Perhaps not in the park. In high heels I might be too tall for you.
BB: I can jumping. Latin lover always find solution.

As I handed back the phone, I said, 'At least he is sort of funny. Are you going to meet him?'

'No,' Frankie said. 'Not today. But that'll probably mean never. This app's like that. Mostly if you don't take up the opportunity straight away the flame burns out pretty quickly. Always the next thing and the next thing.' She put her phone down on the side table. 'I think my confidence is blown. The other day I met up with this guy. He said he didn't have a popular look so he extended his age range to see what would happen, and when he saw my picture he thought surely I'd swiped right. It's thrown me. I thought I was putting out some sort of interesting image of myself, but really are they just thinking, I can probably notch up that one?'

Notch up? 'Wait, wait,' I said. 'I really need a cup of tea.

Let me go make us one and then we can get to the bottom of this.'

'Okay,' Frankie said.

In the kitchen, I gazed out the window as I waited for the kettle to boil. The drug-taking teens had gathered early today, talking their nonsense. The words from one of their tracks drifted up to me: *I'm here for a good time not a long time.*

What did they take? A few days ago I'd overheard a girl in the queue at the supermarket tell a friend that she'd been walking in Görlitzer Park one afternoon with her mother, 'a typical Scottish lady in her dress, a bit round, and with a string of pearls around her neck', and a dealer approached and offered to sell her some marijuana. It was nice that they didn't discriminate, the girl said to her friend.

I pushed open a window, and the air felt cool and inert without any sea-breeze to blow it around in this inland city. I thought of that skirmish I'd witnessed on my first day. The small struggle for power down below, as if everybody in the world was scuffling for their little bit of sway, whatever that amounted to. All these ways people were trying to make themselves feel better by making others feel worse. What was wrong with just being nice? It felt like something had happened to the world, to the way the world was being led at this time, that niceness had become the weaker deputy to personal advantage.

Back in the bedroom, Frankie had a magnifying mirror up in front of her face and was conducting a close inspection of her skin. She quickly put the mirror down to hold both cups while I climbed back in beside her. 'Quite often those boys call me pretty online,' she said, handing back one of the teas. 'Hello pretty. That's the most common opening line. What a beautiful smile you have. Some write that I have lovely eyes, even though I'm wearing sunglasses in my profile picture. Some of them think that God must have been working on his last angel when he made me. They say things like, Setting my eyes on your picture, my heart hushed, and my lips whispered what a goddess.'

'Does that ever work for them?' I let myself imagine them all as pandas and raccoons who'd somehow got themselves online and were either guilelessly fumbling their way towards their wants or sneaking around dark-eyed and alert to opportunity.

'I doubt it. One claimed I owed him ninety-nine cents because he had a Snickers bar in his pocket and when he gazed at my photo it melted. I delete all of those. Sometimes I respond to How's your day going? Or, You look interesting, will you talk to me?'

'And then...' I asked, never having had cause to choose which way to swipe in my own life.

Frankie explained it becomes addictive, and that if you are on dating apps too much you start to see the world in terms of that community. 'It's actually just a kind of microcosm,' she said. 'A set of people who're mostly just stepping up onto the carousel here and looking for hook-ups, not long-term relationships. And while they're looking for the next best thing, perhaps they have a vague idea in the back of their head that they might find something worthwhile, but nothing worthwhile comes as easily as hook-ups come on those apps. So, I meet up with them and I listen to them talk for hours. Mostly they're from somewhere else, possibly lonely in Berlin but not admitting it, in IT jobs or engineering jobs, or quite often working on their art project. They think it's exotic that I come from Australia. So far away, they always say. And usually: I've always wanted to go there. I tell them I think their country is exotic too. And at some stage they lean forward into a kiss. And then, as soon as they've finished the whole thing, they pull up their pants and leave and often I don't hear from them again. Not even, 'Thank you that was fun.'

'Really? So rude.' I worried, although I didn't say so, that it all sounded like letting piranhas tickle away at your toes until you look down and notice they have taken more than you bargained for.

'I know,' Frankie said. 'Honestly, I'm tired of it. What's that about? It's almost like when it's over they need to get out of there fast because they're starting to think, What kind of dirty girl lets me do this to her?'

Sunlight was creeping through the bedroom window, edging its way towards a pile of discarded clothing on the floor. 'Do you ever think about what you're really getting out of it yourself?'

Frankie took three long slow considered sips from her tea. 'Well, honestly, I think I get some sort of kick out of it all,' she said, but her voice contained some doubt. 'I think I like the feeling of being taken out of my own life and doing something without boundaries with somebody who has a different way of seeing the world. But then that one from the other day carries some secret disapproval or something, some buried anger, and drops an idea into the conversation to make you feel small.'

'Please don't let them make you feel small.'

'Okay,' Frankie said. She put down her cup and slid down the bed, bringing the duvet up to her chin. 'I guess it's sort of attached to the expat thing, the foreigner in a foreign town on some sort of search for a connection. Although sometimes lately I get stuck in a complicated cycle of thoughts about whether I'm pandering to some wolfish desire in these men. Or am I the wolf?'

Everybody has their phantom nag in some form or another, I realised. Some people take great lengths to keep themselves well out ahead of any Fionas from Townsend who have suburban domesticity nipping at their heels if the pace isn't kept up.

Frankie was pensive for a while and then added, as if this was the biggest confession of all, 'I keep having dreams that the German authorities find me hiding in my own bathroom, and they drag me into an interrogation room and ask about my association with that guy from Kosovo. I lie, and tell them we didn't have sex. I insist that he's making it up. They keep asking me questions, examining me for good character, deciding whether they'll let me stay. They tell me he is only fifteen in my dream.'

Further down the hallway the toilet flushed, and Frankie and I glanced at each other. Today we didn't have to worry about our shadowy one. Alive, at least.

'Would you ever do it?' Frankie asked.

'No, well. I don't think so. I sort of have somebody back home.' When Frankie described being taken out of her own life and doing something without boundaries, I'd felt a slight resonance, the possibility of this as a valid, broken way of launching into living without attachment to the future.

'What? Why's this the first time I am hearing about this?'

I couldn't answer.

'It's a man? What's he like?'

'He's kind. Very kind.'

'And?'

'I don't know. Right now, it's hard to talk about him.' I

got out of her bed and straightened the duvet in the place where I'd just been. 'Why do you think yours are mostly not from here?'

'Sometimes I think it's because the locals are harder to meet up with. They have their established lives, and their friends, and I guess in a city like this they've seen so many outsiders come and go they're a bit jaded about it. The decent ones prefer to stand back for a year or two to see if you're really going to stick around. But also the other thing is, I'm attracted to meeting people from places I haven't been to. I like it. You learn things about the world.'

'Like?'

'Well, like… Latin lover always find solution.'

What's he like? I went back to my own room, lay down, and hurt myself by imagining how I would even begin to explain him to Frankie. Honest as the day is long, I might say. That's what he's like. So honest that he is almost incapable of a compliment. If you ask him, say, How do I look? he will say something like, Fine, but I liked the dress you had on yesterday better than that one. If you laugh, and tell him he's the worst in the world at compliments, he will tell you the story of the time a girl asked him, on their second and final date, if he thought she had fat ankles and he said yes.

He never pretends to be fancy either, I could say. His idea of a relaxing time is to lie in bed and look at instructional chess videos online. Or sometimes he'll watch some American guy doing wood-working projects. He admires that guy because he even makes his own machining tools. He also likes to watch videos on micro apartments, which is not the same as tiny houses because those are usually about travellers' caravans or just ordinary caravans, and micro apartments are about clever use of space, where everything doubles as something else. If you point out how inconvenient it would be to have to refold the table every day so you could make it into a bed, he'll simply agree and carry on watching anyway. He really likes the idea of walls that shift, and he'll often say he'd be happy living in a house on wheels. If you point out that living in a house on wheels would be like living in a caravan, he'll nod his head in agreement.

And he was allowed to watch far too much television when he was a child. He will often make a conversational reference back to *Friends*. He'll say, That reminds me of the time Joey put a turkey on his head, or something like that. Often, you might know exactly the episode he's referring to, but will never tell him that, and instead say, Didn't your mother ever tell you to go outside and play some sports? I played sports, he'll say, with a defensive note in his voice, but it's cute that he's not afraid to be so uncool that he refers everything back to *Friends* in his head, and then says it out loud.

And when you're walking anywhere together, he'll always loop his arm in yours and that it isn't at all a signal to others of possession, it's only that he is very tactile and likes to be so near that he can quietly say stuff that might make you laugh. When you reach the side of the road, he'll say, *Careful*, and look both ways for both of you, because he knows that a person can be a bit dreamy and is known to nearly walk into the pathway of oncoming cars.

There are a lot of things he isn't, I could say, but there is one thing that's certain. He is the sort of man who can't be told the real reason the person he loves ran away. Because it's in his nature to insist on good possibilities, and once the person he loves lets him do that, they will not be able to resist him. So yes, the person that he loves might hurt him in the shorter term, and maybe even forever, but they won't be condemning him to the kind of marriage he didn't bargain for, and would never allow himself to imagine how unbearable it might be. But also, the person that he loves knows that in order to release him, at least until they can find the courage to work out which side of the half chance they fall on, they will have to strenuously tamp down the part of themselves that wants to have him loop his arm through theirs and say *Careful* forever.

Almost as if he knew I was thinking about him, he sent a message: *Thought you'd like to know I've bought a lathe and installed it in your office.*

9.

Bozorgmehr was once more sitting at a table at the café across the road. Outside so he could smoke, but sheltered against a wall. Over coffee I discovered he was from Shiraz, where his father was the curator at a museum, that he liked to slow cook his food, caressing it with spices, that he was looking for a new apartment because his current housemates didn't like how long he spent in the kitchen or the smell of his spices. He didn't consider himself religious, he said, although he had a fondness for the rituals, the 'unthinkingness of it', and he spoke not only his mother tongue, Farsi, but also English, French, German, some Arabic, enough Urdu and Kurdish to be understood, and passable Spanish. He sometimes worked as a translator, he said, and he didn't think there were enough words in other languages for all the expressions Germans had about their favourite thing, shit. He also had a bit of a rant about how he was beginning to hate the German word klar. 'This word of theirs,' he complained, 'they say it all the time. It means okay, it means I understand, it is a question, it can be aggressive, it can be casual. Klar, klar, klar. What is this fucking need for clarity all the time? It is very German.' He took a deep drag on his cigarette and then blew the smoke out towards the street with such a long, hard exhale it was as if he was trying to enact a minor form of civil disobedience.

Under his floppy fringe he had a faint, jagged scar on his forehead that cut through one eyebrow, bisecting his general aura of refinement and hinting at some sort of fugitive, street-level violence. I wanted to ask about it, the scar, but I also wanted to be careful about the curiosity I radiated. I'd once been to a reading by some international guest authors, and during the panel discussion afterwards a woman put up her hand and asked them to comment on the *diaspora*. The three authors, none of whom were particular experts on the subject, had all gulped and tried to mumble something intelligent, and I'd glanced over at the woman who'd asked the question, and was struck by the way her earnest face seemed to exude a repulsive greed for an important insight.

When I'd arrived at the café Boz had a newspaper spread out in front of him, and now in a lull in our conversation, he said, 'I was reading about these right-wing marches and so forth. Those neo-Nazis who think that foreigners are ruining their lives. There have been incidences where they chase people in the street and pick fights with those that look different.'

I nodded carefully. 'Does that make you uneasy?'

He smiled at me as if I was a bit simple, as if I should've known that he'd seen so much in his life it would take more than this to unsettle him. 'It says in this story that what is happening in these populist movements cannot be understood without knowing some of the history.'

'And that is… ?'

'A kind of complicated, broken pride, it says here. Saxony, for example, was one of the most industrialised economies here, the first to have a car factory, but after the war it became part of the GDR, and forty years of communism wore them down. When reunification happened they were made to feel like people in the West had rescued them from behind the wall, and they have this accent that other Germans like to make fun of. So now their young are abandoning their townships for better jobs elsewhere and parts of the population feel unappreciated and unable to get ahead and focus on this idea that the cause is too many foreigners.'

He folded up the newspaper. Now that he had summarised this for me, he had no further use for it, and placed it on the edge of the table, available to other customers. 'Have you ever met any of these neo-Nazis?' he said.

'Not really. Not officially.'

He smiled as he began rolling a cigarette. With the white filter in his mouth he said, 'I have.' He liked a little conversational drama. He left a sense of suspense hanging in the air as he completed the first rollie and started on a second. 'I was visiting at a university down south of here,' he began, licking down the seam of the second. 'I had gone for a few days to volunteer on an archaeological dig. I spent some time helping brush dirt away from old pieces of leather, scraps of pottery. Afterwards some of us went for a drink in a pub. A nice German girl, a couple of guys and me. There was a bunch of these skinheads there. They kept looking over at me. After a while one of them started asking me questions, but I pretended I didn't understand. He switched to English. Why was I there? Where had I come from? When I said I was from Iran he said, Ahh – Aryan! and hitched up his trousers to show me a tattoo on his leg. The girl ushered us all out of there. It was funny – she was the only one who reacted. The two guys did nothing. Just sat there with their beers, looking into space.'

'What was he trying to show you?' I asked as he handed me a cigarette and a lighter.

'You do not know this connection? The Persians were the original Aryans. Those Nazis have a relationship with this. They wanted to show me a symbol.'

Three young people slumped down at the table next to us and started talking loudly about visiting Bowie's house later that day, as if he was a mate they were going to drop in on, as if they wanted other people to hear. I mentioned to Boz that I was going on a research trip soon.

'Where to?' he asked.

I told him I intended to visit the place where Count von Luckner had lived in Halle. 'There is a trail you can do around the city – the house he grew up in, the shop where he used to buy his cigars, that sort of thing. I thought I might wander around to see if I get inspired.'

It was a surprise when Boz, who had only ever asked about my work in the manner of an indifferent academic asking a student what she was going to do for her end-of-term essay, said, 'Ahh, this weird Count of yours. Might I come along?'

'Do you really want to? It's in Saxony.'

'Yes,' he said. 'I will enjoy to see what will happen.'

We checked out schedules on my phone, opting for the bus, mostly because it was substantially cheaper than the train, which mattered only in that Boz made no particular move towards contributing to any fare.

As he stood to go, he said, 'Do you know that in 2004 the German football team came to Azadi Stadium in Tehran for the first time. Some Iranians tried to show their connection to the opposition by doing the Hitler salute. It was a big scandal. And so embarrassing for us.' Then he added, 'Tschüss,' and walked off down the road.

10.

The gene that causes Huntington's disease was identified in 1993 but as yet there is no cure. However, there are several approved therapies to help manage symptoms and maintain patients' quality of life. Furthermore, research is continuing into the mechanism of the disease, which could lead to the development of new and innovative treatments. There are a number of experimental therapies currently being investigated in clinical trials...

'What are you up to?' Mel asked on the phone.

'Just looking at some research online.'

'Sounds boring. Feel like coming shopping with me? Jonah's coming over from London soon and he wants to take me to a... club. I need something special.'

We met up at a shop that was laid out in two halves. One side was dedicated to sex toys that ranged from obviously useful to quite alarming, and on the other was wearable gear – black leather, straps, latex and lace. The assistant was extremely brisk, a little scary and utterly no-nonsense in her suggestions. Mel picked a latex dress off the rack. Caught up in the spirit of things, I began sizing up an only slightly more tasteful brocade bodice for myself.

As Mel was struggling into the dress in the changing room, she said, 'It's not that I don't want you to come, or anything, it's just that we're sort of hoping to try having, ah, you know, sex there together, so...'

'Yeah, I get it. I don't want to see that.' I put the bodice back on the rack. I hadn't really intended to invite myself along but now I wasn't even going to pretend anything.

Mel emerged from behind the curtain, and we both grimaced. She was tall and lithe, but the latex clung to her in an unflattering way.

'Did you want to be a sort of fetish cliché?' I asked.

'Not really,' she said. 'And this horror is so fucking hot already I don't know how anybody could enjoy wearing it.'

'Is enjoyment the point?'

Across the road was a smaller boutique dedicated to the corset. The assistant here seemed more interested in how to make a person look sexy. She took a tape out of her pocket, measured Mel's bust and waist, and then went out the back to find a piece for her to try.

'Couldn't you just make something?' I asked, after looking at some of the price tags.

'Hell no,' Mel said. 'I don't want to spend my down time sewing. Also, I don't have a machine here. And also, it's just not exciting.'

The woman came back with a corset that boosted, but didn't cover, the breast area – allowing for the option to go completely tits out or to wear a lacy bra underneath. While Mel tried it on, I went outside and sat on the front sill to wait.

After Mel left home, she'd offer up glimpses of the life she was living. She had girlfriends, she had boyfriends, she was singing in a band, she was going on a yoga retreat in Bali, she'd become vegan, she was starting up a fair-trade clothing label, she was performing as a character in a friend's music video, she was learning 3D design, she got a scholarship, she got a tattoo, she got more tattoos, she got a piercing that she wasn't going to show, or I could see it if I wanted to but I probably didn't want to, she got a job in

Wardrobe on a short film, on a feature film, on the *Lord of the Rings* set, she was moving to London, she won an award, now there was a reputation, jobs were coming more easily, somebody – who again? – convinced her to invest in a cheap Berlin apartment, she had girlfriends, she had boyfriends, what were their names again, this one took her to Paris, this one fucked her on a beach in Greece, this one was always asking her to bring along a girlfriend, this one wanted to take her to get her nipples pierced, this one got her a strap-on. Lately such things were dropped in a tone of voice that implied this was all so regular, and living with a guy who liked to watch chess videos for pleasure was not.

A woman biked past towing a wooden box on wheels containing two small twins and an older kid who stared at me balefully as they passed.

It occurred to me that Mel and Frankie might have more in common than I had with either of them. But then again Mel's drive was actually quite different from Frankie's. Frankie was the latecomer, inventing a new self, forcing herself out of her own conventional tendencies with… what?… this new identity so open and explorative and self-searching that it was most definitely a freshly adopted thing. Mel on the other hand had always had some form of perverse resistance in her system. Bucking against moderation wasn't anything she thought about, or named, it was just part of her nature, part of the flow.

After a long while, Mel came out in a garment that was fitting, understated, flattering, and with just the right amount of strappiness and buckle to be only suggestive of discipline.

'That one is sex on legs, Mistress,' I said.

'God, it feels great too. Everything is lifted in the right kind of way.'

It cost hundreds of euros, but Mel just shrugged and said she would get a lot of wear out of it.

As she took my arm and steered me towards Galeria Kaufhof at Alexanderplatz, where she had yet another item to buy, fishnet stockings, she remembered to ask how the research was going for my book.

'I don't know,' I replied. 'I'm beginning to regret the whole thing.'

'Why?'

Mel felt she had at least a tiny amount of investment in the project because she had joined me on a research trip when I had first begun thinking about the idea. She'd come back home to take up a short-term job in Christchurch as a favour for an old friend, and I had flown down to visit her and to take a side excursion to a nearby island where the Count had been briefly confined. Ferries to the island were cancelled after the earthquake, but an official told me 'off the record' it was possible to scramble over rocks to get to it at low tide. And in the green barracks building at the back, he'd said, I could see some writing on the wall in von Luckner's hand. 'But be careful of any loose wrought iron,' he added. 'And I didn't tell you any of this.'

Mel offered to drive me there on her one day off from the shoot, but as soon as we set off it became apparent that she wasn't exactly an indefatigable accomplice. Just outside Lyttelton she pulled the car over and said, 'Do you see how far we'll have to drive? That's Diamond Harbour on the other side over there, and we'll have to wind right around this coast. And who knows if we can even get across to Ripapa when we get there?' She would've preferred to turn around and order a chardonnay from a cosy wine bar in Lyttelton.

'I really want to try,' I said meekly, and Mel huffed the

car into gear and drove on through all the lonely little bays on the leeward side of a range. The late-afternoon sun was glinting off cottage windows behind us, and though it was all quite beautiful, Mel chose not to notice, complaining instead about the job she was on – 'They're s'posed to look like a community of pure Mennonite types that have risen up out of the rubble and chaos, so the whole thing is starching and bleaching these friggin' white dresses ready for another day running around in the mud.'

We drove for forty minutes, down past Diamond Harbour, and could see the tiny island jutting off the shore across an inlet. Where the road forked at the bay we weren't sure which direction to take, so we stopped and I got out of the car to ask a man walking his dog on the shoreline. 'And can you get across to the island at low tide?' I asked.

'I don't think so,' he replied, but when I got back in the car I told Mel that he'd said it might be possible. Finally, all hope was dashed when we discovered there was a farm on the headland between the road and Ripapa Island, and it was surrounded by a six-foot-high deer fence. When the official had said 'scramble around the rocks', he must have meant the approximately two-kilometre coastal walk from the bay to the head of the peninsula.

'I'm game,' I said, but Mel said, 'That's totally bats. It'll be dark by the time we get there and imagine if we got trapped by the tide on the way back. You'll have to come back another time. Hire a kayak, I reckon.' We drove back to the other side of the bay, got out of the car and looked across at the island and its tin sheds, and I told Mel about one of the Count's bizarre escape plans. How he was going to throw himself into the channel in an oil barrel, and when a ship came alongside and took him on board he was going to somehow pop out with a knife in his hand and seize control. Mel shivered in the wind and said, 'Crazy talk. Mad old bastard, I can see why you like him.'

Now as we stood outside Galeria Kaufhof I could only reluctantly answer her question.

'It turns out the Count had quite the talent for exaggeration,' I said.

'Like what? What did he exaggerate? Did that whole daring escape from… what island was it again? Did that not happen?'

'No, that definitely did happen.'

'So what?' Mel asked. 'What did he exaggerate?'

Could I explain it to Mel, who'd gone to Seville to work in the Wardrobe department of an English-language drama that was set in the Spanish Civil War but who couldn't sum up the film's storyline for me? 'Okay. There was this, for example. Before they first got captured, when they were still marauding in the Pacific, some of their crew were starting to show signs of scurvy, so they headed for one of the Society Islands to restock. They found this atoll where there were a couple of locals and an island full of fruit, and wild pigs, and coconuts, and decided to all go ashore on lifeboats for a jolly picnic, but while they were away from the ship the wind changed and, because they had anchored badly, the ship scraped against the coral and was wrecked.'

'Oh no. But that wasn't true?'

'No, it was true. But he claimed that a forty-foot tsunami had come along and dashed them on the reef.'

'Come on! That's fantastic. I love that. Especially that he must've decided that if he was going to lie, he had to lie big. A forty-foot tsunami, that's fun!'

'I know. Apparently a one-and-a-half metre tsunami

was documented there years later and it swamped the whole island.'

'But is that so bad?' Mel asked. 'As exaggerations go, you can surely work with that somehow. It's typical of him, isn't it?'

I had not told her everything yet. The unsettling, unclear accusations of sexual misdemeanours. But more, how lately I couldn't stop myself thinking about how the history of history had mostly been written by men for an audience of men, and so the history of history revered great feats, and the more I sat with this sailor's story of men amongst men, the more I thought about all those greats atop their pedestals while the women sat around their feet with lyres and their breasts exposed to all the wandering hands.

'So what else?' Mel said. 'That doesn't sound like much. What is actually bothering you? You do seem kind of… tighter than usual.'

'Tighter than usual?' I repeated.

The security guard who was standing in the alley between the outer weather door and the inner store door was staring at us.

'So?'

'Well, there is something quite big I…'

'Are you doing that thing you used to do?'

'What thing? What are you talking about?'

'That thing you used to do before you met Jay, where you stayed in your pyjamas all day and let your house get really messy, and obsessed over what you were writing and kept asking me if I thought you were wasting your time, until finally I felt cornered enough to say that maybe you were, and then you'd slam everything into reverse and start defending your shit, saying I didn't understand anything.'

'I used to do that? Before I met Jay?'

'Yes, you did,' Mel said. 'Don't you even remember?'

I sighed. 'Meet up with me after you've been to that club with Jonah? Tell me what it was like?'

'What is this? Vicious living?'

We both laughed. A standing joke of ours, derived from one of Lorelei's many malapropisms. We had collected others into our private glossary too. Being made an escape goat. It's a doggie dog world. For all intensive purposes. It's not rocket surgery.

'Promise?'

'Oh, okay.'

11.

I didn't feel like going back to my laptop, so I walked and walked until I came to a line of rusted metal poles, trace representation of the former wall, start of the Berlin Wall Memorial or, as the plaque said, the Monument in Memory of the Divided City and the Victims of Communist Tyranny. There were information ports scattered throughout the park, and by the time I climbed up the metal tower at the visitor centre on Bernauerstrasse to look across at one of the few sections left standing, I'd come to understand that it hadn't been a single wall. There was the familiar concrete construction that faced West Berlin, and many metres back there was a signal fence that set off an alarm when touched. In between had been the death strip, overlooked by watchtowers with searchlights and trigger-happy twenty-year-olds with Kalashnikovs. The Anti-Fascist Protection Rampart, as it was known in the GDR, seemed so crazy and overzealous now. Those increasingly cruel methods to prevent comrades crossing towards capitalist decadence. Carpets of steel spikes, trip wires, automatic guns, patrols of unfed dogs.

On the other side of the road I put my hand on the grey concrete that had once been the west face of the wall, and thought about a school-leavers party a long time ago in Titirangi, and the guy who lived there showing off the prized chunk of nondescript concrete that his father reckoned he had chipped off in the eighties with a Swiss Army knife.

A few of us had crowded around to look, impressed, even though the chunk itself was so undistinguished it could just as easily have been chipped off the low concrete wall in the back garden. We were all such innocents – living in an island nation about as far from Berlin as it was possible to get. We'd still been children when the wall came down, and had only a rough idea of its menace or even its purpose.

Further down towards Nordbahnhof I stood looking at all the faces of people who had perished trying to cross over, their photos set into a cast-iron frame in date order. At the eighties end were the mostly young men who couldn't have known it would be possible to wait until the end of the decade for freedom. All those boys with hair down to their collars, their eyes animated and searching, looking like they wanted to be in a rock band, to wander distant lands, to just smoke pot and follow their every whim. An English-speaking guide wearing a bright yellow beanie came up beside me with his small group and began recounting some individual stories. He pointed to the impish face of one of the few girls there, young Marienetta Jirkowsky, explaining that she had tried to escape with her boyfriend, Peter, and another friend. 'So they snuck out at night and used a folding ladder to scale the signal fence near Hohen Neuendorf S-Bahn,' he told his group. 'She was the last one to go over but she accidentally triggered the alarm. They ran, shots were fired from a watchtower, but the two men still managed to get the ladder over to the outer wall and drop down. Marienetta's boyfriend leaned back over to help her because she was too short to grasp the top of the concrete. Some border soldiers ran towards them, firing their guns, and she fell off the ladder and later died in hospital from a bullet through her abdomen.'

'Died! Oh, sad story,' somebody said.

As I walked away I kept thinking about that dash for the wall. Leaving everything known behind. Risking imprisonment, demoralisation, death. What was courage anyway? Did it rise up out of some kind of counter-pressure? In Marienetta's case, the counter of having to live a limited life when you were essentially free-spirited. The courage of not doing nothing?

The Count, when he was lauded, was lauded for his courage: his legendary trip across the Pacific in a small lifeboat with a skeleton crew after his ship was wrecked, disguising themselves as Norwegians and making it all the way from the Society Islands to Fiji. But was it courage or necessity? The raconteur's counter-pressure of being otherwise obliged to live a life of unbearable oblivion among the bountiful pigs and coconuts?

And what then was the opposite of courage? Defeat? To surrender to the circumstances? Remain behind the rampart. To exclaim, per Dieu, we are lost! Although, thinking about it, maybe there was a kind of courage in that too. To take in information, assess, refine, summon up some resolution in the face of absolute defeat. To accept being escorted to the brig, and just summoning up the dignity and grace to survive.

Perhaps courage exists, or not, in your blood as a sort of DNA largesse. Have they found the gene for that one already? If I let myself believe in that, then I would have to consider that maybe I, the girl who couldn't even confront her own father about her mother's suicide, probably did not have that particular gene. And if I looked further back, then it was hard to see the courage gene in the previous generation, with a mother who couldn't summon up the will to live, and a father who would rather drink himself to death than talk about the past.

By the next morning I was beginning to intensely dislike this idea that I probably lacked the courage gene. Maybe there was another way of looking at such things. Perhaps suicide, my mother's suicide, was actually – within her difficult frame of reference – an act of daring.

The confused climate was giving off another erratic spike of fine weather – warmer, I thought, than anyone could reasonably expect this time of year when the days were getting noticeably shorter. I opened the doors to the balcony and stood outside.

Christoph, who was up above on his own balcony, leaned over his balustrade and said, 'Hallo. Nice day.' I agreed, and he added, 'How spontaneous are you feeling? A swim in Krumme Lanke? Meet downstairs in ten?'

'A swim? You're joking. Won't the water be cold?'

'Last chance of the year? Let's just call it bracing. Good for you.'

I went back into the bedroom to put my bathing suit on under my clothes, doubtful he'd be able to persuade me to go in. Ahh, but courage.

On the U-Bahn we sat side by side in the carriage, facing the other passengers, and I asked him what he actually did at the film archive.

'Well,' he said, 'for example, lately I have been cataloguing everything from Jürgen Böttcher for a small film festival.'

'And he was?'

'He is a painter, but also made documentaries for DEFA.'

'DEFA?'

'The film studios of the GDR. He also made one feature

film, *Jahrgang 45*, about a couple who are considering a divorce and idle their time away around the streets of Prenzlauer Berg. It wasn't released at the time because the Party banned it. They locked it up in storage.'

At the next stop a woman got on and took the seat next to me. She seemed to arrive in a cloud of sweet rose perfume and was wearing high strappy stilettos, unusual footwear on the U-Bahn.

'That must have been devastating,' I said to Christoph. 'But it's been seen now?'

'Yes. It was shown for the first time just after re-unification.'

'Why exactly did they ban it?'

'Well, it was sort of about the generational war in the 1960s. When he showed the rough cut to the Party, they became angry and decided that the film was antisocial and did not properly reflect the youth of the GDR. He once said that a Party functionary shouted at him, We don't have slums! and he replied, But it was filmed around the streets where I live in Berlin.'

The train pulled into the next stop, and two men wearing bulky jackets over their cotton tunics stepped into the crowded carriage. There was only one seat left, opposite us, so one of the men commanded the other to sit, and he went and stood near the door. The standing man seemed jumpy, edgy.

'He wasn't even allowed to show it to the people who were in the film,' Christoph continued. 'One of the characters was played by his next-door neighbour, another by a DEFA driver. When it got banned, he found out that some of them felt like they were just humouring him and they never really expected it to be released.'

The man seated across the aisle, the one who had obeyed the command to sit, had a wall eye and misshapen posture, and sweat was beading on his lip as he sat in the overheated carriage in his ill-fitting jacket. Were they brothers, perhaps? The standing one resentfully tasked with having to look after the less able one?

'So did he try to leave after that?'

Christoph didn't answer immediately. 'You know, not everybody tried to get out,' he eventually said.

I could feel myself blushing. His reply made me feel naïve. 'Is that just a very Western view?'

'Well, he grew up in postwar Germany. There was a lot to try to understand and come to terms with. As a young man he went from his village to Dresden to study art. Can you imagine what Dresden still looked like in the fifties? It had been totally bombed out at the end of the war.'

The train lurched briefly and the man standing near the door swayed on the vertical strap he was holding on to.

'He was fourteen when the war ended. He'd been one of those boys who had worn a uniform and gone to see the weekly Nazi Party reels, and then at the end he could see more clearly that they had been part of a gang of thugs. And from where he lived, they could look further east into Poland and Lithuania, those countries where all the killings had occurred, and he felt, he said, a certain kind of responsibility to atone. I think he thought it was more enriching to stay,' Christoph added, 'and try to understand hard things than to just go off to the West to make money.'

The sickly–sweet perfume of the woman next to me overlaid the general smell of body odour on the carriage. A post I'd seen on Free Advice Berlin had once asked why nobody wore deodorant on public transport in Berlin. Some people said they did use deodorant, but they avoided ones with aluminium because this causes breast cancer and unfortunately the others don't work that well. One person suggested it was cos Germans didn't wash every day, and tempers flared and they were hounded for prejudice and ignorance and told to go back to wherever they came from. It all began to get angry, and others said it was because the trains were full of stupid, sweaty tourists. One person said that she took some deodorant on the train with her and sprayed it all around herself. This attracted some strange looks, she said, but she didn't care.

'I think I would like to see that film,' I said.

'You can come to the archive one day if you like,' Christoph offered.

As the train was slowing for the next stop, the standing man signalled for his companion to come to the door. He took a set of prayer beads out of his pocket and wrapped them around the other's hands.

The woman next to me put her hand warningly on my arm. 'Oh my God, brace yourself, it's happening.' Her voice got louder. 'It's happening, it's happening. What shall we do? Oh my God. I can't believe it. It's happening.'

Everybody looked at her, then followed her line of sight to the two men. The train pulled into the station, the doors opened, and they got off.

The woman, embarrassed now, said, 'It could happen like that. You are on a train and two men get on. I mean, you could see, couldn't you, that they were from... from... somewhere else. They could've blown us all up.' She was addressing these comments directly to Christoph and me in English. 'I'm a doctor,' she went on, loud enough for the whole carriage to hear. 'I've worked with refugees and most of them are very nice, very humble, but some of them, they have problems... and it was what he was wearing, that baggy jacket, and, well, some people you can see are just fat in a normal way—' She waved her hand towards a man sitting opposite who had a big round stomach, and an uncomfortable expression of hurt came over his face. 'But that baggy jacket,' she went on. 'That's the sort of thing you might wear if you had explosives underneath. And then did you see the other man put the prayer beads in his hand. They do that, don't they? They get a man who is a bit simple and they put the explosives on him and detonate him. I don't mean to overreact but, don't you think?'

A heavy silence fell over the carriage. Everybody, including Christoph and I, averted their eyes. The train slowed for the next station, and the woman got up and stood near the door, swaying unsafely in her high heels. As the doors opened, she turned back to stare at the two of us with something like accusation before stepping out.

We got off at the last stop and began walking towards the lake. 'I suppose that is how it happens,' I commented to Christoph. 'You're on a carriage and somebody does something that you don't want to believe is about to be a terrorist action. Next thing, blown up.'

'Yeah, I was once on a train where a guy was frantically chanting and sweating and swaying. I sat there wondering if I should get off.'

'But you didn't?'

'It put me into an existential dilemma, truthfully. What if I had got off and said nothing and the train was blown up. How guilty would you feel? But then again, what if I had got off and found somebody and reported it and they had stopped the train and the guy just turned out to have a travel-anxiety disorder? I would just end up looking like a racist.'

'So you?'

'Well, I was running late, so… and I'm still here, so…'

It's indiscriminate, the world. You might be tortured to death by a disease or you could just as easily be taken out suddenly.

'Did you see the look on that man's face when she pointed at him and said some people are just fat?'

'Completely ruined that poor guy's day.'

We reached the lake, long and narrow and completely fringed by trees that were now tending towards yellow and brown. The water itself had a greenish tinge that made it look cold.

'Left for FKK?' Christoph said.

'What do you mean?'

'FKK, textile free.'

'Textile free? You mean naked?'

'Genau,' Christoph smirked. 'Too soon for that?'

'I think it might always be too soon for that.'

Christoph laughed. 'Klar. Wouldn't want to make you do anything you didn't want to do, but…' He steered me towards the left anyway. 'It's optional.'

As we walked down the path I imagined what it might be like. Christoph and I taking off all our clothes. Introducing my naked body to him. Seeing his. He had implied he'd be fine with it, and my feeling was that he'd suggested it more for the sake of introducing me to a German habit than for contriving to get me naked. But still, I wanted to keep some distance between us, to keep this uncomplicated, at a friend level.

We selected a spot between some scrubby trees, in an area with few other people. I took my time spreading out a towel before I sat down, while Christoph flopped down on the bare soil.

'I've developed a morbid fear of ticks,' I told him.

Christoph peered around. 'Too late for me. Hopefully they are hibernating already.' He began taking things out of his backpack. Two beers, some bread rolls, cheese slices, a small tub of sauerkraut and some Fairtrade chocolate.

'I didn't realise we were picnicking. I didn't even think to bring food.'

'I think lake, I think picnic,' Christoph said. 'Just grabbed a quick snack from the fridge.'

I liked Christoph's capacity to indulge in every experience with an abundance of ease. He used his keys to flip the caps off the beers. He tore open the bread rolls, used his fingers to stuff them with cheese and sauerkraut, giving one to me and biting into the other himself. A little further down from us an elderly couple were taking off all their clothes – the woman folded her own underwear and then folded his. We were careful not to look too closely at them as they waded into the water as if this was something they made a point of doing every day. They had a small dog that stood on the shore, its cries getting more anxious the further out they swam.

When we had finished our beers, Christoph said, 'Alles gut?' He pulled off his shirt, revealing a tangle of chest hair so lush that I immediately wanted to brush my hand through it. His left nipple was pierced, and he had a tattoo on his shoulder. Lately I had been thinking of language ability as a secret power that reveals itself only in certain circumstances. You are sitting next to someone and suddenly they break from one language into another. They carry that ability quietly within them. Christoph's piercing felt like another dimension of that. A symbol of some secret urges.

'Sollen wir?' Christoph said.

I took a deep interest in the trees to the left of us as Christoph threw off the rest of his clothes and made a quick dash into the water. Once he was submerged I slipped off my outer clothes but kept my bathing suit on, not quite ready for communal nakedness just yet.

I navigated the squishy shoreline, the weeds and the small fish darting about, and lowered myself into the water, squeaking in surprise at the iciness of it. As I swam towards Christoph, he dived under the surface and emerged shaking water off his head. He grunted with pleasure, and I began breaststroking further out to keep warm. Christoph came up beside me, matching my stroke. He didn't comment on the fact that I was so prudish I had chosen to leave my swimsuit on.

'Where are we heading, Captain?' he said.

'Oblivion,' I replied.

Halfway between the opposite shores of the narrow lake, completely surrounded by trees, blueness up above and only a few other distant bathers and the odd duck for company, we stopped and trod water so opaque it was impossible to see anything below the surface.

'Can I ask you a question?' I said.

'Better do,' Christoph replied.

'If you found out your life was going to be foreshortened, would you live differently?'

Christoph slowed for a moment, looked hard at me, and then began turning himself around in the water, around and around, taking in the three-sixty-degree view. I remained a few metres away from him, briskly moving my arms and legs to stay afloat and to keep my blood pumping in the cold. Around he went, around and around.

'Interessant,' he said eventually, not stopping, as if the circles he was turning were helping him formulate his thoughts. 'How short? Are we talking instant death on the train back, oder...'

'Say five to ten good years left.'

'Ah,' he said.

I kept my eyes on the distant shore rather than risk looking directly at Christoph.

'I think my ambition might change,' he said.

'How?'

'I'm trying to figure it out. Either I would start to think about legacy and become obsessed with my epic project, or—'

'Or?'

'I might start to not give a fuck.'

'So which, do you think?'

He stopped turning, started floating on his back instead, his arms flapping loosely at his sides. I rolled over and did the same, floating at an opposing angle so that I was not in view of the parts of him that were now breaching the surface. 'I'm not sure,' he said. 'I think it would take time to adjust to it. But just even thinking about that tightens the sphincter a little. It's an interesting question, because it makes you consider what really matters in your life. I mean, I work in film but only tangentially. When I was much younger my ambition was not so much restoration but making. But now I have worked with so many forgotten pieces of the past that I've lost some of that passion because I struggle with the futility of it all.'

My body was a prickly field of goosebumps and it was taking more effort to keep afloat than I was used to in the sea. Above us, airplane trails criss-crossed a sky that was otherwise devoid of blemishes.

'And relationships? What do you think would happen

there?' I asked, hoping I was successfully portraying it as a random inquiry.

'I think that might go two ways as well.'

'As in?'

'You would really have to decide, wouldn't you? What kind of person are you? I think some people might burrow down with their families and become more loving. They would want to leave their legacy there, be remembered or even missed as a good, kind, loving person. They would want to believe they made a contribution.'

'Some people? Not you?'

'I can't really say, but I think I might go the other way.'

'Which is?'

'Absolute hedonism. I am a bit already, I guess, but that would make me... try everything, experience everything, burn up my entire life in the time I have left. Und du?'

Absolute hedonism. We were now floating head to head, our bodies angled away from each other. What was that exactly? Seek pleasure, avoid suffering. Try everything, do everything. Exhibitionist sex in nightclubs? Or casual encounters with foreigners? Giving in to the urge to brush your hand through chest hair? Never feel guilt? Live like there is no shaky tomorrow?

'I guess there are two kinds of people in the world,' I said. 'The kind who easily dive right in. You might be that kind. And the other.'

He flipped back over and looked at me.

'Go on,' he said. 'Put your head under. I dare you.'

'Nah, I'm okay.' I rolled over onto my stomach for the swim back to shore, wondering if we had actually been negotiating something else between us. He had dared me, I had declined, now we both knew where we stood.

Between the trees on the bank I performed a brisk under-towel manoeuvre to get out of my wet togs and into my clothes, the lake's chill having reached my bones. Christoph, who was also pulling on his clothes, but with much less modesty, said, 'Why did you ask that? You're not—?'

'Oh, just curious,' I replied.

On the train on the way home, Christoph, who if he had had any other intent for the day seemed content now to just acquiesce to friendship, said, 'Did I tell you what happened to the boss of a mate of mine when he went to buy a new car...'

'Do you want to hear an amusing story?' I said to Jay online. 'I'm not sure if it's true. The person who told me said that it happened to the boss of a friend of his.'

'Aha,' Jay said. 'Proceed.'

'So, there is this place in Germany called Wolfsburg where you can go and pick up your brand-new Volkswagen, and they will give you a tour of the factory and so forth.'

'Yes, I actually have heard about that before.'

'Really?' Some men know amazing details about iconography of bands and musicians, and others know things about worldwide car manufacturing. 'So, this guy from somewhere in Rhineland decided to take his family along on an outing. After they picked up the car, they opted to take it on a spin further up north to celebrate, and they went to a safari park. Anyway, it was the kind of park where you can drive through the animal compounds, and they stopped the car to have a look at the elephants, and one came right up to the window and put its trunk into the back seat. Their little daughter screamed and panicked and wound up the window, trapping the elephant's trunk, which also made the elephant panic, so it started kicking the side of the car.'

'Really? The new car?' Jay was feeling the pain.

'Yep. Of course after that their nerves were shattered, so they decided to stay in a hotel overnight before driving back home. The father was especially beside himself about the dents in his brand-new SUV, so he went down to the hotel bar and had quite a few drinks. The next morning they set off, but somehow they ended up in a terrible Karambolage, as they call it here, a nose-to-tail affecting a lot of cars. They had been crunched in the front and the back.'

'Oh man.'

'Precisely. Eventually the police came down the line to take details of the accident, and they took a careful look at the car's brand-new registration and the dents on the side. This is surely not caused by this accident, the policeman said. And without thinking, the father said, No, an elephant did that. The policeman looked harder at him and pulled out his breath tester, which the father failed because he had drunk so much the night before, so now his whole insurance was voided.'

'Ha, oh my,' Jay said. 'That's quite a bad day.'

'Yup.' I had hoped to make him laugh out loud, but he was too tense for that.

'Is that really true?'

'Well, it was not a first-hand account.'

'Who told you?'

'This guy Christoph who lives upstairs.'

'Ah,' Jay said carefully. 'Christoph sounds like a character.' It was a question.

'Nothing for you to worry about.'

12.

The acquisition of knowledge is both random and accumulative. If you hadn't asked speculatively for a linking idea between two countries, you might never have heard of the Count. If you didn't travel to Berlin you might never have a reason to find out that a sign with FKK on it invites you to take off all your clothes at a lakeside. If you hadn't this morning looked up how genetic testing works you might never know that there are three DNA building blocks labelled CAG, and that a person who has an extension of over 40 on a certain gene will develop Huntington's disease, and a person who has more than 26 but fewer than 40 is in a grey zone, or rather 36–39 may or may not get it in their lifespan, and 27–35 do not have a risk of developing it but might pass it on. And if you stopped staring at these numbers long enough to go to the café across the road for the promised debrief, but somehow your head had been shifted towards seeing the world in terms of flailing exaggerations of genes, then you might also begin to think that your stepsister had a greater extension than you of whatever gene it is that pitches a person towards hedonism.

Mel arrived with Perry, some guy who had been the assistant to the sound operator on that film she'd worked on down in Christchurch. He was wearing braces, possibly as an affectation, or perhaps more simply to hitch up his trousers. They had the effect of pulling everything so tight and close around his crotch that the first impression was that he had a huge bulge and was proud of it. He was from Blenheim originally, he said, had decided he needed a break from everything and was passing through.

'So how was it?' I asked.

Mel turned to Perry. 'What did you think?'

So, she had taken this guy with her? This casual acquaintance?

'I'm not sure about it,' Perry said. 'I had a good time. I danced like a maniac, and I had a swim in the pool, and there was tons to look at, and girls were giving me a lot of looks, but…'

'But… ?'

'The thing is that going in I kind of had the idea that I would have sex maybe four or five times.'

'And you didn't?'

He had the slightly goggled-eyed look of someone who'd newly caught a bug – the kind of thing that might happen when a person flies in from a small New Zealand town and finds the city is full of people who have come here to get a taste of personal freedom and that you can swipe left or right without coming to an end of offerings. Frankie's bug. Even in this café, his eyes were sliding over every person there, rating them on his wide-open scale of possibilities.

'Nah, no luck. A few times, when girls were checking me out, I went over and asked them what they were looking for.'

'Straight out, like that?'

'Yeah. Straight out. Like, I'd ask them if they were looking for sex tonight, but they didn't seem interested.'

'You didn't try opening with something like, I noticed you from across the room, or I really like your rubber gear, or something like that?'

'Nah, well, it's a sex club. I thought it was best just to

be kind of straight up,' he said with a good amount of sangfroid for someone fresh out of Blenheim.

'Is it actually a sex club?' I asked Mel.

'No, it's just a club that has a permissive attitude to sex and fetish,' she said.

'I think even in a permissive club,' I said to Perry, 'a person might want to feel something more than just that they were being targeted for sex by some random guy, maybe.'

Perry was staring into my face. He seemed to be deciding that he hated me. Up until that moment, he may have been congratulating himself on his own bravery. He may not have been successful but at least he had gone out there and front-footed the whole thing. Now I was just pissing all over his technique.

Mel was being quiet for once. She reluctantly admitted that she hadn't had a good time. Some of the men were too pushy. They were sleazy. Some of them would come and rub themselves against her but were dead behind the eyes. 'It takes time to fully get the rules of engagement in those kinds of places,' she said.

'Did you have sex with Jonah there?'

'Yeah. That was the point. Well, he wanted to anyway.'

'So, was it a turn-on? Having people watch?' I was trying to keep anything that could be interpreted as me sifting Mel's experience out of my voice.

'While we were doing it, a guy came up and put his cock in my hand.'

'What? Eww. What did you do?'

Perry was smirking.

'What do you think? I stared at him in such a dick-shrivelling way that he rethought his plan.' Mel's voice had a detached brusqueness, like she was making it plain that she believed in the right to be overtly sexual, and that she could easily conjure the sovereignty, if she was in the mood, not to be sleazed upon.

'Could you not just have batted the thing away?'

'Yep, probably.'

How did it all work, I wondered. Do a couple do it quietly in a corner, or do they do it in the middle of a circle of voyeurs, or is there a special room where everybody does it together? I thought of those actors on stage for *Die Fledermaus*, stroking and singing and pretending to hump and lick.

'I'm going up to order us more coffees,' Perry said with an intentionally licentious look on his face, putting out his tongue and panting like a dog. Mel and I turned to see two young women up at the counter. Mel looked over at me, biting her lip. Perry hadn't had enough sleep yet to separate this street café from the club he'd just emerged from. As he sauntered towards his targets, it was hard not to feel he was letting our side down – or the whole nation, in fact.

'Shall we go?' Mel said, and we quickly gathered our things and slipped out the rear door before Perry had time to notice we were gone. As we hurried up the street, I said, 'But the coffees…'

'Fuck him. Dickhead. Type 4.' Mel liked to rate people she decided she didn't like on the scale of the Bristol Stool Chart that used to hang in the sick bay of our old school. Every former pupil knew it by heart. Type 4, like a sausage or snake.

Even as teenagers Mel had introduced me to the seamier side of the suburb we grew up in. The lecherous old guy in the second-hand bookstore who'd comment on her school uniform and tell her she was very naughty and needed to be spanked. And the boss in the clothing shop she worked in on Saturday mornings, who liked to corner her in the storeroom and say, 'Show me your tits,' and she would lift her top and let him tweak her nipples so much that she would be 'wet' when serving customers. Always laughed off as some brand of crazy adventure. But she also knowingly instilled in me the wide-eyed impression that the alternative universe – the one where adults were conducting sexual acts – was a craven, difficult, oily world that I didn't have the strength for. Mel was slightly older than me, prettier, and braver, and more savvy, I thought, so it never really occurred to me to question why things like that happened to her. She burned up my innocence by telling me things I didn't want to know and then that I couldn't unknow. And that, I was beginning to see, was also my real problem with contacting a genetic counsellor about testing. If I took the test and I didn't get the result I wanted, I could never go back to just not knowing.

13.

Boz turned up at the bus station for our trip to Halle with a paper bag with two almond croissants inside. We consumed them kerbside while watching two people, obviously mother and daughter, argue quite ferociously. I couldn't understand what they were saying, their German was too fast, but I began to wonder if their physical similarity was also a kind of repellent for them – the deeper action of the gene, the anti-magnetic force that drives the genetic material to separate itself from the known and mingle with the new. Boz was listening intently, and after we'd boarded told me with an amused expression on his face that the daughter didn't want to go visit the grandmother because her house made her feel sick with the smell of cigarettes and sweet Kaffeesahne and all the racist bullshit she talks, and the mother said but she is old and lonely and the other day her only friend, Frau Müller from upstairs, had a bad fall and can't live near her anymore and she is sad, so the daughter had better get her skinny, ungrateful arse on the bus.

'Ah. Klar,' I said.

We both gazed out the window as the bus heaved its way south.

'I wish I could read onboard, but alas, motion sickness,' Boz said.

'Me too.' Should we have taken the train instead? We could've walked around, we could've read, it would've felt more authentically European, and less... well, ploddy.

Once the bus hit the Autobahn, Boz adjusted his seat back as far as it would go, which wasn't very far, and I did the same. 'So, we have all this time,' he said. 'What shall we talk about? Tell me what you have been reading lately.' People had been looking at us as we boarded the bus as if we were a couple, and now with both our seats in recline, our heads close together, I wondered whether I would need to do some clarifying of the situation with him. But I liked this particular question, this brand of curiosity. What have you been reading lately? was not a question Jay had ever asked. Why? was Jay's question, or When?

'Actually, the last few days, a book about Kaiser Wilhelm the Second.'

'Aha,' Boz said. 'And why?'

'Context.' It was the Kaiser who sent the Count out to maraud the Pacific in the First World War and I wanted to understand more about how that war started.

'Thorough.'

The scruffy old man seated across the aisle cracked a tab on a can of beer. Possibly not his first of the day. He had a pale, sweaty face and his belly sat hugely in his lap, the likely product of a lifetime of patriotic wurst and ale consumption.

'And so?' Boz said. 'How did it start?'

'According to that book, which admittedly was written by an Englishman, it was because the Kaiser was a bit of a duffer.'

'Duffer? Duffer? What is that? I like the sound of that word. What does it mean?'

'Like a kind of fool, I guess.'

'Ahh. The fool. A very Persian concept. What kind of fool was he?'

'He liked a bit of pomp and tomfoolery?'

'Tomfoolery? This word too? You are killing me. Are these Kiwi expressions?'

'No, at least I don't think so.'

'Let me write these words down. I will look them up later when we have WiFi.' He took his phone out of his top pocket and made a note in it. He then reached into his backpack and extracted a packet of mixed nuts. 'We Persians like our nuts,' he said as he offered them. 'So, tell me more about this Kaiser.'

Boz had an odd down-turned smile, and the reason for his faint amusement wasn't completely clear to me. When people back home had asked what I would be writing about in Germany, I would give a few shorthand anecdotes about my adventuring Count, and mostly they would respond in a similar way. Really, he stole the camp commander's speedboat? And made it all the way to the Kermadec Islands? With a homemade sextant and just a school atlas for a map? And then he told everybody in prison that he would be Governor of New Zealand if Germany won the war? Awesome! Without having to talk about it, Kiwis easily understood the sub-characters within the story – the too-trusting camp commander, the eager-beaver authorities in pursuit, the gullibly awestruck locals clamouring after his celebrity. In Germany, though, on the few occasions I was asked, the response was always, 'And why are you writing about that?' It was inexplicable to them. They were used to people coming to Berlin to write about the Stasi, or the fall of the wall, or the decadent Weimar years, or the dramatic Hitler years – but the Kaiser years? The First World War? That old rumpus had been so thoroughly eclipsed. But maybe this was good now, this opportunity to talk out loud. And Boz's slight mockery was even better. I would have to convince him there was something of interest.

'So, the Kaiser's main problem in life stemmed from the fact he had a difficult birth, and was born with a crippled arm. And his mother, who was the eldest daughter of Queen Victoria, found it difficult to love him properly. He grew up craving her attention and hating her too. So that was his beginning, half English, half German, each side despising the other. Do you see where this is heading?'

'He started a war?'

'Well, yes. All that Prussian pride and a large insecurity complex meant he developed a sort of bombastic fetish for military symbolism. He was supposed to have had over four hundred different uniforms. Solid-gold Prussian helmets, you know the ones with the spikes on top, a sword on his hip, a huge waxed moustache... '

'Ahh, so when you say fetish... ?'

The woman in the seat in front of us coughed, and I realised we had been talking quite loudly about German history, in Germany, within hearing distance of actual Germans. 'There was this one story, I'm not sure how true it is—' and I leaned in closer to Boz, telling him about the White Stag Dining Club, where to gain membership a young man had to tell a blue joke and then be patted on the bottom with the blunt edge of the Kaiser's sword.

Boz made a little snort of amusement. 'So, what has this to do with Count von Luckner? Was he one of those young men?'

It was a good question. I didn't know whether the Count had made it into the inner circle but was sure he would've been a total sucker for all that business. 'All I know is he had a thing for the Kaiser, because the Kaiser was obsessed with the Navy.'

'Ahh,' Boz said. 'As Heidegger says, whatever can be noted historically can be found in history.'

This was habit, I guessed, for a philosopher, this dropping in of quotes. I ran my mind over it a couple of times until I could properly extract some relevancy. Except…

'You're quoting Heidegger? Didn't he turn out to be a Nazi supporter?'

'Some say yes,' Boz responded, obliquely. 'So, continue…'

'Okay, so I suppose a confluence of things have to happen for any war to come about. Basically, he started a massive ship-building race and spent so much time playing with his dreadnoughts that he nearly crippled the German economy. And, of course, a man who spends so much energy building up the machinery of war needs to throw around a few threats and swagger. He sometimes made inappropriate speeches that his aides had to scramble to correct.'

'Thank goodness he didn't have Twitter.'

'Precisely.'

The old man in the seat opposite pulled a tab on yet another can, and then started laughing loudly to himself. This, it became evident, was meant as unsuccessful cover for a low fart. Boz waved his hand in front of his face as an impressive drift of rotten giblets crossed the aisle. The old man, who was half senseless by now, noticed the movement, stared glassily at Boz as if registering him, and then raised his can in an almost friendly toast.

Boz turned away from him. 'An old friend of the crazy Kaiser's perhaps,' he said with a sly smile, and urged me to continue with the story.

I gave him the rest of it. How the Kaiser had his cousin George on the throne in England and his cousin Nicky as the Tsar of Russia, so even when the Austro-Hungarian Empire blundered its way into declaring war on Serbia, the Kaiser didn't really think his cousins would mobilise against him if he came to Austria's side. 'Tensions in Europe were so hot that it only took the murder of one Archduke to trigger everything off.'

'Ahh, that is a scary thought. It is like my home region now,' Boz said. 'So he didn't mean to go that far?'

'I don't know if you can say that exactly... but, well, he was rash and impulsive, and it seems he tried to wriggle out of the war on the Franco front but couldn't pull it off. So instead he appeared before his public on the balcony of his palace, pale-faced and trembling, saying, "In the midst of peace we are attacked by our enemy" and something about "defending ourselves to the last breath of man".'

'Oh my,' Boz said. 'How many Germans died in that war?'

'About two million, I think.'

For a long time we didn't say anything more. We ate Boz's salted nuts and looked out the window of the bus. What I hadn't said, what I probably didn't need to say, was that reading that book had made me feel a certain kind of tidal anger towards men. Not every man in the world, but the type who surround themselves with other men, with all their bluster and brinkmanship, and who play with the shiny instruments of war as they played with their boyhood toys, and who get hard-ons for tactics and dominion and the thought of crushing enemies. And it wasn't the sort of anger I could post back to the past either, because all I had to do was turn on the small television in our apartment and there they all were, every day – the fool of all fools throwing out his blithely racist taunts in America, and in Turkey incarcerating any and every voice of opposition, and in Syria sacrificing his own people for his seat on the power-throne, and in Russia mastering the world with his underhanded guile, and that angry man-fight in Yemen for God knows what reason. There they all were, those men who loathe women so thoroughly that they have no affection for such nice things as harmony, or empathy, or pacification.

I'd thought the bus might pass through some picturesque German countryside – slopes and farmsteads and lovely villages – but so far we were taking a seriously workmanlike route down the Autobahn, past trees and trees and signs and industrial estates and more trees, with barely a herd of cows in sight.

Boz yawned and said, 'Do you mind if I sleep a little? I was up late last night.' When I replied of course not, he adjusted his position, making himself comfortable, resting his head on my shoulder. For the next hour I sat with the rigid responsibility of maintaining my posture so that I didn't wake him, but also uneasy with the intimacy which felt a little assuming when he laid his heavy head on me without asking first.

The central Marktplatz in Halle was bordered by many old buildings with steeples, and chain stores, and terrace-fronted cafés that were at the tired end of the season. We stopped to look at the statue of Handel, this town's most famous son.

'He looks very satisfied with himself,' Boz commented.

'Well-fed is the word that comes to mind.'

'A lot of curly hair.'

'A wig, I suppose. All the rage back then. Maybe a bit of a spanker?'

'Agreed.'

'And that hand on his hip. It makes him look like he owns the place.'

'Arright. Shall we go find your Count,' Boz said.

At the Tourismusbüro I inquired about a map for the von Luckner trail in such tortured Deutsch that Boz smirked, though didn't step in to help. The enthusiastic young man behind the counter looked confused, so I showed him the Count von Luckner Society's website on my phone. 'Ahh,' the man said. 'This is the first time I have seen that. I think the best I could do is print out the map on their site for you. Would that be okay?' He seemed embarrassed now, his special combination of professional and civic pride dented by a gap in local knowledge. When he handed over the printout he said, 'I think I'm going to do some research on that. Thank you for bringing it to my attention. Next time you come I will know more.'

'Klar,' Boz said in a tone that was so lightly dismissive it was possible only I noticed, but I overcompensated anyway by thanking the man much too profusely for his help.

As we set off towards the first destination on the map, we noticed a definite sense of retraction in Halle. Many shops were closed, and the street-facing sills of some of the houses had displays of traditional lace and small well-dusted knick-knacks, and these also gave off a whiff of conservatism and narrow values. An elderly couple seated in chairs just inside their front window stared at us as we passed by.

'Terrorist watch,' Boz joked.

'It might be just me, but I'm starting to feel a sense of paranoia.'

'Mmm,' Boz said. 'I know what you mean. You'll be okay though. The ones to really look out for are those that look like me, who rumour has it are looking to drive their truck through another Weihnachtsmarkt sometime soon.'

'Suspected as much,' I said, and our eyes met briefly.

We wandered on to look at the tower of Moritzburg Castle. 'First stone laid 1484,' I commented. 'Pretty old.'

I'd been going for understatement, but Boz said rather too earnestly, 'Old is relative. We had libraries in Persia for over two thousand years by then. Around here they were still running around with wild boars, bashing each other over the head and swilling down ale.'

'Mmm, it seems Persians enjoy a bit of moral superiority,' I said, smiling – although in that moment I saw more clearly that Boz wanted the well-educated and slightly prim side of himself to be deeply identified in the earliest of refined civilisation.

We located the Count's childhood house, and stood together staring at its aristocratic façade and its big blue front door. I'd hoped for something uncanny to happen here, that a vision might light up or, better, a flash of coherence would swing open that blue door and deliver scraps of old conversations directly into my imagination. But as I gazed at the building, just a building, no such gift arrived. Boz commented that this place was uncelebrated, no plaque.

As we stood there the sky greyed considerably and began to rumble in what seemed like a particularly German way, like an omen reaching towards us from the past, or like the collective indigestion of a thousand forgotten barbarians. We buttoned our jackets and moved onwards, around the corner, where the Count's early school had been. As we went, I tried to force an image into my mind of a young boy, perhaps in breeches, running these same streets.

From a doorway opposite, out of the freshly icy wind, we sat on a step and stared at the stone frontage. Eventually Boz said, 'Is this doing anything for you?'

'I don't know what I expected. A feeling, I suppose,

atmosphere. Something. Maybe it will take me some time to process.' I pulled some bottled water out of the side pocket of my backpack, offering it first to Boz, but he declined. 'He was useless at school, you know,' I said. 'It's not that he was stupid. I guess in this day and age he'd have been diagnosed with ADHD and put on Ritalin. His grandmother bribed him into doing better by giving him fifty pfennigs whenever he went up a grade, so he started lying and saying he had gone up a grade until he was top of the class. Then one day she bumped into his school superintendent and commented on how proud of his progress she was and, well, the shit hit the fan.'

'The shit hit the fan?' Boz smirked, taking out his phone again to make a note. 'I need to remember such an amusing expression.' Then he shivered and said, 'If this isn't working the magic for you, can we move on? It's cold sitting here.'

'Of course.' We abandoned other highlights on the map, including the Count's former tobacco shop, and when we arrived back at the central square the day was turning to darkness and young children holding lanterns were lining up behind a red-coated man on a horse. As the horse began clomping slowly through the square the children followed behind, struggling to keep a straight line, singing, *Laterne, Laterne, Sonne, Mond und Sterne, Brenne auf, mein Licht…*

Boz stood watching them for a while as if he was the officially appointed observer at a rustic tribal ritual, and then he translated for me: 'Lantern, Lantern, sun, moon and stars, burn on, my light…' He asked another onlooker what this was all about. 'Sankt Martinszug,' the woman replied. 'Für die Kinder.'

We made one last half-hearted attempt to locate a landmark, the memorial plaque that had been erected to recognise the Count's efforts to save the town in the dying days of the Second World War. We walked around in a circle until at last we found a small, simple brass plate tacked high up on a wall of an unprepossessing building, next to the entrance of a bookstore. The Count had crossed enemy lines to persuade the advancing forces not to bomb Halle, reportedly wearing knickerbockers and with his ubiquitous pipe in hand. He had spent his time between the wars touring the United States, telling his madcap tales and flogging his book, so he was considered to be the resident of Halle most capable of instant camaraderie with the enemy. There was a photo in one of the books of him and the American Major General Terry Allen poring over a map together. Somehow the old windbag had managed to persuade the other side that the only people left in Halle were women, the old, and the crippled. The bombing never happened, but this plaque seemed like a deliberate attempt to minimise the legend with its plainly factual wording thanking the Count – fourth among five names – for saving the town from destruction by their courageous actions in April 1945.

'So, not very heroic,' Boz commented.

'Well, I found out that there was some controversy about it. Some people didn't want it at all because the Nazis had put him on trial for sex crimes in 1939, and with his imperialist background the communists couldn't really be bothered celebrating him.'

'Wait. Back up. Sex crimes?' He dropped the half-bored expression he'd had all day and was suddenly alert.

'Yes, he was accused of having sex with his own daughter, and also of sort of rubbing himself up against the young daughters of his lawyer.'

'Really?' Boz looked like he wanted to laugh. 'That kind of ruins your story.'

'I know. But some people say it was trumped up to discredit him because he'd fallen out of favour with the Nazis. The courtroom was closed, a settlement was reached, and no transcript exists.'

'And so that's what you believe? It wasn't true?'

'Some people do believe that.'

I saw in Boz's face that he now considered this whole day to be a grand act of futility.

When I had first read of the charges against the Count, I was taken aback, but I'd come around to the idea that it might be the enormity of his fallibility that had the most potential for a modern story. The impetus for any great act of audacity is, most likely, the courage of the flawed character. And, on this assertion, his might have been very flawed indeed. How many of the significant men of history were motivated to do their large feats out of pure, burning self-hatred?

Was it true? Pure slander, the International Felix Count von Luckner Society claimed on their website. I'd reread *The Sea Devil*, some of which I now knew to be his exaggerated half-truths, his bluster, his contrivances. In those pages, whether he wanted to or not, he was constantly revealing his capacity to convince himself of his own primacy, his special set of rights, his own irresistibility. I'd gone as far as an active internet search on his daughter, the only person who could really verify whether he did force himself on her at Berlin's Hotel Excelsior. It wasn't that I thought I had the courage to approach her and ask directly, but it turned out she had died in Hamburg in 1955, at the age of forty-one, married, no children. Von Luckner talked a lot about his second wife, the Countess, but never mentioned this earlier family. Could they have become so embittered by abandonment that they colluded in bringing him down? And he had fallen out with some powerful people by then, Heydrich and Hitler themselves, who were more than capable of orchestrating a nasty reputation-buster for the public hero who had streets throughout Germany named after him. I'd filed it all in my mind as an issue of doubt, something that I could run a spotlight over later.

Boz was shivering in the cold. 'Shall we see if we can get the earlier bus back?'

In the window seat, listening to the heavy grind of tyres on the tarmac, I tried to recall what, other than expedience, had attracted me to the Count's story in the first place. The question – especially in the light of the complete collapse of what was, at best, only ever superficial interest from Boz – was not so much about *where* I should start, but *if* I should start at all. Boz had grown almost sulky about my already knowing about the accusations and allowing us both to waste this cold day on my dead-end folly. He sniffed loudly a couple of times to let me know that he had probably contracted a cold too. But I was beginning to see things in a new light. Perhaps what had begun as a story of madcap prowess was really showing itself to be a tale about seriously bad judgement, large falls from grace, and ignominy.

'You know how you quoted Heidegger earlier,' I said to Boz. 'Does it not completely discredit him in your eyes that he was a Nazi?'

'Actually, there are many papers on that. It is a whole field of study in itself. Was he sorry? Not really. He never addressed the Holocaust or apologised. But should the work of a man be ignored because of this? There is so much that he did that is marvellous and groundbreaking, so—'

'Surely, though. I mean, I don't know much about Heidegger except that he was groundbreaking on *being*, but how can that work negate, say, antisemitism? Denying millions. I don't really understand how somebody who can be so stupid as to allow himself to fall for Nazi doctrine can be respected as a thinker.'

'He was the lover of Hannah Arendt. Did you know that? She once said that she considered his Nazism as a temporary perversion. He influenced a lot in the French existentialist movements, Jean-Paul Sartre and Simone de Beauvoir, for example—'

'That makes it okay?'

'No. Perhaps that makes him not irrelevant. Many people are still in awe of him. If you go to the Philosophy Department at the University of Tehran, for example, it is all Heidegger, Heidegger. They love him because of his work on technology.'

'Which was?'

Boz sighed. 'That is a big question you are asking.'

'You don't think I'm up to it? Can you do it in a nutshell?'

'Nutshell.' Boz laughed. 'Okay, since we are in the habit of speaking together in nutshells… basically he offered the idea that the alienation that comes from modern life comes from an excessive emphasis on reason as a way of justifying our existence. His theory is that reason has led us astray from other ways of appreciating meaning such as, say, our use of humble tools, and the way language captures tradition. And so, by investing so much in reason we have been led to a forgetfulness of being, or nihilism.'

'Ahh, nihilism, now we're cooking,' I said, but was trying to concentrate. I liked this. I liked that we were on a bus together discussing this, and that he was rising to his subject now.

'He was interested in the concept of the origins of technology or *techne*, the Greek word, that at one time referred to bringing forward what was true and beautiful through the poetics of fine arts.'

'Okay, so now I am warming to him, a little.'

'So, in his analysis he tries to look to the retrieval of a lost authentic existence from behind history. Do you understand? Through a future-oriented struggle against the smothering forms of universalism, through a revolutionary project.'

'Ahh, so I'm beginning to understand his appeal in Iran is not so benign.'

He smiled tightly and leaned back in his seat as if he had given me all he was going to. This kind of conversation was only fruitful, for a man like him, with people who were already up on the vantage point, with at least some depth of knowledge. I understood that completely. It's too big a job to pluck someone straight out of a southern hemisphere nowhere and let them in on the way philosophical ideas are applied in a complex, hot-blooded land like his.

'All I can say is Heidegger must have been amazing if Hannah Arendt could let him off that lightly.'

'He must have been,' Boz said, settling down into a nap position. He closed his eyes and his hand came forward and found mine. I turned my head away from him and looked out the window as the afternoon fell into darkness, but I liked the feeling of his warm hand in mine. I chose to receive it as an expression of some sort of special rapport, code for the sealing of an extraordinary friendship.

It had never been a matter of writing a direct version of the Count's adventures – others had done that. Perhaps it had been more about the comedy potential of a man whose sense of adventure was so large it amounted to hare-brained insanity. No physical challenge was ever considered insurmountable. That nonsense he had written about throwing himself into Lyttelton Harbour in an oil barrel and commandeering a passing ship – that was the kind of thing you could talk about later only if you never actually did it. And yet there he always was in photos, the pipe-clutching central figure, the first to catch anyone's eye. And a man like that can achieve nothing without others actively colluding in the delusions. What was it that drove the followers? The excitement, the charisma, or simply the desire to escape their own grinding sense of reason?

If Count von Luckner had a dating profile, I wondered, how would he display himself? *Fond of sailing*, he might put. *Very strong. Can rip a phone book in half with my bare hands. Can bend a penny with my fingers. Have plenty of good stories to share. And, er… like 'em young.* And, if he was being honest, he would have to put his current status as *Expired*.

It was only when we were back on the pavement in Berlin, exactly where we had started, that Boz began the negotiation that would ruin the day.

'What shall we do now?' he asked.

'I'm tired. And I need to think. I'm going to head home.'

'Can I come with you?' he asked with a humble, hapless smile.

I said I didn't think it was a good idea. This was a little disingenuous. I hadn't mentioned the across-the-ocean, technically-still-engaged-to reason why. And I didn't mention that I didn't quite trust my current attraction towards him, that I had my reasons for feeling in a generally self-destructive mode, and that I wasn't sure I had the power to resist him if he made a move.

Boz's tone was soft. 'But I just want to be with you. I don't want to do anything. To be with you is enough.'

I knew this probably wasn't completely accurate, but the way he said it made me consider the simplicity of acquiescing. Right then I wanted his desire for me. He saw my hesitation and was emboldened to press further.

'Please, I just want to lie on a bed with you and hold you.'

I said again that I didn't think it was a good idea, and at that point it was still because I knew if I was lying on a bed with him the inevitable would definitely happen. But then he became more emphatic:

'But you let me hold your hand.'

'Wasn't it in friendship?'

'And I have spent the whole day with you.'

'But you asked to come.'

'Why do you think that was?'

All of a sudden there was a turn in his expression. He had taken on a focused intent, becoming a man who had no patience for anything like natural progression; he wanted his wants returned. And right now. On he went, implying that this was something he needed, that I had indicated to him that I needed it too, that he couldn't take no for an answer, that the adventure could end no other way.

Had he considered the whole day only to be a prelude? It all began to feel so disappointing that I said, 'This doesn't feel right,' and turned abruptly and walked away. I couldn't think of any other way to end the discussion.

By the time I got back to the apartment I was feeling shaky and fragile, but also considering how to reframe the slippery thing that had happened. His desire for intimacy was rich and strong, possibly fired by loneliness and some degree of disaffection. And a large part of my being had wanted to say yes to him. Had I made that so obvious that it was available to his argument? All day I had tried to show him some front of myself, and perhaps that could be called flirtation. And I had held on to his hand. And I had let him sleep on my shoulder. And I had not mentioned Jay. And I knew that the thing, the uncertain future nestled in my cells, gave me a slightly unsteady, incautious edge that he may have picked up on. Perhaps right now he'd repossessed himself and was boiling with contrition that, in the heat of the moment, he had debased himself by becoming insistent. Or maybe he was still raging at me for saying no, for misleading him.

14.

Notes on possible ways in:

1. The seafaring story from the point of view of a sub-character, say a cabin boy, or a stowaway on the *Seeadler*. Maybe a girl, dressed as a boy, with her secret viewpoint into the tired excesses of male bluster. Even go further? Unmask the hoary misogyny that buttressed the hero-image of multitudes of great male adventurers.

2. Perhaps a moment in his post-heroic history, say when he was charged with paedophilia. Take on the narrative perspective of one of his lawyer's young girls, who he may have frottaged, or the daughter from his previous marriage who he is alleged to have had sex with 'because she wanted it'. Could be about the deluded monstrosity of his fame and self-regard. Or the story of innocent young women being used as puppets in a bull-headed Third Reich game.

3. Set over the night of the real incident in 1938 when a group of NZ businessmen invited the Count to a boardroom meeting, plying him with aged whisky and cigars, listening to his stories, and then using a soda fountain to put out a fire his pipe started in the carpet. Perhaps an insight into their small-country clamouring and amateur sleuthing as they tried to establish whether

he was really a spy, or not. And the way hero worship is blind.

4. Set on a chase ship after his famous Christmastime escape from Motuihe Island. The pursuit by a volunteer boat of citizen sailors that have at the helm a... Captain Huntington. The Captain's life is falling into tatters and he can only find a reason for living if he actually manages to capture what he is chasing...

15.

Captain Huntington at the Helm

She boarded the boat and they raised the sails to enter the murky virtual waters. She was scared, so scared, but also knew this excursion was necessary, so she slipped a Teflon protector around her heart and installed her Anti-Anxiety Protection Rampart.

As soon as they set out to sea they began to sail through drowning bodies thrashing and contorting and unable to communicate or even cry for help. All were slowly sinking below the surface, and even if the crew took them on board there was little they could do for them. The drowning people were changed beyond even recognising themselves. After a while their faces began to look similar. Haunted, sunken eyes. Their mouths in a grimace. And skinny. They were so skinny. They were terrifying. Captain Huntington leaned back from his wheel, puffing on his cigar, and said, 'I think you should look away now.'

The ship was dragging lines – our DNA lines, one of the crew casually called them. Long chains, with links marked CAG, that had begun extending out from the origin of the trip. Only now it was discovered that some of these chains were mutated. They were going rogue. They were too long. Something weird was happening on the fourth chromosomal lines. They were snagging on things they shouldn't, whipping about and creating gluey toxic protein substances that were crawling up onto the boat and eating the timbers at the top of the mast. 'Cut them off,' she shouted into the wind. 'Surely we can just cut off the extra chains.' But the Captain explained calmly that if they tried doing that now they might destabilise the whole rig. She didn't really understand. It was too complicated.

They came across some anglers with nets. They were catching, tagging and releasing. 'It's the Enroll-HD project,' they explained. 'We take their details. Compare, contrast. We need to see how things develop and change over time. It's all about the knowledge, the possibilities. Twenty thousand, that's our target. We don't know, yet, what we don't know.'

Soon she began to concentrate on a series of buoys bobbing in the water. She could see direction-pointers on them. STEM CELL THERAPY and MIS-MATCH REPAIR and POST-TRANSLATIONAL MODIFICATIONS and FAN1 BOLSTERING. Some with tags like LAQUINIMOD and AMARYLLIS were sitting half-submerged below the surface, and the Captain explained that in previous times they had radiated hope but they had turned out to be false beacons.

There was one buoy, ASO HUNTINGTIN LOWERING, with a series of fat bells attached to it, and it was ringing out across the sea. We're in trial, the tune sang, we're off to cut the proteins…

And way out on the horizon there was a sleek modern cruiser called CRISPR. That boat was packed with scientists, working at an escalating pace. They were using technology so new it was shining like stardust. Looking down their microscopes to assemble the kind of experimental long-range devices that had never been used before. Putting harnesses on bacterial viruses. Loading them up with cutters and splicers and tiny, tiny messages strapped to RNA torpedoes which were pointed at genes. Working within their own containers, each of them eager to release something into the waters, but they were keeping an eye on one another to make sure that nobody got overexcited and sneaked one into the slipstream, just to see what might happen. Their biggest worry was a pirate boat called *Unintentional Consequences*. Their captain was keeping them reined in. 'More experiments,' he was commanding. 'We need to test to be sure. Let's lift some people onto the deck to try this out on. But only if they can still swim. Only if they can still shout. Only if they can take experimental monthly lumbar punctures for two years without complaining. Ahoy there!' Meanwhile ghost bodies and last-gasp strugglers were desperately trying to climb up the ropes on their own, but they had no strength. Some were falling back down below the surface because it was all just too hard.

From a distance this looked like the only boat that could really save anybody, but it was so far out on the horizon, who knew if it could be reached in time.

A small dinghy came floating up alongside. A nurse was shouting happily, 'I've been scanning the sky for alien craft for ages, it won't be long now. They are all going to start landing near us soon.'

What were they all supposed to do? Enjoy the journey?

16.

I shut down my laptop and went out to the kitchen.

'Do you feel like going to a club? Techno? Really loud and hard and unrelenting. Can we find that?'

'What's up?' Frankie asked.

'I just feel like trashing myself a little.'

'Ahh, you've come to the right girl. Need something to wear?'

It was dark, smoky, fleshy, music so loud that it forced a disconnection between self and the world, movement so innate it was involuntary, faces swirling in and out of sight-lines, heat of hundreds of bodies, heat from inside, the booming rise, the almost imperceptible shift, some sort of pleasant communal agreement that the body was made to do this, just this, accidental brushes of others' bare skin, vague awareness that in some other corner, in some dark basement room, people, strangers, furtively going further, these men, women, looking for brief connection, but they can't sustain it with the one who won't hold their gaze, who won't lift their eyes, who is contained inside the tiniest of spaces, between one lash of the snare and the next, within the grinding continuity of the beat.

Frankie danced over and handed me a pill, and after that everything fractured and strobed. Occasional glimmers coming back to me. Over forty repeats of a chemical code. In one small section of a chromosome. Under, and you're probably fine. Nothing yet to abate or even mitigate. The

CRISPR scissors are proving unreliable. Plausible science is a dance of one step forward, one step back. It's all about how the gene codes the protein. Everybody's wrestling with that. But for now still just the half chance. Prince Orlofsky humps and licks. The Kaiser had a Daimler. Its horn played the thunder theme from *Das Rheingold*. Dah-da-dah-de-dah. The Count once seized a cargo of champagne. Drank the hold dry. Boz deleted me from his contacts. The children wander around after St Martin. Singing *Laterne, Laterne, Sonne, Mond und Sterne, Brenne auf, mein Licht...*

It was mid-morning by the time I left the club, and I'd lost Frankie.

On the way home, I stumbled over a cobblestone in the street and had to run over the odds again, had to find enough evidence to reassure myself that it was just normal clumsiness, that I was still just dazed from the club and whatever Frankie had given me.

'Speak English?' a man asked. 'Parlez-vous français?'

When I nodded, saying English, he asked if I knew the way to Ostbahnhof. He had a kind face and I was walking that way, so I offered to take him.

He asked me where I was from and introduced himself as Karam. 'I do not know this area,' he said. 'I come early to sign contract for a job on building site.'

'Congratulations,' I said.

He said he was happy to finally have some work. He'd had to leave Syria, and was grateful to this country for taking him in. Now he was learning the language and making his way, making his contribution.

It sounded like he was telling me what he thought I

might want to hear, but I couldn't blame him for that. 'How long have you been here?' I asked.

'Two and a half year,' he said. But before that, he explained, it had taken him a year of travelling to get to Berlin. It wasn't that he wanted to come here. He spoke very good French, he had cousins in Canada, he didn't really care where he went, but he just had to go somewhere where he could make a life for himself.

'And how did you get here?'

'That is long story,' he said. 'I come first to Turkey and from there I make my way to Greece, then Macedonia, then Vienna. Paying people all the way. Sometimes sleep on streets, sometimes in trees. Have to work out who to trust. I see other boys, so young they never left their mothers before, cry all the way. Once I get to Vienna, I buy this.' He took a cheap phone out of his pocket and showed it to me.

'You need one to keep up with family,' he continued. 'I already travelling for eight month and not ring my mother yet. I have phone number of friend in Hamburg. My good friend, from childhood. When I ring he say where have you been? We ring your home for months to find out where you are. You don't even ring your own mother? I tell him I can't ring my mother. What I say? I sleep in trees? My friend say you come here, it is better, it is good here. But be careful on border, he say. If they find you, they send you back to Turkey. I pay a guy a thousand euro to drive me from Vienna. He went to Frankfurt and took me in his car. When we get there, he give me two hundred euro back. He say you are good guy. Finally, I am here, safe. It cost me twelve thousand dollar.' His story spilled out of him as if any will to keep it in had been broken.

'You decided not to live with your friend in—'

On an adjacent building a man was using a pulley to

send a fresh bucket of plaster to another worker two storeys up, and Karam stopped to watch as if it was now his duty to take special note of how things were done.

'I want to,' he resumed. 'He offer me place to stay, but when I register the authorities say I must come to Berlin. I don't even know where was it. So, I come here. They send me first to one camp. But it is not good place. A lot of crime and people—' He mimed injecting into his arm. 'I hate it there.'

'You moved out?'

'Yes, I am in new place. I have own room, bathroom, and cooking. I do not need anything else. It is much better. Four hundred of us there. Before I was send to another camp with twenty men to one room, in bunk beds. No choice where you go. They just send you. But I am happy enough now.'

We were passing a bakery and I realised I was starving. Karam waited outside while I went in and bought some Pfannkuchen. I took one from the bag and offered him the rest. He accepted with polite hesitance, asking if I minded if he saved them for later, folding up the top of the bag. I tucked into mine as we continued walking.

'And your family back home? They are still there? How are they doing?'

'I love my mother. She is not educated woman, but she is very clever person, very wise. I miss my mother, but she is eighty now and says she would rather die on her own land than leave.'

'And siblings?' I asked, wiping my mouth with the back of my hand in case there were traces of sugar or jam.

'Only one sister left. She is teacher. She prefer to stay and help the children from within. The others, father, brothers…' He moved his thumb across his throat.

'In the fighting?'

'No, they come in the middle of night. Take everybody by surprise. I am away in Lebanon working but they were all three killed that night. We were peaceful family. None of us want to fight. All we want to do is to work on our land. The same land our grandfathers work on, and before them. We have olive trees, so old trunks are like this.' He held his hands a metre apart.

We entered through the back of the station and I threw the rest of my Pfannkuchen into a bin. It was too frivolous a thing to be eating when talking about such harrowing experiences. I helped him find the right S-Bahn platform, and waited with him for his train. He looked at me and said, 'You are nice person, I can see. So open-hearted. I only just meet you and already I tell you my story. Because you are kind. I hope in your life you never get to see what I see.' He took out a small notepad and asked me to write my name. I put down the long form, Virginia, not sure what he wanted it for, and then on a new page he wrote out some beautiful Arabic script. He ripped it off the pad and handed it to me, saying, 'This is your name. The only gift I can give for thanks, for hearing me, for taking time with me. I don't know what you believe but I think someone was looking down on us this day. I am just simple man who ask for directions and you help me and listen to me. That is a beautiful day.'

His train pulled up and he stepped on, looking back at me as the doors slid closed. Immediately I regretted that I hadn't offered more. My telephone number. A more enduring friendship.

Exiting the platform to find my own train I noticed a filthy old man sitting in the wind-tunnel that was the passageway, begging for money. A trail of urine ran from his body and he was shaking, probably from alcohol or drug withdrawal – that was my immediate assumption – but perhaps not, perhaps something else. Something congenital. I dropped some money into his cup, and he mumbled Danke without looking up. What would happen, I wondered, to such a man in a country at war, where even a simple olive farmer struggles to avoid a throat-slitting and where every ailment, minor or otherwise, and especially anything like anxiety or depression or shifty hypochondria, becomes trivial and irrelevant when there aren't even enough hospitals to put back together people who are being buried alive by falling bombs?

17.

Hi. Zelda gave me your email address. She said she thought you were in Berlin. I'm Lena, your cousin, or your second cousin, or however that works (technically my dad, Phillippe, is your cousin, anyway). I'm not sure how you are feeling about family things, but I am passing through and wondered if you'd like to meet up?

The communal area in the backpackers' hostel where Lena was staying reeked of body odour and cheap cooking oil. I bought a couple of Radlers and we sat down at a table in the front bank of windows.

Lena unscrewed the cap from her bottle. 'What even is this?' she asked. 'Radler?'

'I think it's more or less beer with lemonade in it.'

'Okay,' Lena said, taking a sip. She grimaced at the taste, and said, 'I don't usually drink alcohol.' I offered to get something else, but she said it would do. And then she added, 'It must be so weird for you. Being so freshly inducted into this genetic shitstorm. Getting tested?'

Black eyeliner, black clothes, heavy Docs, piercings in her lips, her eyebrow, her ears. Her hair was dyed a raven black, and her skin, by contrast, had the whiteness of somebody who mostly slept through the daylight hours. Her nails, I noticed, were bitten to the quick, red-raw flags of obsessive compulsiveness.

'Um, I think I'm working up to it. You?'

She leaned back in her seat. 'Yeah, I wanted to from

quite an early age. But for a long time I couldn't.'

'Because?'

'They make you wait until you are over eighteen.'

Maybe in her early twenties? She appeared to want to radiate an anarchic fuck-the-future stance, but couldn't quite extinguish the shine of vulnerability in her eyes.

'How is your father? Phillippe, isn't it?'

'He's having trouble.'

'Ahh. I am so sorry.'

Lena shrugged. Loud noises from across the road attracted our attention for a moment. A man with a long white beard and wearing nothing from the waist up despite the cold was standing outside the travel agency opposite, shouting at his own reflection in the window: 'Sie sind alle tot. Ich bin der Todesengel.' Inside people were crouched at their desks, looking uncomfortably back out at him. Lena turned back to me and said, 'I am okay. I don't have it. But I am still the only one that's tested. My sister prefers not to know.'

I breathed out. I'd been holding everything in, nervous about sitting next to somebody who potentially had what I might have, as if it was possible for the disease to connect and activate through some kind of genetic Bluetooth. And I'd been thinking Lena might tell me that she had the gene, and this was the reason she was transmitting some antipathy.

'Really?'

'Actually, that's quite normal,' Lena said. 'Do you know that less than nineteen per cent of people who have it in their families and can get pre-symptomatic testing actually do it?'

I lifted my bottle to my lips, trying not to show that my hands were trembling. It felt like I needed help with this conversation. We had dived in so quickly. I needed somebody calm sitting beside me, with his familiar hand in mine, offering reassurance that I could survive talking about this.

'Why is that, do you think?' I managed.

'Fear.' Lena spat the word out, as if this could be just another term for weakness. 'I had to get away. To escape it all. It's like a vice on our family. I couldn't breathe there. Whenever we got together we'd be looking at the others for slight tremors, or this look you get about your eyes that you can't describe, or a tendency to get a bit manic on it all.'

'Manic? Like what kind of manic?'

'Making lewd jokes, for example. Penis jokes. Dad would do it sometimes, make these jokes, and we'd just laugh tightly. First because the jokes were bad, and second because we all saw it as a symptom.'

'Ah, that must have been hard.'

Lena stared at me and I felt her disdain. Too grand an understatement? 'You have no idea. I would've killed myself if I had it,' she said.

'But you just said... and even if you had... you're so young. And there are the trials – I mean, it can't be long until...' To hear this from her shocked me. It wasn't as if I hadn't vaguely entertained the thought myself, but it felt as if it needed to be ardently defended in somebody else. 'And surely there'd still be a lot of living to do even after...' Saying this made me feel like I was cracking open a door I hadn't been paying any attention to.

Lena sighed harshly. 'Back home they are all so desperate about getting good care, finding good doctors, understanding it, extending the good part of their lives, hoping for the cure. I just want to get away from it. Just be me somewhere in the world without all that shit. I thought about staying here, but all that fucking history everywhere is getting to me.'

'History?'

'It's, like, an industry here. Haven't you noticed? Fucking everywhere you look. In the pavement even.'

'Yes. But for quite good reasons. Why exactly does it get to you?'

'It's so boring,' she said, at once too blasé and too lifeworn. 'I don't care for looking backwards.' She was picking at her bottle, ripping away the label piece by small piece.

Two Polizei were closing in on the shouty, half-naked man outside the travel agency who was now both laughing and making threatening gestures at himself in the window. They moved him along calmly, and a woman with a tight face, probably the one who had made the emergency call, came out of the door of the agency and watched them go off down the road.

'What a fucking nut job,' Lena said.

Her contempt landed on me with a tiny pock that set something in motion. 'You know what they were doing here with people like him, the Nazis, before the war? And, for that matter, with people with genetic diseases?'

'What?' Lena said impatiently.

'They started with a propaganda campaign that labelled people useless eaters. They recruited doctors to tag everybody and put them on a list. The first step was rounding up people and subjecting them to forced sterilisation. Four hundred thousand, imagine.' Lena was looking at me as if she was finding me a bit tedious. A dogged know-all. Which made me plough on: 'And after that they started picking them up in vans and driving them around while they gassed them. They sent the families letters saying that their relatives had died in ridiculous accidents. Having a tooth extracted, or something. After they found they could get away with that, they set up buildings for mass slaughter and started thinking about gassing Jews and homosexuals and Romas and anybody else they didn't feel like having around.'

'And that has to do with me... ?'

'Well...' I faltered. 'It's obvious, isn't it? And if people don't learn about such things and understand what might happen when there is no empathy in the world, how can we ensure it never happens again?'

She looked at me, unconvinced.

'And if it's part of the history of Huntington's, then it is part of our history too, I guess.'

There was a tightening of Lena's jawline, an even more defiant look to her eyes. Had I gone too far? She was only young, struggling with her identity.

'Well, maybe I shouldn't say this but sometimes I wish Huntington's had been wiped out earlier,' she said. 'Grandpa Caspar's mother had this thing, but what she did was carry on with her faulty genes and have three children including your mother, and they had more children who had more children and here we all are. With our fucking fault line intact, potentially crazier than that fucking mad bastard over the road.'

'I don't get it. Are you saying you wish she hadn't done that? That's like wishing your own existence and your entire family away.'

'Is it?' she said. She was holding fast to her stance but there was a flicker in her expression. 'You haven't had to live with the fucked-ness of it all the way I have,' she said.

'That's true,' I said, and to change the subject began

asking about her travel plans. I had wanted to ask her about other things. About her family, about how the disease had progressed with them, about what it was like to take the test. But I also didn't want to know. And I could see that there would be no shade to the answers. Lena seemed to be only looking for ways to move on and annihilate attachment. She thought she might travel down to Jordan or somewhere, she said. Live somewhere closer to danger. It might've been a joke, but I wasn't sure.

'I think I'll go,' she announced, picking up her jacket and her daypack, leaving me with the vague impression that I hadn't given her something she'd expected. But then she fished an envelope out of her bag and handed it to me. 'Aunty Zelda said she found this and you might like to have it.'

'What is it?'

'Some photo.'

As Lena strode off towards the stairwell that led up to the dorm rooms, I opened the envelope. Inside were two colour photographs of my mother and father, taken on a bridge, with a castle in the background that could only be somewhere in Europe. In the first she was kissing him on the cheek. He had his arm around her. She was wearing a paisley scarf, a black shift dress and cowboy boots, and had a blue jersey tied about her waist. He was skinny, and wearing a denim jacket, thick-rimmed glasses and sneakers. In the second photo they were both looking at the camera, smiling in a way that seemed like they were on the verge of breaking into laughter. They appeared happy. In love.

I couldn't stop looking at them. They made me ache. Not just for my mother. For the life she never lived. For the hopes of this girl that were so dashed. But for my father too. For the thing that took away that smile of his. And for me. For the parents I never knew, and never would.

When I got up to leave my legs were so shaky I had to sit down again to collect myself.

From Lena's hostel I walked down the wide Unter den Linden, past the palace that was being refurbished, the same one where the Kaiser had stood on the balcony and made his declaration of war. Past Humboldt on his chair of wisdom up a plinth outside the university, and past the line of brass Stolpersteinen set into the pavement with names and dates of birth and place of death of the people who had been taken from there. Past other square-front historic buildings that had endured falling bombs or been rebuilt from the ground up in their original style. The cold air on my cheeks, the exertion, felt good. I turned left, I turned right, and as if led by some instinct that the way to handle grief is to submit to a greater sorrow, I came up to the Memorial to the Murdered Jews of Europe, the huge, gently undulating field of concrete blocks. I wandered among them, and after a while their big sharp shapes began to seem animated. Their very slightly off angles gave the impression they were tenderly, sadly whispering to each other. The alleyways between the blocks deepened, and I came across people who were kissing, who were playing a chase game, who were taking selfies, and those who were silently absorbing the gravity of the remembrance. Up above, the gloomy day was falling into night already, and I stayed for a long while in this canyon of shadows.

A text startled me. It was Christoph saying he was leaving work soon, did I feel like a drink? I told him where I was, and he said it was on his way, he would try to meet me within the hour. With some time to fill, and feeling the cold, I took the stairs down to the information centre underneath.

At the security check, a group of school children behind me were scuffling and shoving each other, talking in French. Once inside, they quickly became muted and sombre, filing past words scribbled on letters, or on postcards thrown from trains, or on toilet paper hidden in walls, by people who were sent to Auschwitz, or Treblinka, or Belzec, or shot in the forests near Ponary. Short desperate notes about receiving summonses, about being forced to board trains, being scared, doing what they can to say goodbye, trying to reassure themselves and others: it probably is a work camp.

In the next room portraits of entire families chaperoned us, the living, into a haunted understanding of what had been lost through systematic persecution. Looking at them, I was reminded of the list, and felt an icy finger on the back of my neck. What had happened with Lena? I might've let myself become disoriented by her unexpected hostility. Had I ranted at her? Been too earnest? Maybe she didn't want to know all that, maybe she hated me telling her, or the way I told it – but it was definitely how she would remember me. We two connected forever by some terrible facts I'd stumbled across at the foot of the Philharmonie and then forced on her. But also, we two meet and it's not just us. Our mothers and fathers are there, our grandparents, our great-grandparents, all our people. The thread that runs through.

When I emerged into the night-afternoon, Christoph was leaning on a block near the exit, headphones over his ears. He greeted me, 'Na?' Then he lifted off the headphones and said, 'I was just thinking about how a few years ago they had to ban people from playing Pokémon Go here.'

'Really?'

'Ja. Kein Respekt,' he said. 'So?'

'Yup. Pretty heavy,' I said. 'You think you know it, and then when you face the scale of it...'

'I think that's what these big stelae are all about really. Scale. I like that we chose something so surreal to recognise this part of our past.'

His use of the word 'we' made it feel like he had a conscientious stake in it. We watched as a dad assembled his three young children on top of one of the memorial blocks and using a flash took a photo of their grinning, oblivious faces.

'I hate to say this, but I think the burning question that you emerge with is about how a whole nation could have been persuaded to collude in such a truly horrible thing. How could people here have been so collectively evil?' I waved my hand vaguely towards a small crowd queueing to get on a bus.

Christoph looked in that direction. 'Well, let's not incriminate those exact people,' he joked, before adding, 'I think part of the debate has been not to attach labels like evil because it kind of sidelines those that participated as uniquely satanic. It is a more interesting question for history to examine what motivated normal, intact people to commit such indefensible actions.'

'Yes, you're right.' I felt somehow chastened, the clueless one stumbling over the historical traps. 'And have you? Examined that question?'

Christoph sighed, crossed his arms and leaned back. 'You think we live in this country and don't try to get our heads around that? It is a huge part of our education here. Visits to camps. Discussions. Social role-plays. It would be unrealistic for us not to thoroughly examine this part of our past, don't you think? Never heard of this word Vergangenheitsbewältigung?'

He looked at me in a way that felt part warning and part vulnerability. I was just another newcomer poking around in every contemporary German's sore spot, trying to acquire my personal understanding. He was willing to stand up for it, but I could see also that he had some natural reluctance as well. 'Vergang... what? What is that?'

'Vergangenheitsbewältigung,' he said again, more slowly. 'It is our word that describes this process of coming to terms with the past.'

'That's a big word.'

'It's a big process.'

The terrible image of a bulldozer pushing at a pile of naked, emaciated bodies was so freshly imprinted in my mind I felt unable to properly assemble any thoughts. I must have appeared disconsolate, because Christoph put his huge arm around me and gave me a brief conciliatory hug. 'Need a drink?' he said. 'The Adlon is just around the corner. Not my usual style, but we could try a posh cocktail.'

I nodded.

We walked past the American Embassy with its armed guards and metal fence, and turned through the Brandenburg Gate, which framed a fairytale-sized Christmas tree. Everything around us seemed brightly lit and pointless: the people standing taking selfies with the lights behind them, the souvenir traders, the last touring groups of the day with their eager faces open to taking in their bite of history. One group were looking up towards the Adlon Hotel, and Christoph told me the guide was pointing out the balcony where Michael Jackson had dangled wee Blanket.

Inside the hotel we sat near the elephant-head fountain, below a dome of decorative glass, and in the spirit of the surroundings ordered Cosmopolitans from the uniformed waiter. Christoph didn't look entirely comfortable. He was definitely more of a Kneipe kind of guy, but I was grateful for his effort.

'You know that filmmaker you mentioned. The one who wanted to stay and understand hard things?'

'Jürgen Böttcher,' Christoph said.

'Yes.'

The waiter arrived with our drinks on a tray. A little girl came running across the room and watched closely as the waiter put two placemats down on the low table in front of us, and then the cocktails. She giggled in a way that was calculated to charm us, and then ran off again, skipping around the furniture.

'I was wondering, did he make other films?'

'Yes,' Christoph said. 'He made quite a lot of documentaries for DEFA. Some were banned but many were lauded. He made a wonderful film called *Wäscherinnen* or Washerwomen…'

'About?'

'Just realist material following women working in a laundry. But he captured all their humour. A sort of homage to the worker's struggle, I guess.'

'And these are having a resurgence?'

'Neo-realist filmmaking from inside the GDR. What do you think?'

Where were we now? The former West or the former East? The Brandenburg Gate was important, right on the edge, but which side was which again? Who got to stand and look at the horses' faces and who only had the haunches? The piano player on the mezzanine was playing a song that I only just recognised as a flowery, soulless version of 'Thriller'.

'And he is still making films?' I asked.

Christoph's oversized hand didn't look quite natural on the crystal glass, and he took a sip in an exaggerated way, satirising himself. 'Nah. After the fall of the wall he focused on his painting instead. I think it was hard for some of those DEFA filmmakers to make it in the West. Their orienting point fell with the wall. There was no fight left.'

'Yeah, I get that.'

The girl skipped past our table again, grinning broadly, and Christoph smiled back at her in a way that added more bounce to her skip.

'How old were you when the wall fell?'

'Only about eight. Honestly, it didn't touch me much at the time. I grew up about as far west as it was possible to get. We were a long way away from the blunt edge of it all.'

'Behave yourself!' the girl's mother shouted, her loud remark invading our space more than anything her little kid was doing.

Christoph said, 'You know, it's funny we should be talking about this. I was sort of immersed in that era just before I left work today. My colleague was showing me some photographs. A collection about relics of the Cold War, buildings in states of decay, places where they once stored bombs, underground tunnels where they reloaded planes, and so on. Anyway, there was this one photo of an old Stasi interrogation room. Just a table and a chair set against a wall with a grille in it. And all the walls were covered in the kind of wallpaper that was popular in the seventies, with stripes and bamboo leaves, I think. That photo really struck me because it needed nothing more. You fill in the gaps yourself.'

'I know what you mean. Every scene from every film you've ever seen that had a Stasi interview.'

'Genau. But then again, it was.'

It was. The free-spirited ones dreamed of making it to the other side and ended up in a bamboo-wallpapered room. All those people in the world, in history, now, who hold fast to hope as the only way forward. Your grandmother had an inheritable disease in the family but she had three children who all had children. That was another form of hope. And today there was something new to try to understand about proportion. There was a number. Nineteen per cent. Or rather they are the ones who choose to face up to the truth. So eighty-one per cent would rather not. The majority. The vast majority.

'Speaking of photos…' I took the envelope from my bag. 'My parents,' I said, although as I handed it over it felt wrong. My relationship with these images was too fresh and delicate. It was as if I was handing him revealing photos of myself.

He took them out and looked closely at them. 'Ahh, I can see that's Schloss Neuschwanstein in the background. King Ludwig's castle near Füssen in Bavaria. My parents took me there once. Ludwig was obsessed with Wagner, I remember. All the rooms are decorated with scenes from operas. *Tristan and Isolde* and *Tannhäuser*. Very fruity.' As he handed them back, he commented, 'They look like they really like each other. You are lucky.'

I said nothing. He may have sensed in my reserve that I was holding back from him, because he seemed to become restless and suggested we should go. Perhaps he was more in the mood to have fun and was realising that a person who was bent low by their glimpse into a confronting past was not the best companion for what he had in mind. We drained our drinks and gave the girl, who was still squirming in her seat, struggling with her own obedience, a small wave as we went.

Out on the street a tour group flew past on Segways. Christoph's eyes followed them as he said, 'You know, it was really the cold war that advanced the technology we have today. The space race and all that. While they were competing to get ahead of each other, they invented amazing spy stuff like pinhole cameras and recorders and microchips and intranet and rockets to get to the moon.'

'So really we have them to thank for ending up with tours on Segways and Tinder?'

'Yes, I think we do,' Christoph said. 'Thanks, chaps.'

18.

'Big news here,' Jay said. 'Three cows were killed by lightning in a storm.'

Our smiles connected online, but I knew what he meant. It was both big and small news. Unprecedented things were occurring. If it can happen to cows, the awesome power of the weather is writ large. At the same time, there was something sweet about this being the front-page news from home. Weird things were happening everywhere, I said. I'd read that wild boars were a problem here, that a gang of them had once run into a bank in some small German town and the police had to be called.

'So, were they wearing balaclavas?' Jay asked.

'No,' I said. 'But they nearly got away with several thousand euros.'

We laughed. It hurt to laugh.

'Don't be the tallest thing in a paddock on a stormy day,' I advised as we ended the call.

I was acting. Acting like a person who was just taking a little time out to write a book. Was Jay acting too? Acting as a man who had relaxed over the question about when I might be back? I was relieved to be experiencing this easier version of him, but it also left me feeling slightly neglected. Was I, underneath everything, relying on the intensity of his wanting me?

After our conversation I couldn't sleep. Awake. Awake. Tick-tock. The darkest of imaginings. What did it feel like to lose ability? When was a person no longer their self? Had I made jokes that other people thought were off? Could a person lose themselves so much that the loss was unnoticed? Or even immaterial? Jay had once hung a poster on our bedroom door. A Bedouin saying about how the night is divided into twelve hours, each with its own name. I liked it so much I had memorised it. Sunset, dusk, darkness, blackness, the enfeebling hour, midnight, the heart of the night, the disgracing hour, the foretokens of morning, the first dawn, the second dawn, the widespread dawn. Like a spectrum of pre-testing emotional states, I thought now.

In what was perhaps the heart of the night, I tried to make myself imagine pleasant things, best possible things. I had read somewhere that when a geneticist finally located the gene with the Huntington mutation, he sent a one-word message: Bingo. Now, decades later, the mission had moved on. All those things warmongers invented during the space race were leading to something more promising, beyond Segways, beyond Tinder – an escalation in the ability to understand the previously unseen. Mars was no longer unreachable, and the unknown within the minuscule world of any individual's cells was also becoming more and more visible. Even a teeny tiny piece of mutant protein emitted by a mutant RNA message that came out of a mutant gene that was a billionth of a centimetre in size. The enemy was in the cross-hairs. The night sky outside my window was starting to lighten. Bingo, Bingo, I tried to imagine all the way into the foretokens of morning.

19.

It occurred to me that Lena had said one curious thing. *Here we all are, with our fault line intact.* Had she meant that generally, or had she perhaps been lying about her result? Or even about getting tested? As her father's father, Caspar, did? I wrote to Zelda on Messenger and thanked her for the photographs.

> **Z:** *It's a relief to hear from you. We have been worried about you. How are you coping? I hope your meeting with Lena was okay. She seems to be going through a phase. Understandable of course. But perhaps not the best ambassador for our family?*
> **G:** *I was wondering, do you have more photographs of my mother and father?*
> **Z:** *Honestly, there are no more that I know of. I only have those two because she sent them to my mother from abroad. She burned all her photo albums just before she died. I often wonder why she did that. Sometimes I think she was trying to erase herself. I wish I could have a different answer.*

> **Z:** *How are you doing? Do you need to ask anything else? I feel that our news must have come as a big shock to you.*

> **Z:** *Okay. We are here when you want to talk more.*

Having reached out, I wasn't exactly sure why I couldn't continue. Zelda must have stared at the three animated dots, wondering what was to come, but I couldn't get over my reluctance to formulate any more words. I was glad, in a way, that Lena had been the way she was. It made me feel that not being a hundred per cent empathetic was a valid response.

20.

Frankie was meeting up with a friend from back home and invited me along. Yvette, wearing a thick winter jacket with a fur-lined hood, was waiting for us in front of the Lucia Christmas market at Kulturbrauerei. As soon as she laid eyes on Frankie, she enveloped her in an enormous hug. She paused, perhaps only because she read my hesitation, before she embraced me too.

'At the other end of the market is this tepee thing that you can squeeze into to drink Glühwein,' Yvette said. 'Up for it?'

We shouldered our way into the crowd, jostling past all the wooden huts selling sugared almonds, and Nutella crepes, and Raclette, and sizzling bratwurst, and gingerbread hearts with Frohe Weihnachten iced onto them, and wooden toys, and glass decorations, and winter hats with pompoms, and Glühwein and Feuerzangenbowle and, because this market was Scandinavian, also stands selling Glögg. Where the market widened in the centre the tiniest of children were whizzing around on a swing carousel under twinkling lights. The grandmothers, the great-grandmothers, the great-great-grandmothers of some of the people here had probably eaten a sugared almond at a Weihnachtsmarkt similar to this. Even the Count probably cherished a seasonal Glühwein or two.

We bowed our heads to enter the tepee just as some other people were leaving. 'Quick, grab those seats,' Yvette said. 'I'll get the drinks. Mit?'

'Mit?'

'Mit Schuss,' Frankie explained. 'Meaning do you want your Glühwein with a shot. Rum or brandy?'

We settled on rum, and Yvette went to order as Frankie and I sat down near the burner on seats which were really just fat rounds cut from a tree trunk with a cushion on top.

As Yvette handed over the hot mugs she explained that she'd come to live in Berlin because she'd recently married her German boyfriend. 'The first thing we did when we came here was go to stay at Moritz's parents,' she said. 'Over breakfast on the first morning his mother said, I think it is time we start with your Deutsch, and after that she'd only speak German to me. I just had a sprinkle of words, so I spent the whole weekend feeling exhausted and confused and really quite fucked off with her.'

'What about Moritz? Did he do anything?' Frankie asked.

'Not enough. His mother is fucking terrifying though,' Yvette said cheerfully. 'Anyway, so I'm learning now. It's really, really hard. All that der, die, das. I thought I'd pick it up quite easily, but I have no ear for pronunciation. I worry all the time about my terrible accent and my terrible ability to absorb.'

'It is hard,' Frankie agreed.

'But you can do it now?' There was an amount of desperation in Yvette's question, like she needed to believe that other people could surmount it eventually.

'The best thing is to surround yourself with Germans, probably,' Frankie said. 'At work I have to speak it, so it starts to come more naturally.'

'I have a German at home, but whenever I say anything he corrects me, so it just makes me feel a bit shit,' Yvette said. 'Und du?' she asked, looking at me.

'A year or so at school but that's not enough,' I admitted. 'But I'm probably only here for a few months, so…' I could feel the strong Glühwein and the stifling heat coming off the burner making my cheeks glow. Also, I was feeling a little disengaged. The more I found out about my family, the less I knew myself.

'Sometimes I think it's quite funny in class,' Yvette continued. 'Some of us have this slight fear, I guess, of the clashing consonants. When we practise talking to each other, saying, Woher kommst du?, we sound insanely aggressive.'

'But you've made friends in the class?' Frankie asked. 'Or a tandem?'

'Not exactly,' Yvette admitted. 'I'm older than most of them. We talk all this shit together about what we did on the weekend – Wie war dein Wochenende? – and what we like – Was magst du? – and then try to formulate answers.' She licked some sugar off the edge of her mug. 'There's this one boy that comes in late most days, or quite often not at all, and he doesn't really even try. I mean, he paid all that money. Or somebody did. Anyway, he keeps coming in with new tattoos and trying to sell us drugs on the breaks, and he just wants to tell us all what he did on the weekend but he doesn't even do it in Deutsch. The other day I heard him saying to this lovely Korean girl that he likes: I never go to parties unless they are at least two days long, otherwise there's no point. You should've seen the one I was at this weekend, he said. Everybody was handing out GHB and at five in the morning there were just guys everywhere, sucking and fucking, nobody was using condoms, nobody cared who was watching. I'm not gay or anything, he said, but I think there's a lot to learn from those guys. They love to live in the moment. He said it all in English, but I'm not even sure she understood. She just sat there blinking really hard.'

Frankie laughed. 'That probably didn't get him far with her.'

'Not at all,' Yvette agreed. Then, looking around, added, 'Isn't it cute here? I came here once a few years ago on my first visit with Moritz and it has barely changed at all. Shall we have another?'

It was cute. Much more authentic than back at home, with our snow scenes spray-painted on store windows in the middle of summer, and our Santas sweltering in red nylon inside shopping malls. I offered to go up to the counter and get the drinks, saying I could practise my Deutsch, but all I really needed to do was hand over the empty mugs, hold up three fingers and nod my head briefly and receive three more. When I returned to the seats Frankie was saying: 'I really like the literalness of German. The way they put words together to try to describe an exact thing. Like Lebensmut.'

'What does that mean?' Yvette asked.

'Lebensmut literally translates to living-courage. It's a word for something like the courage to face up to life.' She glanced at me before saying, 'And I discovered another great one the other day. Schwanzgesteuert – it means cock steered. For a certain kind of tourism here.' A woman sitting beyond Frankie's shoulder turned her head and glared. Frankie had said the word Schwanzgesteuert particularly loudly, with an amount of glee. 'And once when I first came here,' Frankie continued, 'I wanted to buy some gel, but I wasn't sure I had the right product, so I put the words während des Geschlechtsverkehrs off the label into my app and it translated it so stupidly into during the gender traffic.'

We all laughed, and the woman behind moved her body further away.

'Gender traffic!' Yvette said. 'That about describes the sex Moritz and I sometimes have these days.'

'That doesn't sound great,' Frankie said.

Yvette shrugged. 'We've been together for over five years now, so…'

There was a short moment when nobody said anything and then Yvette jumped in with, 'Oh my God it's so nice to see some friendly faces and just relax. Even when I've been talking English it's mostly been to people with English as a second language so when you drop certain slangy words you have to explain them.'

'Like what?' I asked.

'Oh, like let's see, like um, fuckwit, or dickhead, or douchebag, or hissy fit, or shirty, or, um, pack a sad.'

'You're dropping those words in your Deutsch class?' Frankie said.

'No, mostly at home,' Yvette said breezily.

'The shit hit the fan is another one,' I said. 'Or is that a Kiwi expression?'

Frankie looked at me as if I wasn't exactly getting the game, and then said to Yvette, 'Maybe I can arm you up with some good ones in Deutsch you could use. Like Arschgesicht – that means arse face. Or Stinkstiefel. That translates directly to smelly boot, but it means a person in a bad mood.' The woman behind Frankie got up and guided her elderly partner out of the tepee. 'And Warmduscher means a person who likes to take warm showers, but you might pull that one out when you want to accuse someone of being a wimp. And then there is my personal favourite, Backpfeifengesicht.'

'Which means?'

'A face that is asking to be slapped.'

'Ah, perfect,' Yvette said. 'I had uses for all of those words when Moritz and I went to the movies to see this animated film the other day. There was a woman behind us with a whole lot of kids, and they were talking and laughing, and then when the movie started they continued on so loudly that we could hardly hear anything. So, after a while I got really irritated and turned around and went shush. Next thing I know the woman is standing beside me and yelling that it is a children's movie and they have the right to enjoy it and the whole point is that they have fun, and on and on, and suddenly I was caught up in this avalanche of abuse from her. And Moritz didn't do anything. Afterwards he said, Were you angry at me that I didn't defend you? and I said, Yes, a bit. But what I should have said, was, Yes, you Arschgesicht, you Warmduscher!'

I said, 'That reminds me of the movie *Force Majeure*. Have you seen it?'

Yvette shook her head and I explained. 'It's about a family who go on a ski holiday and while they're having breakfast on the balcony an avalanche starts coming down the mountain. At first they think they will be okay, but then they realise that it's coming for them. While the woman is gathering up their children, the father runs off. The whole movie is about their struggle to get over his selfish instinct to save himself.'

'And this movie reminds you of my story how?' Yvette retorted, fairly aggressively.

I thought it was obvious, but while Yvette had – accidentally or not – been revealing these moments of frustration with her partner, it seemed she didn't want anybody to introduce the word selfish.

Shortly after, I mumbled something about needing to

go and do some research in the library. While Frankie knew this probably wasn't true, she didn't say anything and encouraged me to go.

On the tram I sat next to a man who took out a piece of string and a small booklet about knots and began practising, his long, thin fingers working away with a natural dexterity. What for? I wondered. Sailing? Magic tricks? Cargo handling? Bondage? I thought about the way Yvette, and Frankie too, had looked relieved that I was leaving, and began to wonder if my inner world was so awry that I was beginning to show some outer malfunction. My ability with language was possibly being distorted by the new vocabulary I had been silently absorbing but not using with anybody else. Chorea = uncontrollable muscle movements, from the ancient Greek word for dancing involuntarily; anosognosia = a lack of awareness of symptoms; dystonia = sustained muscle contractions that cause abnormal posture and torsions or twisting; oculomotor apraxia = eye movement abnormalities. All words that could be names for knots.

The corner of Rosenthaler Platz, where I alighted, was bustling. Feeling a hazed internal warmth from the Glühwein I walked over to a place that sold pizza by the slice, and sat down at one of the long tables out front to eat it off a paper plate. There was one other person at the far end of the table just finishing up his slice and looking round now for distraction. He was perhaps in his twenties, his head so closely shaved his hair made only a black pointillist pattern on his head. There was something content and gameful about him as he leaned towards me.

'Pizza,' he said. 'Perfect for soaking up the booze.'

'Tell me about it,' I said.

'Tell me about it? You're a Kiwi?'

'Yep.'

'Been there once. Your accent is so cute. Lag.'

'Lag?'

'An ex of mine used to like doing these Les Mills exercise videos. She'd watch these big muscly dudes say things like luft your lag and I was always laughing in the background.'

'Luft your lag?'

He lifted his leg onto the seat next to him.

'Oh. Lift your leg?'

He nodded. 'Yeah. Luft your lag.'

All around the world random people were finding our accent hilarious. He introduced himself as Pascual. Here for a series of seminars for his master's of education, he told me. 'Actually, the last was yesterday, a really interesting talk.'

'About?'

He slid along, moving directly opposite me. Around his neck he was wearing a single bead on a thin leather cord.

'It was sort of a future-focused thing about how scientific developments might change teaching in the future.'

'Like?'

'Well, we talked about holograms and AI and things like polygenic scoring.'

'What's that?'

'It has to do with how they've discovered that certain traits to do with your ability to learn are fifty per cent governed by your DNA.'

A passing truck picked up some fallen leaves and swirled them about in the gutter, and a crow flew down out of nowhere and landed on the edge of a nearby rubbish bin. It felt, for a moment, as if the universe was delivering portents.

'Fifty per cent?'

'It's not an absolute thing. More evidence of a probable tendency. Sort of half nature, half nurture.'

Nature had delivered him very dark eyes, very long lashes. Perhaps it was more nurture that had created the kind of body language that said he knew, deep inside himself, that he was loved, or at least lovable. I looked at him for signs of something else speaking through him. For an alignment of fates so uncanny it felt unreal. But no. Just another person passing through, killing time

'But like what kind of traits?'

The crow flew up to the top of the U-Bahn entrance with a crust in its beak. It had obviously adapted its traits to become minorly successful at big-city scavenging. 'Mostly we talked about things like a tendency towards creativity. Intelligence. Or being good at maths, say.'

'That's governed by DNA? How do they even determine that?'

'Twin studies, mostly. Looking at people who had similar genetic material but were raised in different families.'

'And what about more negative qualities then. Like, say, a tendency to be controlling or sociopathic?'

A wave of people came up out of the U-Bahn station and a queue was starting to form for Cosmic Kaspar a few doors up. One couple sauntered past us, entangled in a tongue kiss. Pascual's eyes wandered to them and then back to me again.

'I guess, although we didn't exactly talk about that. We mostly talked about the potential to guide education towards an individual's strengths.'

'But would that require that all the pupils you were teaching take a test to show their—?'

'Polygenic scores? Ideally, yes.'

'But couldn't you also be getting into something much more ominous with that? Like a kind of fatalism, say? The indicators have already pointed to the future of an individual and therefore they don't strive for a different future or even competence in certain areas?'

'The research suggests it's just a genetic nudge more than anything. So, the entire theory is more about being all you can be. If, for example, you find that a child has an inclination to be a struggler at maths or, say, spatial awareness, what's the point of putting them into a stream that has them failing to learn well?'

A group of over-excited teens came up from the U-Bahn tunnel, all in fancy-dress costumes, relatively innocent by Berlin's standards – angels and crazy cats and a squirrel. They were laughing and teasing each other as they joined the Cosmic Kaspar queue for what was presumably some under-age gig. I wondered if there were polygenic scores for being good at making friends, good at nights out, good at innocence.

'Can't you simply tell they're a struggler at maths when they fail their maths test? And actually, that all sounds a bit dangerous. If everybody's scores were available and then some kind of totalitarian regime came into power, imagine what they could do. They could stream the population into those who were worth investing in and those who weren't. Isn't that getting scarily close to modern forms of eugenics?' Were these pioneers, these young pioneers, opening up the back door in the name of science, without looking all the way down the path? Were those people on the CRISPR boat doing the same thing?

He stretched out his hand as if he was reaching for an answer. He gave it a good consideration. 'I hadn't thought about that. But wouldn't they find a way to do that anyway, some other measure?'

'But isn't it putting a new instrument into their hands?'

'I dunno, we just talked about it in terms of individual betterment. It seemed quite innovative and brilliant to everybody in the room at the time. Do you think I've just been drinking the Kool-Aid? Is that the expression?' He looked down at my paper plate, empty now except for the crust. 'It's my last day here in Berlin. The programme I've been on is finished. I've bought all the presents I need. I just feel like getting some beers and sitting in the park. Wanna come with?'

'A bit cold for the park, don't you think?'

'Who's making the rules? Anyway, you have a warm coat, haven't you? I just want to sit and look at the night sky for a bit.'

The whole conversation made me feel hopeful. If scientists were spending their time on this, on knowing what genes did what, on trying to understand whether a gene made you good at maths or not, then of course there were others who were also able to dig much deeper, to find the gene that kept all the other genes in line. Surely any new understanding was leading somewhere promising.

We went to a Späti, where he spoke fluent German to the woman at the counter. Or at least something that sounded like fluent German to me. Invoking his magic power. One minute English with a Spanish accent and the next... He loaded the four beers into his backpack, and we found a spot on a bench seat overlooking the lily pond, which had a thin layer of ice on its surface. Pascual casually flipped the cap off the first beer so that it flew in a small arc, landing on the ground near a discarded chess piece. Nearby, a couple of dogs were playing, fighting over a large stick, growling and tugging. A third dog came running over, and the first two instantly dropped the stick and started sniffing the newcomer's rear.

'The canine form of DNA testing,' Pascual joked.

One of the dog's owners threw a tennis ball from further up the slope and all the dogs raced off in its direction. Pascual took a sip of his beer. 'Would you take the test?' he asked. 'That DNA blueprint thing?'

I could only shrug. 'You?'

'I think so. It would be interesting. But also, I would be scared of finding out that I had some tendency towards, say, cancer or heart disease or something like that.'

We had been in near territory the entire time but now it was edging closer. 'I know exactly what you mean,' I said. 'But what if you found out you had a risk of being a selfish arsehole?'

He laughed. 'I guess that is the reason for doing it. You could do something maybe. Modify your diet, say, if you knew you had cardio risk. Know yourself at least, if you tended to selfish arseholery.'

'Surely only a negligible percentage, but,' I said, smiling. Our breath had been steaming as we spoke. Someone in the park shouted, 'Apollo, nein!' I took another sip of my beer. 'But what if the risk of something horrible and life-limiting was so high there was nothing you could do?'

He thought about this. 'I dunno. Enjoy life in the moment? Don't you think?'

Enjoy. Life. In. The. Moment. So easy to say. I shivered and pulled my hands up into the sleeves of my coat. 'I know exactly what I would do. Worry. Angst over it. Become indecisive and crippled by procrastination.'

He became alert. 'That sounds like you've had reason to think about it.'

'Well…' Because I was not looking directly at him but at the frozen lilies in the middle of the pond, and because I had glimpsed the back of his neck which was as soft and downy as a duck's, and because I was a bit drunk and also no longer sure why I was keeping it secret, I told him about my cousin and the news she had dropped on me. It was like puncturing a hole in the hold and letting a little pressure out.

'Huntington's? What is that?' he asked.

'Think of Parkinson's, MS, Alzheimer's and cerebral palsy all wrapped up in one disease.'

He turned his body towards me. 'But you haven't tested for it yet?'

I shook my head.

'Too scared? It does sound pretty scary. But isn't it better to know?'

'Is it?'

'Of course.'

'What then? I modify my diet?'

'What is the chance you have it, again?'

'Fifty per cent. The magic number today.'

'Fifty per cent, so still a big chance you don't have it.' He put his arm around me and pulled me close to him. I turned my head and found myself trapped by the empathy of his gaze. We were locked into that stare for a long time. It made me feel known. Slowly he strengthened his grip and pulled me even closer. He put his lips on mine, more an act of compassion than anything else.

He moved his head back but kept his eyes on me. 'Sorry,' he said. 'I just wanted to do that.'

'No, it's… I mean, I quite liked it.' The dogs were still

playing their games nearby, cars and trucks and trams were still rattling by on the adjacent road, but for a few seconds he had made it all – everything – disappear.

'Yeah, sorry,' he said. 'I can't help that I inherited the DNA for being, like, a pretty sexy dude.'

He kissed me again and I let myself give in to the niceness of feeling desired. I'd surrendered my secret up to him and he now knew me in a way no one else did. And he was going back home tomorrow. Without saying anything, we both got up and started walking towards my apartment. I got the key out of my pocket, and we stood kissing in front of the main door.

'So I am coming up?' he asked.

The angles of the surrounding buildings had blurry, indistinct edges and I realised I was too giddy from the mix of Glühwein and beer for any good decisions. 'I'm not sure,' I said.

He kissed me again, more intently. 'You're killing me,' he whispered. 'I'm dying here. I want you.'

Desire for him passed through me like a further melting of soft ice. 'Um, the thing is, technically I am still engaged.'

'Engaged?' he said. 'A pretty historical concept. Come on. He doesn't need to know.'

I managed to pull myself back. Used my key to open the door. Just beside the lock I noticed a new piece of graffiti, *Fuck you*, written in small but clear handwriting. I started to close the door on him. But I made the mistake of looking once more into his brown eyes. Not desperate, but not indifferent either. Warm.

'I'm dying,' he repeated, and my hand, by itself, went forward and grasped his and pulled it towards me through the door.

There was a half-bottle of red wine in the kitchen that

was so vinegary it was only used for cooking, but I stalled our moment of entering the bedroom by pouring us each a glass before leading him down the hall.

'How many languages can you speak?' I asked as I closed the bedroom door, trying to mask nerves and regret.

'My mother tongue,' he said as he looked around the room, picking things up and putting them down again. 'And German, English, a little French. Some Portuguese.'

'I am so envious,' I told him. He was already slipping out of his shirt. His chest was slightly concave and covered in a thin sprinkle of hair, an anti-hero's body. I kept talking: 'The other day I was walking in front of some guys speaking French and I was thinking that you could listen to a man giving you instructions for how to connect your printer to your computer in French and it would still sound sexy, but if you heard the same thing in German it might tend more towards sounding quite forceful.'

'They love that word *muss* here,' he said. 'Du musst.' He gulped his wine in a voracious, hungry way, not seeming to notice how terrible it was. 'Du musst take off your clothes now,' he said.

I obeyed. I wanted to obey. Or at least to be so lacking in responsibility that I let myself be commanded. But I felt shy enough to get under the covers before wriggling out of my clothes. He joined me in bed, by now down to his boxers. And once he was under the covers he wriggled out of those too.

'You want me to speak French to you?' he asked. 'Or German? What about mother tongue?'

'Okay. Say something.'

He spoke in Spanish, or perhaps a dialect, and I said, 'That just sounds like you're trying to charm me. What did you say?'

'That is for me to know,' he said, suddenly snapping back the sheets, rolling me over and giving me a quick sharp slap. It was playful enough that I could go along with it: 'Mmmm, try again.' The sting resonated through my whole body. We continued lightly. Some smarting slaps. Biting. *Du musst* had excited a game in both of us. It began to escalate, and there was an electricity to knowing that it could spin out of control. He tugged on my hair and in return I bit his shoulder. I had the feeling, although it was only a brief intuition, that what he was really trying to do was challenge me to convince myself that I was fully alive. Or worth defending, at least. Or probably it was more animalistic than that. His face took on a primed expression, then, holding both sides of mine, he gobbed up some spit and shot it out at me. I was shocked for a second, and then the sordidness of it appealed to me, landing as it had in such a way that it successfully touched a bit of my self-loathing. I slapped him quite hard in a manner that invited him to hit me back again. He groaned and we continued for a bit, but his pupils seemed to dilate, invoking a new risk that he was so drugged with excitement he could take us both all the way over the cliff edge. It made me pull back a little, quieten.

'You're not that good at getting out of yourself are you,' he commented, and I felt defeated, suddenly, that I hadn't been able to disguise that I was unused to this play, was into it more with my mind than my body.

When it came down to the next act, he struggled to get the condom on. 'We don't really use them,' he said.

'We?'

'Me and my girlfriend.'

The vulnerability in his effort, struggling to disguise the sudden flaccidness of his cock, made him momentarily dear to me. Eventually he got it on, and we started. I no longer knew why I was participating in this at all. I was not turned on, but now that we were here it seemed rude not to go on with it. He had changed into something more like an enthusiastic puppy. Maybe he was just wanting to take something back with him. A secret. Or maybe he just wanted to satisfy an urge. It had nothing to do with us cementing the friendship. I knew already that I would never hear from him again. He was not Jay. He would be a barrier between me and Jay, and maybe that was what I really wanted. He knew my secret. I would never learn his last name and he would never learn mine. We would just pour ourselves into this moment.

After, he asked if I had any cigarettes. 'I'm not that much of a smoker but some moments call for it,' he said.

I wrapped the sheet around myself and went into the kitchen and found the *emergency unforeseen circumstances pack* that Frankie had once pointed to on the shelf above the microwave. Back in the bedroom, he lit up and we lay naked in bed, passing it between us. He told me that he had got talking to a guy the other day about how wolves were having a renaissance in Germany. They were coming into the east from Poland and forming packs. This guy had a whole theory, he said, that it had to do with urbanisation of populations. The smaller country towns had emptied out of people and the wolves were feeling more emboldened to roam. They were attacking sheep and sometimes pets, and now people were wanting to have them culled. We were hesitating between the moment of having finished the sex and the moment he would put on his clothes and go.

'Maybe you should have told me that while we were doing it,' I said.

'Yeah,' he said. 'I could've bitten you on the back of

188

your neck.' He tenderly ran a finger over a bruise that had formed on my arm. 'You bruise easily,' he said. 'Hope I didn't trigger any shit for you.'

'Trigger? Don't think it works like that.'

He kissed me goodbye. 'Be well,' he said. He shut the door behind him, and was forever out of my life.

Lying there alone I couldn't help the feeling that I had actually triggered something. Whatever was coming my way was gathering speed now.

At around midnight I heard Frankie come in through the front door and close it quietly behind her. By that time the impulse that had let me feel exhilarated enough to enact on the desire (drunkenness?) had turned in on itself and become something else. I took a rusty old gun out from under the bed and fired a shot of blame in Frankie's direction, and Mel's, and all the other reckless ones, and then Zelda's for upending my life, and then finally in at myself. Most specifically, I decided that if I had left Jay it was okay; if I had not left him it was definitely not okay.

21.

'But you'll be away for Christmas,' Jay had said, back when he was pleading with me not to go.

'It's just a day,' I'd said. 'We'll survive.'

Now that Christmas was here, the insult of my dismissiveness had been compounded a thousand times, and I could feel a dog's paw of guilt pressing down on my chest. I woke late as if my body was trying to stop me from returning to cognisance. By the time I looked at my phone, the day was already over for Jay. He had sent me a photo of lunch with his family, him seated at the table between his sister's two boys, all of them wearing flimsy Christmas-cracker crowns, three paper princes. He was smiling, holding up a glass for the camera, so it would take an expert in knowing him to see that he was also quite bereft.

Mel and I had agreed to have lunch together at the Swiss restaurant in the park. She'd spent the previous week in London trawling second-hand shops for vintage clothing for some upcoming biopic set in the sixties. Now she was dressed in what she called her find of the century – a Pierre Cardin mod cocktail dress. Original, she said. As we discovered on our entry to the restaurant, it was definitely a head-turner, even in Berlin, though on her it also looked like style. A person who dared wear such a thing looked as if she might be famous.

The restaurant had arranged the day into sittings, with long tables strewn with candles, nuts, mistletoe, glass icicles and small chocolates. The terrace outside was being used only by smokers huddled up in their coats. The park beyond would have looked pretty if it had snowed, but this year the ground was scorched brown by frost and appeared a little undressed. The pond at the bottom, the same lily pond that Pascual and I had sat by, was still frozen in place by ice.

The steamy family festivity in the room was not really Mel's idea of a good time, and neither was it balm to my own fresh remorse. This might not go well, I thought.

After we'd finished our first serving, slices of fruit and sweet pastries, I took the two photos out of my bag and showed them to Mel. She stared at them for a long while.

'You look a bit like her,' she said eventually. 'Something in the eyes.'

'God, don't say that.'

'Really, why not?' She examined me for the reason. 'Do you think if you look like her then you will do what she did?'

'Kind of. Something like that.'

We were elbow to elbow with the other people at the table. The man next to me had squeezed back into his seat with his plate piled high, committed to getting his money's worth out of the smorgasbord.

'You look a bit like your dad too, actually,' Mel said. 'It's the mouth. Luckily, not the long nose. It's almost like you got the best of both of them. Her nice eyes, his nice smile.'

'You think he has a nice smile?'

Mel must have noticed something like gratitude in my face, which forced a small shift. 'It's weird, isn't it. To see him like this. He looks happy. He never looked happy when we were kids. The most we ever got out of him was a dry joke when he was a bit pissed.' She glanced up at me for agreement and then returned her attention to the photo. 'And she isn't what I imagined. In this photo she appears like she might be fun. You can't see why she might have done it. From how she is. From how he is.'

I was incredulous. 'From how he is? You're still implying that he caused her to kill herself?'

'Well, I mean…' Mel became conscious that some people in the room had their eyes on her. She always dressed to gain attention, but at the same time despised those who stared at her too readily. She took a small compact out of her bag and checked her lipstick. I didn't want to watch, surveyed the room instead, and noticed that Christoph was standing near the entrance talking to the maître d'. I waved and he came over to our table, saying, 'I'm coming in later with my brother's family but I forgot what time I booked so just dropped in to check.' His eyes landed on Mel, and he said, 'Christoph Becker. Upstairs neighbour.'

'Mel. Sister,' she replied. Her eyes flicked over him and her posture suddenly became coy as she slipped her compact back into her handbag.

He was still dressed for outside, wearing a grey woollen hat and a heavy double-stitched coat that made him look handsome in a rugged way. His big frame hovered over us. There was no room even to invite him to sit. He was looking at Mel. Taking her in. 'I don't want to interrupt. You looked like you were having an important conversation.'

'Not at all. Stay. I'm sure we can squash up,' Mel offered, but no, he said, he really had to get back home and wait for his family to arrive.

Only seconds later a familiar mischievous look came over her. I braced myself. 'Oh, hang on,' Mel said. 'Upstairs neighbour. So you're the one?'

Christoph was taken aback. He blinked slowly. 'Sorry?'

She gleefully noted the warning look I was sending her and continued anyway. 'It's just Ginny mentioned she suspected you might… like a bit of fun.'

'Did she?' he said, giving me a sort of joke-accusing glare that was meant to be slightly charming but also had counter-inclinations. 'That hedonist comment at the lake?'

I nodded. Mel appeared confused by this, but didn't actually seem to be on the verge of telling him that it had anything to do with noises I'd heard coming from his upstairs flat.

'Good to know she's got me properly clocked,' he said before leaving. He took one quick glance back. Not at me, at Mel.

'Jesus, Mel!' I said as soon as he was out of sight.

'Jesus, Mel,' she repeated sarcastically. 'The lake? Hedonist comment? What's going on there?'

'Nothing. We're friends.'

'Friends,' she snorted. 'Nice work. I wouldn't have thought someone like you had it in you after sitting all alone in your flat downstairs listening to him root – what was it you thought again – prostitutes?'

'Someone like me?' I said, and Mel snorted again. She knew too easily how to mess with me. But she didn't know me anymore. I didn't even know me anymore. It suddenly felt too clammy in the restaurant. The saccharine Christmas songs. The greedy man tucking in next to me. The over-excited children playing a peek-a-boo game amidst the tables. And that pond at the bottom of the slope, that knowing eye.

'You're into him?' Mel asked.

When I said no, she said she thought she might be into him. She said it in a flippant, joking way that I immediately knew should make me concerned.

'How's Jonah?' I asked.

'How's the pleaser?' Mel replied.

I recoiled, and we held each other's gaze in a charged coalition for a moment. The excessiveness of Mel's dress suddenly annoyed me. It was just another way she turned everything into a vortex swirling in towards her. Right from the beginning I had set an impression about Jay that gave Mel what she believed to be the right to be quite forceful about not wanting me to be with him. *The pleaser.* Mel said it in the same way she'd call the children that Lorelei used to help in her teacher's aide job *the specials.* 'There's one of your specials over there,' she'd say to Lorelei out on the street, and there was always some distaste in it. She never wanted Lorelei's devotion, but she didn't want anyone else to have it either.

Mel looked around and said, 'I've had enough of this. Let's go somewhere else.'

As we made our way out, a man whose face was glowing red from the effects of festive drinking pointed one of his fingers at Mel's dress and said something neither of us quite understood. Something cheerful, maybe something stupid.

'Idiot,' Mel muttered.

We walked down the steps into the park and she abruptly changed her mind about going somewhere else. 'I need a lie-down after that. See you later?' She saw the expression on my face and added, 'Sorry to throw a spaniel in the works.'

Danke, Mel, Dankeschön, Bitte, Vielen Dank, Gerne, Tausend Dank, Herzlichen Dank, Bitteschön. Why had I let her do this to me? I walked through the park back towards the apartment, aching with the desire to tell the one person in my life who really, truly understood how complicated this was that I had somehow managed to let my stepsister scuffle the upper hand as usual. But then again, I remembered, I may have forfeited any right to rely on him.

When Jay and I had arrived at the stage of our relationship where going to bed together was imminent, he confessed that he had something of a foot fetish. It had stopped me taking it further for a while. 'What did you say to him?' Mel wanted to know after I'd confided in her, and when I told her that I'd said that wasn't something I was into, she'd responded, 'I would've said how interesting.'

It was the potential obsequiousness that I didn't really like. 'He's already such a pleaser,' I said to Mel. 'The idea of Jay worshipping my feet seems masochistic.'

But Jay knew how to talk about things. He explained that for him it wasn't so much a toe-sucking thing, more just about liking the form. One afternoon I let him take off my boots and my socks, and he did little more than rub his warm hands all over my feet, and kiss their soft underbelly, and then kiss my heels. It made me feel that if he could like this part of me, he could like every part of me. The next time I saw him I told him he could do whatever he wanted to with my feet, and he took off all of his clothes, and I saw for the first time the muscled hardness of his body, and he took off all of my clothes, and then he picked up one ankle in each hand and rubbed my feet over his taut stomach and, one by one, over his penis, and then his balls, and then his penis again. I found it surprisingly erotic, and he lay down beside me and stroked my whole body with his hands, and kissed every part of my face with his hungry trembling lips, and we had the warmest sex of my life.

By that time Mel had left for overseas and there was a

void. But I soon found I made a gentler space for myself with him. He showed me the way towards kindness. Not the type of overbearing kindness that Lorelei had given us as children, but seeing kindness. And he was set up to notice the essential good. And after that first time he only occasionally paid attention to my feet, so that I eventually forgot that it was ever a thing. I forgot.

22.

The city emptied out between Christmas and New Year. Frankie had gone off to party for the week in Prague with friends. There were no footsteps coming from the flat above, and even ghostly Florian did not seem to be around either. It felt like there was nothing to be done, no decisions to be made, nothing much was open, nobody to talk to, nothing to be inspired about.

At night loud explosions came from the park, so booming and resonant they shook the walls of the apartment. Fireworks, I hoped, but they could have just as well been bombs. If they were bombs, how would I know?

In the dark the bare trees beyond the window started to appear spooky, like constructions of bones or standing skeletons risen up out of the earth. One night I looked out over the balcony and saw a quick movement in the rose garden, a fox, stealthy and sly, checking to the left and right, Stasi officer on a clandestine surveillance mission.

At midnight on the last night of the year I stood on the balcony to watch the fireworks. The entire sky exploded like the celebration of the end of a war, all the people with their parties and fun, firing their salvos from their rooftops and balconies up into the night sky. Everybody saying good riddance to the year of dubious politics. The year there was no snow at Christmas. The second-hottest year in human history, when children admonished us all for being such wasters, and parts of the world caught fire under the hot, hot sun. And tonight all the pyromaniacs were celebrating by filling the sky with rockets and making the air so heavy and thick with gunpowder that it all began to feel like planet-ruining excess. Goodbye, terrible year.

I sent Jay a heart emoji and the champagne-popping one.

It was becoming harder and harder when I opened my eyes in the mornings to remind myself the reasons why I was waking up alone. What had once felt possible to rationalise now felt more like exile and deprivation.

During the days I alternated dry-docked efforts on the page – my illusion about completing anything on the Count clinging on by the thinnest of threads – with long, solitary walks around the chill streets, worrying that my inability to make any real progress might have something to do with my brain not turning over properly. I had been searching to find out what happened to the Count after the court case and had come upon a news item from 1941 when a group of journalists were having lunch at the Adlon and the Count approached them, saying, 'You are Americans?' They invited him to join them and showed him an article from *Time* magazine that speculated he was once again raiding in the South Seas. 'The story is foolish,' the Count said, but after admiring how he looked in the photos he asked if he could keep the article. 'I was some man then, eh,' he said. He told them he still liked to keep fit, then stiffened his biceps and plonked his arm on the table for them to feel how strong he was. Like a tree trunk, they thought. Shortly afterwards, a man wearing a Nazi badge came up and tried to draw the Count away, but he batted the man off and stayed at the table, drinking more beer and showing photos of boats he had sailed.

This was after the trial, and after the Nazis had banned him from public life. Why then, I wondered, did he choose to travel all the way from Saxony to drink in a place where, it seemed, he was effectively under Nazi supervision? Just so he could chance upon some English speakers who would listen to him telling his tall tales, with his version of charm?

Outside, the sky was low and grey, the days were short, and the rows of apartment buildings felt like they were snubbing the world, crouched inwards around their central heating. Church bells rang out, calling people to worship, and those who had fallen out of their own lives stood in their places with their paper cup out. I began to recognise some faces as I wandered my circuits: the woman in her hijab who positioned herself outside the bio market every day, the man with no teeth who swung open the door that led to the ATM machines, the skinny boy with pink hair and massively dilated pupils who had a spot near the Bäckerei, the old man with the perky-faced dog who sheltered in the warmth of the U-Bahn entrance in a sleeping bag. If I was lonely, they were lonelier. It was a kind of privilege, I realised, to spend time worrying about what might happen within ten years when some people could barely make it through the day.

Sometimes I paused to browse postcards on a rack outside a Späti with sayings I struggled to interpret with my word-to-word translation. *Das macht Dir so schnell keiner nach.* This makes you so fast nobody after. *Totgesagte leben länger.* Dead said live longer. I bought one to glue to the front cover of my notebook: *Angst macht den Wolf größer als er ist.* Fear makes the wolf bigger than he is.

I tried not to think of Pascual on these long winter walks, but when I did I could only remember him saying,

'You're not that good at getting out of yourself, are you?' If I had to lodge a plea, then I guess I could say it taught me at least one thing: I was no hedonist.

I had barely seen Frankie since the tepee night, but when she came back from Prague she seemed at least pleased to see me. We met up at the bathroom door. She was holding her make-up bag. Only just off the train and already getting ready for a night out.

'You go first,' I said.

'No, you,' she replied. 'I can wait.'

'No, really. I'm not going anywhere or anything. I'm okay to wait.'

Frankie laughed. 'This reminds me of the Iranian custom of Taarof.'

'What is that?'

'Oh, I think it's like a kind of ritual politeness. One person says you mustn't pay for that, and the other insists they should really pay, and it goes back and forth like that a few times until it is settled, and somebody says something like, I am forever in your debt. If you go there a taxi driver will insist, say, that there is no need to pay, but he doesn't really mean it precisely, it is more something like decorous manners, so you have to try and understand this custom so as not to abuse their notion of hospitality.'

'How do you know about that?' I asked, and she told me some guy she had once dated had told her about it, offered up as advice in case she ever went there.

Had I just misunderstood at the bus station after Halle? Had I just turned my back on some kind of ritualised playful negotiation? And had there been other cultural transgressions? The holding of hands not as innocent as I had received it? But, no… 'That guy. His name wasn't Boz, was it?'

'Boz? No. Why?'

I said nothing and stepped back to let Frankie get ready for her night out.

23.

My dearest Publisher, here is the essential problem:

He comes from a land where wolves roamed wild and men surveyed the landscape with the eyes of alphas and the musculature of boars. I come from sheep outnumbering people, chooks running free in the backyard, and acknowledging all-comers with the heart of a kitten.

And inheritance for him is a long line of cavalrymen with expectations of dominance and brooking no weakness, and having 'Count' bequeathed in front of their name. My only birthright, just quietly, is a curse carried within the walls of the body like a clandestine secret.

And he comes from ideas about women being mostly decorative and men entitling themselves by sucking on their pipe through acts of bravery at sea or war. And quite frankly we, the women of the world, are so over this kind of carry-on.

So, as you see, I am having some trouble with the Count. At my most confident I thought I could be some kind of excavator of truth, zeroing in on the difference between the lie of self-preservation and that of false elevation – but the transcripts are missing. And it's not just that. At a time when we are turning over the old stones of dominion, the Count's legend has taken on a certain whiffy obsolescence. I probably should have thought about that before I started. Too late I've realised it's not so much muscle and bone that matters but what runs between, and even then it's not so much what is conveyed but what it is made up of, right down to the cellular level, and not even that, it's what is deep inside the cells that really matters...

Frankie came storming in through the front door, not acknowledging me sitting at the table, and went straight into the bathroom. She was in there a long time. I reread the letter, which had mostly just been a form of procrastination, and deleted it.

Frankie emerged from the bathroom with a terrible look on her face. 'I've been stealthed,' she said.

I closed the lid of my laptop. 'What does that mean?'

'It's when a guy pretends to put on a condom but then slips it off and comes inside you.' Her hand raked through her hair. 'It's a form of rape,' she said angrily, pacing. 'He had no consent. He explicitly did not have consent for that.'

'Can you report him somehow?'

'I don't know. His profile has totally gone already, and to be honest I only knew his first name and that probably...' She shivered. 'Oh, I feel so dirty and so stupid.'

'He's the stupid one. What do you want to do?'

Frankie flung herself down on the old sofa which creaked under her weight. 'I guess I need to go to the clinic in the morning. Get checked out. Maybe PrEP. If he's done it this time, he's probably done it before, and who knows what...'

'Do you want me to come with?'

She didn't reply immediately but sat looking down at her hands while a single tear slid down her face. Without looking up, she nodded.

We walked up some nondescript backstairs inside a nondescript office building on a nondescript street, and arrived in a room full of young people who looked hungover and full of regret. We were oddities there, older, and the others stared at us as if they were wondering what kind of sex mistakes we could've made at our age. I took a seat opposite a poster that displayed the warning signs of syphilis – cankers in intimate places, rashes on hands and feet – as Frankie gave the receptionist a name that wasn't her real name or her nickname.

Frankie hadn't said much all morning, and as she sat waiting for her number to come up she tried to do Sudoku on her phone. Her legs were jiggling, and my stomach was churning. This was nearly too proximate and too sudden to bear. This anxiety about testing. I understood it too well. I understood all the bargains and calculations that go on inside a person's head...

If you live in a city of nearly 4 million people, and P equals the Percentage of the population who are sexually active

And M = percentage of those sexually active people who are sleeping with Multiple partners

And C = the percentage of those who are Carrying an STI

And S = the likelihood that the Stealther is one of those

And T = the Transmission rate between women and men, taking in moderating factors (x) such as roughness of sex etc

Then 4 million x P x M x C x S x T (x) = ?

We had to wait a long time for Frankie's appointment to come up. Every now and then I touched her, giving her hand a squeeze, just to assure her she was not alone. Frankie felt frail and too loosely held together under her skin, and I wasn't sure whether I was exactly transmitting strength either. I'd started to think that had there been a slight adjustment in the personality of Pascual, this could just as easily have happened to me. To distract myself I googled the name Lowell Thomas, author of *The Sea Devil*, on my phone. I had always thought he was just some proxy who had written a fairly lazy translation of the Count's German memoir. It turned out he had written dozens of books, had become one of America's best-known broadcasters, and was most famous for publicising the life of Lawrence of Arabia. I found a speech his son had given at his father's funeral. 'He had a pretty big ego and Mother was the only one who could really catch him on it,' he said, going on to describe how his father liked to surround himself with important men, to the detriment, it seemed, of paying attention to his only child. The son said he remembered only one of those men well: Count von Luckner, who he described as a giant of a man, very jolly, always laughing. 'He was very good to me. He had a little dachshund named Susie and the three of us would go hunting for woodchucks.'

'There was this thing that happened last year,' Frankie

said. 'My bank rang me, and it turned out someone had stolen my card details from an ATM and was withdrawing money in some American town I had never heard of. The bank paid me back, but it freaked me out for a while. That the world seemed so full of these malign forces who were trying to find complicated ways to commit crimes against you.' Her voice was unsteady. 'But this is next level.'

After a few moments she added, 'I think I need to go home for a while.'

'But you haven't had your appointment yet.'

'I meant home home.'

'Oh,' I said. Something selfish inside me wanted to persuade Frankie not to go. I could see that she needed to do it, though, to align herself up against familiar, easy things. She had been skipping along and now the grim side of this city's face had revealed itself to her. But at the same time, Berlin… unthinkable without her in it too.

Frankie said, 'There was this one moment when I glimpsed that guy from Kosovo in the mirror as he was hugging me. He didn't know I could see him and he was looking over the top of my head. The expression on his face was that he was not really that into it. He'd dropped his usual act because he thought I wasn't looking, and I knew then how desperate he must be, or innately open for whatever chance might come his way. I had thought it was attraction, but it was just a kind of opportunism driven by dire need. Ich liebe dich really meant I'd love you to give me one chance at a different life and I will do anything you ask to get that chance.'

Her number was finally called, and as she stood up she said, 'That's horrible, isn't it? To always have such a thing, such a person, on your conscience. I almost feel I deserve what's happening now because of that.'

24.

There was a new story in my feed. I had already done so many searches that Google knew what I was looking for. And Google told Facebook. And Facebook delivered it conveniently into my feed, as if spying on my obsessions. And so with no more effort than scrolling my finger down my own homepage I could read about the latest discovery, written in layperson's language, from a website that specialised in simplifying complicated scientific research on Huntington's. Whoever wrote it was a minor genius at metaphor.

The story explained that this new study targeted proteins that are 'in charge of capturing cargo destined for disposal in the cell'. Autophagy is an orderly way for cells to recycle unnecessary or damaged parts. The unwanted parts are swallowed up by big bags of digestive juices, and broken down, just like garbage bags left on the kerb are thrown into a city garbage truck and hauled away. Imagine, the story implored, if we had a set of molecular 'handcuffs' that could tether the mutant huntingtin protein to the garbage truck? 'Like the garbage collector who hangs off the back of the truck, methodically picking up garbage bags around the neighbourhood and dumping them into the compactor.'

The tone of the story was both hopeful and measured. This was a new idea; it would take years to know for sure. It might work, it might not. But if only, I thought. If only it was so easy. And while the garbage collector was at it, maybe they could also pick up all the rubbish men in the world and stick them into the compactor too.

25.

'For a month or so,' Frankie said. 'Maybe more. I don't know.' She'd found a cheap last-minute flight and decided to take it.

When she went in to farewell her work colleagues, I went shopping for eye masks and chocolates and facial mist and lip gloss and a couple of magazines and other things that were nice for a long flight, and slipped them into her hand luggage.

She said she hated airport goodbyes but I went to the airport with her anyway. She was okay, she assured me, she was over what had happened already, but it had been a long time since she was last home. After she had got through the chaotic luggage drop and checked in, we went to a juice bar and talked for a while about Florian who seemed to have a new boyfriend. Things had been appearing in the kitchen. A blender. Some coffee beans from the expensive Nordic café down the road. Some bio kombucha in the fridge. Frankie said that she had glimpsed him lingering at the door saying a long, tender goodbye to a man. She had heard the man say 'Be good' as a parting remark, and they had both started laughing in a way that was also double-edged. While for us living with Florian was like living with a feral organism that made only occasional scratching noises, it was nice to know that there were other people in the world who knew him better.

'Drink it,' I ordered, pointing to Frankie's smoothie. 'Your body needs those vitamins for that flight.'

She took a long slurp through her straw. 'I've been thinking a lot about the last time I went home,' she said. 'I had a hysterectomy. Did I tell you that? Fibroids, out of control, too much oestrogen or something.'

'No, you didn't say.'

'I've begun to think that might be the real reason why I've been on such a fuckfest the last couple of years. I think I just wanted to convince myself that I was still a hundred per cent female, or something.'

Fuckfest? Frankie's galloping horse had been well and truly put down now.

We were interrupted by a loud multilingual announcement about not leaving your bag unattended.

'It was pretty weird,' Frankie continued. 'Somebody cuts you open and sees the inside of you in the way you never have and never will. And takes parts away. I remember when I had the pre-op consultation with the surgeon, I could tell that he was gagging to do the operation but he was trying to appear as if I was making the decision in my own best interest. He said to me, I see you've been living in Germany. Do you like cars? They make the best cars. After that I could only imagine him driving around in something flashy, with the top down, paid for by my medical insurance.'

'Why did you let him operate on you?'

'He had come highly recommended by my GP. After the operation he used to come into my hospital room, trailing nurses with clipboards. I was there for three days and each morning he would tell me how well the operation had gone, what a good job he'd done. He wasn't really interested in how I was doing. He just wanted to know if I'd had a bowel movement, because as soon as everything was working they could release me and he wouldn't have to deal with my pale face or my insecurities.'

For days now the only way I could imagine responding to Frankie's sense of resignation was to hug her, but we were both such high-tensile units it also felt like too close a touch might have us flaying to pieces. 'Something like that probably takes a long time to recover from,' I said.

Frankie nodded. It was noisy in the airport, people walking up and down, towing their trolley bags on the hard floors. The clatter of small wheels felt cheap and clumsy and meaningless: dizzying amounts of cash being thrown at frivolous circular junkets.

'For a long time,' Frankie said, 'I thought I was fine as soon as the scar healed up, but I'm only now realising that it was taking longer for me to get my head around it.'

The departure board ticked over and the status of Frankie's flight moved up the listings and I felt a suspended panic about all the things we hadn't yet talked about.

'And you know what else?' Frankie said. 'About six weeks later I had a post-op meeting with him. I wanted to talk to him about these particular pains that had started up. He said, Oh yes, I'd forgotten you were a worrier.'

'Bastard.'

'He asked me to lie down on his consulting table, and all he did was put his warm palm on my abdomen and tell me everything was fine and I was good to go. Afterwards he wrote a letter to my GP that began: We had a delightful meeting...'

'He sounds lovely. Are you going to look him up when you get home?'

Frankie smiled wanly. The juice bar's machines ground into action again as a new order was taken. An animated young couple, each clutching a glass of something so green it looked like garden mulch, took the seat next to us, angling in their bags. Before they'd even taken a sip she pulled his head towards her and they started kissing deeply. It felt a little invasive, an affront to our parting conversation.

'How's that book of yours going, anyway?' Frankie asked.

There was the option to lie and deliver some platitude, as I usually would, about it coming along, but—

'I'm not sure about the Count anymore,' I admitted. 'I'm distracted by another story.'

'Really? What?' Frankie asked.

I hesitated and then with an impulsive surge said, 'It's about this woman who finds out she's at risk of a terrible genetic disease and she runs away from her life to try and work out... well, I guess, her future.'

Frankie went very still and focused. 'At risk?

'Well, there's a fifty per cent chance she has it.'

'But she doesn't know?'

'She could take a test.'

'But she hasn't?' Frankie had already hit on the flawed logic of the narrative. I had to try to remind myself what the plausibility was for the protagonist not to have simply taken the test.

I sucked in a few mouthfuls of vitamin smoothie. 'Well, if the test is positive then a really challenging decline is coming her way, and she – my character, I mean – isn't sure how a person lives with that because there is no cure, only a chance of something in the pipeline, and she can't decide whether it's better just not to know for now.'

A question was burning through Frankie's gaze. She appeared to be weighing whether or not to stay in the game. The opportunity that hovered in that moment was lost as the information board turned over once more. 'I can see that this is an interesting fictional dilemma,' she said, 'because it doesn't sound like a decision that can be made once. I mean, I suppose there are waves, and backtracks, and maybe slowly the person will move to the space where it will be better to know than to suspend themselves in fear.'

Nobody really gets it. I was talking to the one who had marched right into the clinic the morning after because she wanted to know. But then again she knew there was something that could be done. She could take a preventative pill. If I could take a preventative pill I would march straight to the nearest clinic too. Would Frankie have responded so certainly if the sexual risk was like things were back in the eighties and nineties? The potential death sentence?

'How does the story end?' she asked.

'I don't know.' Maybe I was the one not really getting it.

Frankie's flight status had changed to boarding. She gathered up her things and we began walking to the gate together, more slowly and reluctantly than we should have, given that she still had the security check to get through.

As a final goodbye, Frankie hugged me, and the transference of energy between us was so warm and material that I was reluctant to release her. Into my ear she whispered, 'Talk to somebody about it.'

I watched her go through to the gate, and it was suddenly inexplicable to me why I had hunched myself over my secret like a squirrel hoarding an uncrackable nut when all along this person had been available to me. Now it was too late. In this city that could sometimes be hard and unforgiving and transient and uninterested, Frankie had provided the filter that made staying possible. Without her, living with Florian made no sense, eating alone in the kitchen made no sense, struggling to speak German was nothing to laugh at. The Palomino had left the frame.

Jay had gone quiet on me too, and this unsettled me more than I liked to admit. I thought I didn't want the pressure of his waiting for a sign from me, but now that he was not replying to my messages, I couldn't sideline the feeling that I was piloting a craft on which the cargo had seriously shifted below decks and I didn't know how to keep a steady line.

26.

Talk to someone about it. Those words were burning against my sternum. There was only one person in Berlin who knew me well enough that I wouldn't have to fill in any backstory. She wouldn't allow me any self-deception, but her taste for unstable ground was like entering into a quake-zone. Still, I had been trying to talk to her ever since I arrived and, well… Lebensmut.

As soon as I walked into her place I could tell she had been up to something. Her apartment, her behaviour, reeked of sex.

'Okay, he was here last night,' Mel admitted.

'Who?'

'Christoph. You don't mind, do you?'

Immediately I was plunged into a complex cataloguing of responses. What was reasonable here? It's not that I wanted to have anything with Christoph, but it felt like Mel might have wanted to do this to take something away from me. She knew I could hear things from the floor above, so at least she had contrived this dalliance at her own place where I didn't have to listen. But in doing this, inviting him over, she had changed something essential about one of the few things I still had left here. That friendship. Those casual discussions about things Mel was not all that interested in: the history of being nearly forgotten.

The door to what could only be Mel's bedroom was closed, which made me imagine that there were things to see inside. I didn't admit out loud to minding, but I knew

Mel could read it on my face. 'How did you even get in touch with him?' I asked.

'He introduced himself, remember. Never heard of friending someone online?'

'You did that behind my back?'

'Don't be like that,' Mel said. 'You were never going to do anything with him. You've got whatshisname back home.'

'Whatshisname?' I glared at her.

It's not as if I didn't remember Christoph twisting around to get one more look at Mel as he left the restaurant. The man who liked a little personal sport. Recognising the one with edge. And it's not that I'd had anything particularly enduring with him, but had it crossed his mind at all, I wondered, in the midst of his entanglement with Mel, whatever it amounted to, that he might be harming our friendship? Did he care? Or was it just this city, where friends were made and let go too easily?

'Actually, why are you so cross?' Mel asked. 'You've been acting super-weird ever since you came. You don't talk about Jay. You're so touchy. What am I supposed to think about that?'

There are moments when a person has control and moments when a person loses it. I strode over, pulled open the bedroom door and stood looking at the allure Mel had created in there. The bedroom was a separate island inside the apartment and the bed itself a caravan belonging to some bodacious harem. A four-poster with its billowing canopy and piles of colourful cushions surrounded by Turkish rugs and wooden Moroccan side tables.

Mel came up behind me. 'What were you expecting? That he was still in there?'

'I don't know. Where do you stow your gear?'

'Gear?' Mel laughed. 'I have a big trunk under the bed. Actually, I've cut Christoph up into little pieces and I have him stowed under there too.' She laughed again. 'Jesus, what do you think I am?'

The immediate impulse, I suppose, was for some kind of act of invasion. Abruptly I walked to Mel's bedside table and pulled open the drawer.

'Wait!' Mel shouted. Too late.

I don't know what I had been expecting to see, but it was definitely not a used pregnancy test, with only one line, and an ovulation kit. I was so surprised I couldn't immediately take in the implications. Then I picked up the test stick and waved it in the air. 'What the hell? Are you trying to get pregnant?'

Mel folded her arms. She didn't speak.

'Are you?'

'I wouldn't mind if it happened.'

I threw the test back where it had been. After that it was like following whispered directions coming from offstage. Close the drawer gently. Turn and face the other party. Ask the most appropriate question you can muster: 'Are you telling whoever you are doing it with?'

Mel mumbled something unintelligible.

'Pardon? What did you say?' My voice was full of such inert indignation that I sounded like Lorelei.

'Sort of,' Mel said sheepishly, and left the bedroom.

The duvet on Mel's bed was so voluptuous it promised to absorb anybody who lay there. I dropped down onto it, and stayed for a long while looking up at the fabrics she had draped from the ceiling, swathing towards the corners. What exactly had inspired her to create this? It was like being inside a tent, and made me think of the one time we had camped together, beside a lake. Our parents, who were in the nearby cabin, had just got married and my relationship with Mel was new and untested. We had woken to heavy breathing, and weird rasping noises, and saw some strange slug-like shapes sweeping over our thin canvas roof. While I had drawn my sleeping bag up to my chin, Mel had crept to the tent opening, slowly sliding up the zip, and then shouted, 'Shoo!' and laughed. 'Cows,' she said, looking back at me, the scaredy new stepsister, then she rolled herself out of the tent and disappeared for the rest of the morning.

Back in the main room, Mel was sitting in a window seat, flicking through a magazine. It was easy to tell she wasn't really taking it in, that she was enjoying this almost spiteful display of insouciance as she flicked through the pages.

'What happened to Jonah?' I asked.

'We had a fight. It was that spare cock in the club. I'd just wanted him to take care of me a little in that situation and he... blamed me.'

'So did you try with Christoph?'

'Sort of,' Mel said.

A blast of fresh anger hijacked me. 'Mel, you can't do that. It's not right.'

Mel sighed and put the magazine down. She patted the space next to her, and I sat there. 'It's okay, Ginny,' she said. 'We kind of talked about it.'

'Kind of talked about it? What does that mean?'

'I told him in a jokey kind of way that I had been thinking a lot lately about having a baby, and I gave him the option to use a condom if he wanted to, and he chose not to, so...'

I searched my stepsister's face. What was this? Just another impulsive act? But no, there was something new there, or maybe it had been there for a long time but I hadn't noticed it before. Or hadn't thought to look for it. Because it seemed that Mel might have really been thinking about this. Maybe she really wanted this, had been planning it. Maybe, as unlikely as it seemed, a need had grown within her to find a way, even if it was unconventional, to have an elemental love in her life.

'Not all of us have our own personal cheerleader,' Mel said, with maximum sarcasm – and I couldn't absorb it anymore.

I spun out of her apartment, walking blindly through the courtyard, through the heavy wooden double doors and down the street. Where to go? I had nowhere. My legs were weak. My breathing was shallow. My heart banging in my chest. What was going on? Was I going to randomly die of panic now? At the edge of the canal I planted myself on a low concrete wall. Tried to steady myself, steady my breath, steady my mind. I looked around for something to focus my eyes on. I looked at my feet. And down past my feet. At the still icy water. At the place where the Spree directly contacted the bank. At the plastic bag that was slowly moving around under the surface ice like it was trapped in amniotic fluid.

Would a child of Mel's come to hate Mel's impulsiveness as much as Mel hated her own mother's stoic reliability? That anti-magnetic force working its magic. Then again, what if I had been allowed to know my own mother? Would there have been things I resisted? What would she have been like as a mother, anyway? Soft and maternal and bland like Zelda? Or an earlier-generation version of Lena, throwing punches and angry at fate?

And what kind of mother would I be?

A boat was chugging through the water in the middle

of the canal. Not a tourist boat – they seemed to be tied up for the season. Just one lonely boat, thin ice breaking at its bow. Three children stood on the rear deck, wrapped up warmly, waving at anybody on the shore.

It came to me that I had already accepted I would never have children of my own. It was half there before. Jay and I had been trying for a long time and nothing had happened. We'd had the tests and there was no specific reason. I'd taken the follicle-stimulating drugs, but was caught up in the idea that I was putting synthetics in my body and thinking too much about this made me feel as if I was creating an unrelaxed environment further down. All the thinking around it was so complicated. If it was me, then I was stopping him having children. If it was him, then he was stopping me. There were some unlovely bigger-picture remedies that we had been tending towards. Invasive procedures and, if that didn't work, somebody else's sperm, somebody else's egg. And perhaps… was it?… part of the reason why I'd run away? Had I let it all be enveloped by the bigger, more ominous threat?

Would anybody want to be a mother if they knew they couldn't be there for all of it? Even if they knew that the egg was disease-free? I'd never had my own mother when I was growing up, but I'd had somebody else's mother and hadn't been unhappy. Not really. Or maybe I had, but never really noticed because some part of me was snapped shut at an early age.

A community-minded tagger had sprayed words on a wall near our apartment: *Let's leave a better planet for our children*. Underneath, in a different hand: *Let's leave better children for our planet*. And I'd felt myself siding with that, because I was part of a group now, the non-parents who could, if they wanted, take up a position of moral uppitiness: we are not the overpopulators, we are not overusing the resources, we are taking everything with us when we go. Planet, you can thank us. In the meantime, we will do our best to recycle. The history of our history will soon be forgotten. Wiped out by Sturm und Drang. Nobody will even know, or care, that we were here. Nobody will be left to link back to our imprint on DNA.com. We, the non-parents, are just a blink in time, a short moment in history, that will soon become dust.

27.

I was existing more online than in the real world, and overnight my friendly algorithm had been gathering in news for me. A story in my feed segued from images of melting ice-caps into an item about scientists at a conference exploring how genetics could be used to fight climate change. One of their targets was plant "extremophiles", drought-resistant and salt tolerant species. Those clever minds were looking for ways to genetically manipulate the survivor traits so these could be applied to crop plants. They were using all the tools in the kit – genome sequencing, population genetics and CRISPR technology. Also probably bargaining on the fact that we, the population, will be less concerned about the potential unintentional consequences of genetically engineered food crops when all the bees have died out and the temperature regularly tops the thermometer. Those GE crops are called something else in future scenarios. They're called sustainable adaptions to harsher climates.

One day soon, one of those geniuses will look up from their microscope and say, 'I have it. That problem is sorted.' Here, eat this food that we've adapted just for you. Don't worry, there's plenty more where that came from. And hey you, human extremophile with your +26 CAG extension, here, take this injection that will sort out those rogue proteins of yours.

In the same way someone solved the problem of infection by inventing antibiotics, and someone eradicated

Polio through vaccination, someone will save life on earth too. That's all a person needs to believe in the future – a conviction that all problems can be solved by science. We can turn around the planet's demise, we can adapt against all threat, and we can dump a few horrible genetic diseases in the garbage while we're at it. That is all I need to hold on to. So what is there to talk over, Mel? It's simple isn't it? I just need to take the steps. A clinical consultation. Genetic counselling. But where?

28.

Everything in the world seemed urgent. I rolled my mouse over clinicians on YouTube. Why does this one have such mad hair, such clownish make-up? It makes her look half insane when I want her to be something else. But here she is speaking with her empathetic tone and her warm effort to share what she knows: *'Even before an individual with HD begins to be affected by motor dysfunction, we now understand that the disease may first manifest in changes to the personality. Large-scale observational studies, such as Enroll-HD, have helped us monitor how the disease first appears in different people. Earliest symptoms may include moodiness, rashness, greater difficulty recognising emotions in others, and hypersexuality...'*

Oh God oh God oh God. Were they all symptoms? The sex with Pascual? Hasty flight from Jay? Failure to get words down? Not properly relating to Boz? Or Lena? Or Frankie's friend Yvette? Unreasonably angry with Mel? No, no. I had my reasons with Mel. I had my reasons for all of it. I could rationalise everything. Couldn't I?

I made myself get out of bed and walk to the supermarket. *Geschlossen.* Had I got the days mixed up? Sunday already? This was a strange feeling, to be so much of a surface-dweller I didn't know why people in this country, this city, were taking a day off. Oh God oh God oh God. But no. Wait. I could see workmen inside dismantling shelves. Renovations? So back up the path to the café across the road from our apartment instead.

Suddenly, out of nowhere, some guy seemingly off his face on drugs came running towards me through a gang of fat pigeons pecking at some dropped chips, waving his arms and yelling, 'Ick hab keinen Bock zu heiraten.' The birds lifted off and flew at me in a panic. I dropped into a crouch as their dusty bodies flapped past me, and when I stood again my heart was beating too fast, and the idiot guy was still running, still yelling something about his marriage. He's mad. I'm not mad.

It would be just my luck now that the café was closed too. But no, it was busy. Everybody in Berlin was there. Hardly any seats, but Christoph was over on the long bench at the back. I took my Bircher muesli and squeezed in beside him.

'Na?' he greeted me.

I'd briefly forgotten he'd had sex with my sister, and wasn't sure whether to let him know that I knew.

Christoph introduced me to a man called Björn who was seated opposite. The two of them carried on talking, and I zoned out, not in the mood even to try to understand with my rudimentary grasp auf Deutsch. After a while Christoph told me they had been discussing a friend of theirs who had just started fostering a kid, but unfortunately he was called Kevin, so they were joking that the first thing their friend should do is change the boy's name.

'Why unfortunately?'

'Where we grew up, those names like Justin and Kevin tended to be given to the kids from lower socio areas and they nearly always ended up in the Hauptschule. They once did a study that became famous here, because they found that if a boy was called Kevin then the teachers made an adjustment and lowered their expectations.'

Björn leaned forward into the conversation and asked

me where I was from. When I told him he said, 'Ah, so far away. I have always wanted to go there.' He had a round, friendly face, blue eyes, and teeth that appeared to be too large so that his mouth's natural repose was a broad unclosed smile.

'Why?' I asked.

'I have been told that it is very beautiful.'

I was too bored with this to say what I ought to say. 'I always thought Björn was a Swedish name.'

'I grew up here and it is not an uncommon name here,' he said. 'But, yes, my mother was Swedish. My father was German. He was a photographer. Ever heard of the Elk Test?'

I shook my head, and he told me that Mercedes Benz used to take their top-secret test cars up to the north of Sweden and trial them by driving fast on the winding, icy roads. 'Maximum hazard area, including elks,' he said. 'It used to be a job that photographers would hide on these roadsides to try to capture a photograph of the new cars before they were released. But it was dangerous. If the drivers saw the photographers, sometimes they would stop the car and beat them up to get the film. And sometimes the photographers beat each other up, because one photo could be worth a lot of money.'

'Björn's father was a photographer,' Christoph explained.

'Yes, and my mother was a Swedish nurse. So that was how they met.'

'He got beaten up?' I asked.

'Yes, quite badly,' Björn said.

Was he making this up? 'Is that still his job?'

'No, these days it is done by drones.'

Out through the window I noticed Boz sitting at a

smoker's table underneath the awning. I happened to glimpse him at the exact moment he was leaning over with a cigarette in his hand, no doubt asking the young woman sitting nearby if she had a lighter. Flustered, suddenly, I needed to get away. As I was leaving, I said to Christoph, 'Careful she doesn't ruin you.' He looked astonished for a moment, and then he laughed. The room shifted. Oh God oh God oh God.

Not letting Boz see me, I walked to the park and plonked down on a bench near a tree. I needed air, a place to think. Was the fact that my mother had done something so aggressive and irrational as using her toe on the trigger of a gun in the kitchen where my father would find her actually just proof that she had the disease?

All these stick trees around me – unrecognisable in their seasonal nudeness. But actually, even if they were fully green would I know how to name them? At home I would, but here this kind of knowing had to be acquired. I had no labels for anything. At this time of year back home there would be long grass and cicadas singing and fantails bobbing charmingly along branches, and not far away the sound of the waves or, if I was in my own garden, the sound of the rustling leaves of the palm tree.

I looked at my phone. He still hadn't replied to my last three messages.

Jay had never liked that palm tree. He insisted that it was not native and I should take it out.

'But I like looking at it,' I'd said.

'But it's a foreigner here, and it's unhealthy for you,' he said.

'I don't care,' I replied. 'It blew in here as a seedling. One day I noticed that it just started to grow and now ten years later it's become that magnificent thing. So I guess it likes it here. It's thriving. It chose to live here and I'm never getting rid of it.'

'It sucks the water from the ground. Did you know that?'

'I don't care,' I repeated. 'It's good to look at, and there are some local doves that like to sit inside the branches and coo.'

'They aren't native either.'

We had exchanged an amused look then. I was aware that although we had grown up in the same country, some of his templates were from another world. Once when he wanted the monopoly on cleanliness he'd said to me, 'We invented soap long before your lot had even heard of it.' After he'd heard himself telling me to get rid of my tree, he had laughed and started talking and talking, going on a long riff about what he was going to do with five hundred grams of mince and an aubergine and how he was worried he'd forgotten the garlic but then he found some in the back of the fridge. 'That's such an interesting story,' I'd said. 'One day I might write a book all about that. It was so interesting.' He laughed again, and then his hands were all over me, because he found being called on his own bullshit a turn-on.

I looked down at my phone again. Still nothing.

29.

Somebody posted on Free Advice Berlin, panicked about losing her dog. She had gone onto the S-Bahn platform and the dog had stepped into the train and the doors had closed. Mostly people replied with helpful suggestions, links to missing pet groups, or, if they lived near that train line, offers to keep a look-out. One person wrote: Such things will happen if you do not keep your dog on a leash.

Another person put up a photo of a baby bird they'd found in their room. What is it? they asked. What shall I do about it? Most people replied with useful contacts for bird rescue centres or suggested ways of feeding it. It was a baby pigeon, the consensus was. It must have fallen out of its nest. One person suggested roasting it in butter and serving it with potatoes.

And another person wrote about putting a cardboard box in the recycling. It was from IKEA and had his address on it. He had filled the box with other paper. The next morning the box was back on his doorstep with a small, unpleasant note that he was not recycling correctly and that all boxes should be folded down flat. This was a very popular thread. Many people had had an impromptu lesson from one of their neighbours about the correct way to recycle. Never put anything with your address on it in the recycling, one person advised. Some people wondered why others had a problem with recycling correctly. The thread then turned to the way in which correcting the behaviour of others is part of the culture here. A barrage of amusing examples of passive-aggressive notes left on doors followed. It seems many newcomers had not understood that it was common for residents to share the duty of sweeping the buildings, but they had been corrected in surprisingly forceful ways.

What is this world? I really needed to stop looking at Free Advice Berlin. And get myself out of bed somehow.

30.

After an entire week of silence, and just when I was starting to feel really scared, Jay sent a surprise text: *I am in Porto. Join me?*

This was a calculated risk. He knew I probably wouldn't say no. And that I would be surprised. And perhaps touched that he'd made such a gesture. Travelling close but not directly to me. Giving me the choice to come. Seeming to be impulsive. Portugal had always been high on his list of places he wanted to go after his sister passed through there on her honeymoon. He'd liked the photos. Even so, some part of me was annoyed as I booked my expensive last-minute ticket. I was annoyed later, too, when he messaged that he wasn't going to pick me up from the airport, but rather would wait at the apartment. This was another kind of gesture. He was making me come to him, not wanting to be the anxious, uncertain face in a draughty airport hall. I did understand why. Some reserve was required. Now I was the one who'd have to knock on the door, ask permission for him to open up to me.

On the plane I struggled to keep hold of my thoughts as I rehearsed how I might explain myself to him. The girl next to me was reading a paper called 'Passive Attitudes to Bulimia' and halfway through the flight went to the toilet and didn't come back. The older couple across the aisle were drinking and flirting in such a way that they appeared like two separately married people heading off for a weekend dalliance together. The man summoned over one of the crew and purchased a bottle of Prada Candy perfume for the woman. After that he placed his jacket on his lap and her hand reached under it. As we neared the destination, the captain announced that unfortunately we were about to go through a rainstorm, the seat-belt sign came on, the crew rushed to put their trolleys away, the plane started jumping around, and the girl from next to me finally slipped back into her seat. Soon more than one baby was crying, the man's champagne spilled from his glass, his girlfriend had gone pale and was whimpering, and in the row behind I could hear someone being sick into a bag. By the time we were on the ground all the words I'd decided to say to Jay had skittered away like birds spooked off a tarmac.

On the taxi-ride in from the airport I switched my phone back on and there was a message from Mel: *Where are you?*

It gave me some satisfaction to reply, *Porto.*

Whaaat? Why?

Just because.

Are you that upset about Christoph?

Not everything is a response to your shit.

The taxi driver took a call and then began arguing with whoever was on the other end, stabbing the fingers of his right hand in the air to make his points. By the time I was on the footpath outside the apartment building I'd managed to re-summon my annoyance at Jay. I forgot about it the moment he opened the door, though. He spread his arms, and I walked right into his bearish embrace. My body relaxed into the familiarity of him. He smelled of fresh soap, while I was afraid I might have been exuding a musk of guilt from every pore. He had grown a small beard, only a little more than stubble, since we had last spoken online. I put my hand up and touched it. An attempt, I wondered, to show me he was a changed man? He took my hand from his face and kissed my fingers.

'It's so good to see you. Thank you for coming,' he said with a formality that foreshadowed how much work we had yet to do together.

Behind him was the open door to the bedroom. How easy it would have been simply to fall into the bed together – but then I'd be naked in front of him and I wasn't ready. I had things I needed to tell him first.

Off the small living room there was a second bedroom. 'I'm in here,' he said. 'You can choose the one you want.'

I put my bag down where I was standing.

'Shall we go for a walk? Maybe get something to eat?' The intimacy of this apartment was too much. Better to be outside among other people, walking and talking, eating and drinking.

'Sounds like a pastel de nata is calling us,' he said.

'What is that?'

'A sort of small custard tart. I've already discovered that's the thing here.'

He linked his arm through mine as we walked down the narrow lanes toward the river. One long street seemed to be almost exclusively hardware stores, their dusty, dark interiors, piles of wooden planks and not much else, men at work, like something out of earlier centuries. In every direction we could see signs of renovations going on, but also of dereliction and decay.

'The guy that owns the B&B was telling me they've recently changed the laws here,' Jay said. 'Before it was impossible to put up rents or evict tenants, so over decades the landlords just let the houses go to ruin.'

'The buildings are so beautiful, it makes you want to do one up yourself.'

'Shall we?' Jay said. 'Shall we buy one and do it up, and live on port and small pastries?'

'Okay. Which one shall we get?' We looked around at all the crumbling frontages, the shabby iron balconies and the gnarled wooden doors that had absorbed the long histories of their inhabitants.

'Hmm,' Jay said, standing still, his eyes searching, as if for a moment this was deadly serious.

Further down he guided me into a confeitaria and ordered us each an espresso and a pastry. We sat at a table with a view out towards the small park opposite. 'You already know your way around?' I commented.

'I had some time to look about while I was waiting for you. See that crowd of people there?' He pointed further down the street. 'They're waiting to get into the bookshop where J.K. Rowling wrote the first chapter of *Harry Potter*. It used to be a place where locals gathered and discussed literature and politics but the fans ruined the atmosphere. Nobody inside could read or think or talk with the clamour of teens taking selfies, so now they've started charging people to enter, and it's the second biggest tourist attraction here after Museu Serralves.'

'Really? Can we go?'

'There's always dozens of people in the queue, but if you really want to, my love.'

The pastry was delicious, sweet. 'How do you know all that stuff? About the shop? Did you read it somewhere?'

'Did a walking tour yesterday. It was three hours long in shit weather. But I know everything there is to know.' He took a moment to sip his coffee. 'About Porto, I mean.

Not about you.' There was gravel in his voice. He looked into my eyes for a moment, but quickly shifted his gaze back out the window. 'Do you want to go and visit the port caves down by the river after this?'

I'd forgotten he had this basic competency. That he could fly himself to some foreign country, and in a matter of hours find his way around, talk to locals, figure everything out. He'd worked really hard in just a few days to make himself into the man whose arm I could lean on.

Steep, winding, cobbled streets led us towards the river. Now and then we had to flatten ourselves against buildings to avoid passing cars. All the way we made light-hearted, jokey remarks to each other, bearing the weight of the conversation to come. Down on the strand some young girls were standing in a circle, singing earnest folk songs in their school uniforms. A group of men were edging closer to them. Some kind of drunken stag party, dragging around a man who was wearing what seemed to be a giant condom, his very hairy legs exposed and covered in goosebumps. A sign had been hung around his neck with words that were no doubt humiliating. Earlier we had passed some women wearing flower crowns on their head, perhaps the matching party. As the drunken men scrambled towards the singing girls, who were the very personification of innocence, it seemed like something terrible might happen. But one of the drunk men just beseeched the girls to sing a particular song, and they made the groom kneel down in front as they all joined in. Some sort of local song, with some sort of comic lyrics.

'I'm sorry I ran away,' I said to Jay as we watched.

'Are you?' he said. 'Because it…'

'Hurt?'

He sighed heavily. Perhaps relieved he could admit it.

'I've been totally… lost. Really. And confused. And, okay I'll admit it, pretty angry sometimes.'

'Can we sit for a moment?'

Behind us was a glass-fronted bar. The outside tables were mostly folded up against the wall, so we took some seats just inside the door. I picked up the menu. 'Look, you can get a jug of sangria. Shall we order one?'

We sat for a while, fruit floating in our drinks, watching people promenading along the water's edge, and my last resolve melted away. It was possible to maintain the idea when I was away from him that there was a virtue in not burdening him, but when I was sitting in front of the hurt face of the man who couldn't himself lie, I had to choose between saying nothing at all or the absolute truth. Previous thoughts about withholding information and limiting his choice in the matter no longer seemed noble but flimsy, panicked and badly thought through. Dishonest even. Evasive. And, oh God no, irrational.

I told him everything about my cousin coming to see me. Everything I now knew about the disease. I tried to frame my flight away from him as a need to have space to think. And perhaps to gather courage. Attempting to sound logical and reasoned, I explained about how I hadn't wanted to commit him to having to look after me. How I thought this meant I loved him in the purest of ways. But telling Jay was different from telling somebody I'd met in a pizza bar. My chest became so tight I couldn't keep my voice even, and after I said I didn't want to be his invalid, tears spilled out.

Mostly he had listened without saying anything – his body language was taut and contained from the moment I started – but now he reacted in a way that surprised me. He seemed to be boiling with anger.

'Was that all just your decision to make? See, this is what makes me feel hurt. You go away. Just like that. You push me away, thinking you want to sort it out for yourself, but you don't consider how that affects me. You don't think that this is a two-way street. That my life didn't change completely that day you fell off your bike. I picked you. And I had been preparing to say it in front of everybody. You didn't think about that?'

'But it… hurts me to…' I was floundering suddenly. 'It hurts me to think you might waste your beautiful life on me.'

He sat back in his chair, leaned his body out away from me. 'You've always thought that. Don't you know? Remember how persistent I had to be in the beginning. I kept turning up, and you kept saying to me you don't have to do this.'

'Did I?'

'Yes, you fucking did.'

Suddenly I wasn't sure what I was experiencing. It felt like shame. Shame mixed with relief. And a sort of pity for him. He hadn't been able to absorb it all yet. There was much more to be done. I drained the sangria from my glass and refilled it.

'The thing is… let me ask you this… what would you have said if I had told you?'

He looked towards the river, towards the port boats that were moored there, bobbing gently in the water, waiting for tourists to board.

'I would've talked it through with you. I would've tried to help you think it all through.'

'But… would you have made me take the test?'

'I don't know. I wouldn't have forced you. But… isn't it better to know?'

'See, I knew you would say that.'

'Is that so bad? So that's really why you ran away? You don't want to take the test, and you thought I would make you?'

'No, not exactly.'

'What, then? I want to understand this.'

Somebody in the kitchen had turned the music up and was singing along to an Afrobeat song.

'What would you do if you knew I had the condition? Really had it?'

A vein in his neck pulsed. 'I don't know. I guess I would help you find the resources you need. Help you get treatment.'

'Currently there isn't really anything that can turn it around. So everything becomes all about me? About looking after me? But what is the point of that?'

'What are you saying?'

'See, what if I thought it was better for you not to make your life about watching me lose who I am? What if I loved you so much that I don't want that for you? What about children? Look at you, you're a born father. You want it so badly. It will be the making of you, being a father. In fact, I want to do it now. I want to say you are free to pursue that. Now. Without knowing anything. I'm already too old. It's already in doubt. I love you. I want you to find someone to have children with. I hereby release you.'

'Okay, see ya,' he said. He got up from the table and walked away. It was obvious from his stride that he was in a rage.

Had I finally touched on his raw inner truth? My heart was thumping so strongly at the sight of him walking off that I knew he had made his point. That my life was completely diminished without him.

Not knowing what to do, I just sat there. The jug of sangria was empty and I didn't order another one. The waiter was now treating me with slight contempt. Even though the restaurant wasn't busy, he didn't particularly want me taking one of the tables if I wasn't going to order from him. I was hungry now too, but still I didn't order anything. I just stayed where I was, confused about Jay's response. Perhaps I had expected him to hug me, or at least pat my hand. Instead he was intent on maintaining his hurt about my going away.

As the afternoon wore on the rowdy tourists pouring out of the port caves began to seem more and more disrespectful – trashing local traditions by making them nothing more than a commodity for group drunkenness.

I began scrolling around on my phone. Lena had posted some new photographs. From Berlin she had obviously travelled south. There were some selfies in front of a Metro entrance, and on a bridge over the Seine with the Eiffel Tower in the background, but after that she seemed to have picked up some friends and gone down to Greece. The beautiful, lonely framings gave way to blurry group photos in Tavernas, with jugs of wine and always her and the same two companions with various other people. She'd lost a lot of her dark energy, posting a photo holding out some grass in the flat of her hand as a goat with rubbery lips nibbled on it, and another taken by somebody else of her writing in a notebook while sitting in front of a wide window with a mountain view behind, a close-up of a couple of hands clinking milky glasses of Ouzo, and one of her standing in the snow laughing with an airborne snowball about to land on her. Every single posting was liked by her father Phillippe. Sometimes he added little comments on too: *Wow, what a beautiful spot, I'm jealous* and *haha, careful that goat looks hungry!* She didn't reply. There was no text on any of her postings, but she hadn't completely pulled up her anchor from home. At least in this way she was keeping them in touch with what she'd been up to.

From her page I began looking at what the rest of the Canadian family were doing. Zelda's sister, Margarethe, had been busy reposting any advice she could find about alternative therapies. A natural compound found in strawberries could slow the onset of motor problems. Stay off coffee as more than the equivalent of two small cups a day has been linked to earlier onset. Acupuncture can help to maintain the connectivity of brain cells and nerve cells. Chinese herbs that help strengthen the kidneys and dispel wind could be used to treat tremors and muscle weakness. I clicked on a few of the links, thinking mostly about the pureness of Margarethe's hope.

When I next looked up, Jay was coming in the door, his face both ragged and determined. He sat back down in the same chair. 'Can you tell me why you don't want to take the test?' he said.

The desire to be as truthful as possible fought with the desire to just run away from any kind of accounting at all.

'I don't know. It's not that I don't want to take the test, I guess, more that I'm terrified of the absolutism of knowing. It might be different if there was a cure but… I'm not alone. Do you know that only a small percentage of people who can take the test actually do it? It's completely normal not to want to confirm that this unbearable thing is coming your way.'

I understood as this came out of my mouth that it might not be all that normal. By refraining from taking the test I was suspending our lives in such a way that I was committing a disservice towards him. Also I understood now that if you spoke up about the dilemma, then people, especially those who love you, are always going to say to take the test, mostly because they are impatient to know your fate for themselves.

'Is it?' he said. 'But don't you see what you're doing? You're already pushing me away from you, planning for a shit future. Maybe you don't have it. Fifty–fifty, those are the odds. Imagine if you don't take the test and you get to be old and you have to look back on your life and realise you made a whole lot of bad decisions when you were thirty-six because you thought you might have it.'

I looked into his dear, loyal face and said, 'I'm tired. Can we go back to our room and just lie down together.'

As we were walking back up the hill, a football match was starting and locals were crowding into bars. The whole town had the air of a potent moment, the future mood depending on the team's performance. At another time it might've been fun to sit amid that atmosphere, but we were both too wrung out.

Inside the apartment we flopped down fully clothed on the bed. The furniture in the room had a baroque tone: a heavy, carved wooden bedhead, lots of velvet, and floaty curtains that were tinged pink so that the room was effused with a girlish late-afternoon light.

'Let me ask you this,' Jay said, looking up at the ceiling fan. 'I used to smoke. What if I found out I had, say, lung cancer tomorrow. What would you do?'

'Probs take the fastest train to somewhere neutral. Switzerland. Bahamas.'

'Bahamas? What?'

'Oh look, I'm joking. Of course I'm joking. But you're

trying to manipulate me by manufacturing this pretend scenario. It's unfair. Also, don't jinx shit.'

'Why is it unfair?'

'Because.'

This was not a conversation that could be done quickly. It required perspectives to sink in. And in this moment I doubted my capability. I was drunk. The sangria had gone down so easily, seeming just mild and refreshing, and now its true effect had snuck up, making everything edgeless and dulled.

'The point I was trying to make,' he tried again, 'is that you don't necessarily have the world monopoly on a fear of mortality.'

'I know,' I said sulkily.

He sighed. 'Shall we just have sex then? Me with my fatal cancer and you with your terrible degenerative disease?' He ran his hand down the length of my arm, looked into my eyes, and my impulses became unreliable. Somewhere in the back of my mind I felt like I needed first to confess to him that I'd slept with someone else, but instead I put up my hands and slowly pulled his face towards mine and kissed him on the lips. 'Okay,' I whispered. 'Let's have sex as if we are already half dead.' And we began. Long, slow melancholic sex, like it was the last time, a meaningful goodbye, a final celebration of our beautiful bodies. We ran our hands over familiar places. He had never seemed more lovely to me. There was no hitting, no firing out spit. All our senses were boosted in a beautiful way, everything we could bring to it.

Afterwards we fell asleep and I dreamed I was cutting down trees in a forest, but as I rose to the surface I realised it had to do with Jay snoring beside me. I'd hated his snoring when I first started sleeping with him, but after a while it had become familiar and something like a reassuring presence beside me. Now I rolled towards him and placed a hand on his belly, and as if I had drawn it up, it started gurgling. All we had eaten all day was that one pastel de nata.

Jay opened his eyes and said, 'Hungry?'

'Starving,' I said.

He told me that the guide had recommended a restaurant down on the other side of the river in Gaia. 'Authentic,' he said. 'He recommended the octopus rice with fried octopus. Shall we?'

*

We edged into a small restaurant that had white paper coverings on the tables and an industrial fridge humming away in the corner, and was packed with so many local diners we felt like clumsy intruders. We ordered the recommended dish and a jug of vinho verde. When the octopus came, prepared by the motherly cook we had glimpsed through the swing doors to the kitchen, we discussed how the size of the tentacles made us feel especially guilty – this creature had lived a relatively long, sentient life under the surface of the sea before it was dished up for us. We were so hungry, though, that we ate greedily at first, spilling some of the dish onto the table and shifting the plates around to cover up the stain. Quickly sated, I began to pick at the rice and look around the room. Next to us were two men and two women, all middle-aged, possibly family, making their way through a shared meal of battered fish and chips and a big plate of chopped tomatoes. They had nothing to say to each other as they chomped away. On the far side of them was a family with little twin girls in identical dresses. The girls were behaving gorgeously, trying to be grown-ups seated in a room of adults. Jay noticed where I was looking and waved at the girls, who waved shyly back, glancing at their parents for permission.

'You want that, right? You've always wanted that,' I said.

'Children? Again?' He put down his knife and fork. I had already gone against an unspoken rule that we would try to have one meal without getting into it all again. 'I thought about it a lot today. After I left you, I walked to the middle of Ponte de Dom Luís and stared at the water and thought about it. And the truth is I don't know. I don't know if I really need that in my life. I am already an uncle. That might be enough.'

'The Ponte de Dom Luís? You know the name of the bridge?' An uncle. It occurred to me that I might be on the way to being an aunt, if Mel's plans were working out.

'It's famous, designed by Gustave Eiffel.' He ground on with a lot of dull, possibly made-up facts about spans, and the tonnage of steel, the manpower it took to build it and the volume of water passing beneath. He smiled to let me know that he was just satirising my attempt to derail what we were really talking about. He put his hand out, palm open, in a gesture to ask what my real response was.

'I don't think it is for you, though,' I said, seriously. 'It's not enough.'

He shifted his hand on top of mine. 'But we have always been living with this. It's something I have already come to terms with. There was never any guarantee that IVF would even work, was there?'

'That's the thing. I don't know now if I even want to do that. Even if I was… healthy. And I'm getting on. And even if I was not – well, these eggs of mine are probably just not all that good. I mean, it hasn't happened yet, has it? And it's not like we didn't try.'

'It's not that I haven't thought about all that,' Jay said. 'I think at some point I decided that I love you more than I love the idea of myself as a father.'

A wave of warmth washed over me but I couldn't meet his gaze. He was being more generous than I deserved, providing this velveteen landing. It was too lucky, too easy to just let go and fold myself into him.

'That makes me feel sad,' I said. 'Shall we go somewhere and adopt a whole tribe? Shall we steal one from somewhere? You can bring it up. You're spilling over with all that love.'

'We could get a dog.'

'Dogs. Can we get a whole gang? Little dogs that we carry everywhere with us. That we call our furbabies.'

'Little? Forget it. We're getting a big dog. A big sloppy dog that sniffs butt and chases shit and snores and slobbers everywhere.'

'You mean a dog that takes after you?'

'What? Yeah, snore, slobber, but have you ever seen me sniffing butt?'

'Well… I've got a butt.'

He playfully sniffed the air, as if he was receiving a pheromone-laden scent, but stopped when the proprietor came to our table and seemed to be asking if we were enjoying the meal. He started lifting away some plates, revealing the spillage we had made earlier, and we looked at each other, feeling exposed for making the mess, and for our pathetic attempt to hide it.

While Jay was sorting out the bill I sent a message to Mel: *Did it work?*

What?

The babymaking

No response.

Walking back, we discovered it was possible to take a cable car right up to the top strut of the bridge that would take us across the Douro. We bought our tickets, got on, and whirred along quietly, rising up alongside the river. The lit-up tourist boats on the water beneath us looked slow and dozy from such a height, and I blurted out, 'I slept with someone.'

For some long moments Jay did not move. He was looking down at the river. I could feel an instant heat rising off him.

'Only once.' His silence was torturing me. 'I want to say it didn't mean anything really, but that sounds like a cliché, so…'

He turned to me, his face as hard as I had ever seen it. 'I slept with someone too,' he said. 'More than once.'

'Really? Who?'

'Does it matter?'

'Do I know her?'

The cable car was nearing the top, the stress-inducing bit where we would have to quickly jump out before it turned the corner and headed back down. The conversation felt urgent, like we needed to wrap it up before we got out.

'I don't know.'

'You don't know? So, I probably do?'

He hesitated. I stared into his face, not giving him any concession. 'She works in the café,' he admitted.

Ha! I knew he wouldn't be capable of withholding anything. 'Which café? Our local? That girl with the blonde dreads? But she's…'

'Twenty-two.'

A guy was standing on the platform, ready to stop the

car from swaying as we exited. We hopped out and moved sullenly down the alleyway to the stairs. Jay did not take my arm, as he usually would. Once we were out through the main doors we paused for a moment to look over the strand in Gaia from where we had just risen.

'Are you still?' I wanted to contain my anger, my jealousy, but I could feel that my face was flushed with the effort of trying to tamp down any kind of overheated reaction.

'No,' he said. 'No. It was just you had left so suddenly, basically jilted me, and you were being so evasive, and I didn't know... and... well... she was up for it. And I think I needed—'

'A distraction?'

After a long silence in which I felt a seed of confused fury that the liability for this had landed so squarely on me, I said, 'Are you still?'

'No,' he said. 'It was never gonna last.'

'I didn't even find out the last name of my one,' I said, as some sort of appeasement, but he looked appalled. Somehow in his worldview it was worse to sleep with a completely random stranger. 'He was a nice person, though. From Spain.'

'Good to know,' Jay said sarcastically.

Our walk back to the apartment was long and quiet. We didn't sleep in the same room. I had the pink room and he went back to the smaller one off the sitting room. Before I got into bed I saw that Mel had sent a message that I had missed before: *Not yet.*

31.

I got up early. When I looked in on Jay he was only half awake, so I told him I would meet him at the café later. I could barely breathe in the apartment.

The town was getting ready for its day. Women who seemed to be a thousand years old were sweeping their front porches. Shopkeepers were opening their shutters. Ominous clouds were tumbling about overhead. An old wooden tram was parked down by the river. A sign indicated that the first ride would leave at 9am, so I sat alone and waited for it to start up, thinking about Jay and the girl from the café down the road from our house. I believed him, really, that he had mostly done it as a response to my going away, and this co-existed with some complicated relief that he had a mark on his side of the balance sheet too.

A few more people, tourists, joined me at the stop, and when the tram shunted into life we all bought tickets and got on, transporting ourselves into some imaginary yesteryear as we rattled along beside the river.

The couple behind me seemed to have only just met, and the man was telling the woman that back in his country he sometimes had to walk through waist-high snow to get to school. 'I come from home of five hundred books,' he said. 'At breakfast my father reach over to shelf and take one. He thumb the pages as we eat, look at us. Years later I realise he can't read. But I read. I read every of those five hundred books.' Then he started talking faster and faster, saying something about what he had learned from his ancestors going back centuries, and how they had once given a friend salvia and sent him on a hallucinatory journey back through time and he met his ancients, and when they woke him up and showed him a picture of the original mother he cried because that was exactly who he'd met.

The woman said, 'Really,' sounding sceptical and a little wary, and next he started on his theory that all people inherit everything, including diseases like cancer, from their mothers, because it all comes from the umbilical cord. 'And the cancer, it's all about the stomach. Know why Americans the fattest people in the world? Their mens don't give them enough orgasms. Women need orgasms.'

The woman cleared her throat and had nothing to say, and I looked out the window at a fishing boat puttering along the river.

There was a ping on my phone. I took it out of my pocket, expecting it to be from Jay, but it was from Boz: *I had a dream last night that I was appropriated as a character in your novel, and I decided to write my part myself without letting you imagine it.*

Before I could think of a suitable reply, the tram came to the end of the track near where the mouth of the river met the sea.

The waterside path was edged with tall palm trees that were being seriously disturbed by a strong breeze. Further along I came to a low concrete seawall jutting out into the mouth of the estuary. Behind me was an ancient fortress, at the end of the wall was a lighthouse, and on the seaward side was a surf beach. The fishing boat I had seen earlier navigated its way out through the mouth of the estuary, reached the wide open Atlantic and began to bounce on the waves. It appeared brave, intrepid, and made me think of those early sailors for whom whatever lay beyond the horizon was unknown. It must have taken bravery to leave everything behind, to face years without any real attachment to homelands, to bunk down in the company only of men, with months of nothing but blue to the eyes and salt on the skin, far from mothers or grandmothers or doctors or childhood friends or favourite tobacco shops.

A spit of water landed on my nose and the grey clouds above seemed to be lowering, so I returned to the tram stop. When the next tram arrived, the driver got out of his seat and manually turned around all the wooden benches for the journey back the other way. This time I was the only passenger, and as the driver took up the controls at the opposite end from which he had arrived I imagined J.K. Rowling might have been on this thing at least once.

Jay messaged: *Coming soon?*

I sent back a photo of me on the tram, and he replied that he would meet me at the last stop. What was I going to say when I saw him? Whatever it was should be reasonable, but I honestly didn't know if I still had a grip on reasonableness. And I also couldn't quite put a finger on the right thing to write back to Boz. *I'm sorry if my holding your hand gave you the wrong idea.* Or, *I give you full licence to write your version of that story.* There would probably be a large margin, I thought, between his and my versions. Then again, wasn't that the point Boz was trying to make? That any writer's version of another's life would involve some creative licence. There was probably a very great margin between, say, the Count's version of himself and that of Lowell Thomas. The American egoist would surely not have been able to resist some spin. All the other writers had since climbed into those margins too. Some said, as if it was fact, that the Count's boat capsized under a tsunami; others said that in fact it didn't. Some wrote blithely that he was a sex offender; others were emphatic that he was not. The truth was hardly definitive and the further history moved away from the time, the wider the margins grew.

So what was the true historical record between Boz and me, two writers who happened to meet? Some people might say he was definitely inappropriate. Others that I could have been clearer.

Go for it, I messaged.

By the time the tram reached the city centre it was pouring with rain. Jay was waiting nearby, sheltering under the eaves of a building. His face was tense and drawn, and perhaps mine was similar. A few shops down we found some red plastic raincoats and put them on. We took photographs of each other looking like Portugal's most inept tourists. The coats were so thin we might as well have been wearing rubbish bags, we said to each other. 'Rubbish bags might have been better,' Jay said, as the left seam on his coat ripped apart after only a few steps. We tried to duck under sheltered doorways as we made our way up the hill, but soon our shoes were wet and slippery, squeaking as we walked along. In part, it was a relief – this business of trying to get on in adverse circumstances meant we had simple, non-loaded things to talk about. We noticed other tourists in more sturdy white PVC raincoats and began to discuss how we could find out where they had got them. They looked better. A genuine barrier against the rain.

'I always knew you fancied her,' I said.

'Genius,' he responded, then added more seriously, 'It's

over, you know. It's done. It can't be undone. I'd like to say it didn't mean anything really but that sounds like a cliché, so—'

'Did you… I need to know… did you do something with her feet?'

He stopped walking and pulled on both of my arms until I was directly in front of him, looking straight at him. The expression on his face was a request.

'Okay. Let's never speak of it again,' I said.

He nodded. 'Justo.'

'Portuguese?'

'Also Spanish, I believe.'

'Ahh, I see.' Something in my heart lifted. I realised that he was, more often than not, one step ahead of me when it came to a gracious pardon.

We went back to the same café as the morning before, although it felt like it had been much longer. The longest twenty-four hours in the history of the world. We sat with our coffees and our pastries, looking out at the miserable weather.

'Can we talk about what would happen if I had it?' I said, so compulsively that I feared I might be about to pull our whole rickety detente down on top of us.

Jay's hesitant nod suggested he would rather not.

'Can I show you a photo?' I took out my phone and started scrolling. 'See, this is my uncle before he developed it.' It was the image Margarethe had posted in her feed. Of Caspar. Holding a big golden retriever in his arms, looking robust, playful and wonderfully good-humoured. There was another one of him jogging along with the dog at his side.

'I can't see the resemblance,' Jay commented.

'That's not the point,' I said, searching to find another

photo. 'This is twelve years later.' It was the photo of him in the hospital. Even in the photograph it was easy to see signs of dystonia where his body had gone rigid. His eyes had taken on a spooked look, his mouth was a crooked line, but it was possible to see that he was trying, trying so hard to smile for the camera.

'In the late stages they all get like that,' I said. 'I don't want to see it but it is there. With that haunted, twisted-up, skeletal look. The chorea burns up calories and they have difficulty controlling the muscles on their face, and speaking, even swallowing.'

There were more photographs in Margarethe's feed of our cousin Phillippe, Lena's father, looking healthy and energetic and high-spirited. From before. These posts had a serious intent, I knew. Margarethe wanted people to be able to look at our cousin and see what used to be there. She needed people to relate to him not with bland sympathy, but to find his true self, his personality within the unsteady mess his body was starting to become.

Jay had become very still and quiet.

'Within a few years he probably won't be able to feed himself,' I pressed on. 'He'll barely be able to talk or think clearly, not be able to clean himself or go to the toilet. Would you want to live like that?'

'But even if you had it… it might not go like that. With this gene-therapy thing.'

'Maybe. That's possible. But it is also possible that it will come too late for him and too late for me.'

'Or maybe you don't have it. Or maybe you have the late-onset kind that means you have time. Or maybe they find a treatment within the next few years. That seems likely. They're making progress, aren't they? Aren't you catastrophising a bit here?'

'Catastrophising?' I sat back in my chair and glared at him. 'Fucking catastrophising?'

Even as I spat this back at him I was scaring myself by being too angry. It could be that I was teetering between what felt in the moment like justifiable rage and that rage tipping over into becoming a firm indicator that I was actually pre-symptomatic. He was only trying to apply some sensible logic and he knew he wasn't getting it right. Right, I thought, might be getting up out of his seat and running for his life. And I could hear how annoying I was being. Refusing to accept even a hint of optimism. Letting myself become entombed in this fatalism. Obsessing about the end-stages. There was still half a chance, after all, that I was fine, putting both of us through all of this for nothing more than fear of what might happen. And even if I wasn't fine, science was moving so fast, who knew how far out the end game could move?

We sipped our coffee in silence for a few moments. But I couldn't let it go: 'You didn't answer my question. Would you? Want to live like that? If it happened?'

'I don't know.'

'You don't want to say no?'

He considered this. 'But how can I? This is all projected. Like that thing I laid on you about lung cancer.'

'But don't you see? It's not just a physical decline. It's the brain. It eats the brain. It takes away your autonomy, your identity. What are you without that? So if it came down to this, if I couldn't do anything for myself, if I didn't even know myself, I mean this point does seem contingent to our future, and what I want to know is would you… help me to…'

He looked unsteadily into my face. He knew what I was asking. 'I'm not sure,' he said. 'Maybe. If that's what you really wanted. But the thing is, at what point? Even if your capacity is failing, maybe the will to live kicks in. So at what point do you say, I'm ready? Does your cousin? Your uncle? They live within their capacity. They are still them, as much as they can be. Maybe that's all you need to do in life.'

A group of five French tourists, two young women, three young men, came through the front door and began noisily ordering coffees and pastries. All tall and young and thin and buoyant. They were in holiday mode, teasing and joking with each other.

'But what about all the other nice girls in the world,' I whispered to Jay. 'There are thousands of more suitable girls for you. Look at them. What about her, or her? Choose someone else. I'll be okay.'

He looked over towards the women at the counter and said, 'Well, yes, those two do look very nice. Shall I go over and ask one of them if she wants to marry me?'

I let out a broken snort of laughter. When I looked back at Jay, I noticed that his hand was trembling as he brought his cup to his mouth, and I understood how much he was struggling to keep himself together. We were like two people travelling along the deep ocean in a submersible, able to perceive only what our searchlight could reveal of the sediment bed, sea monsters to the rear.

'I keep thinking about that film of the book, *Still Alice*,' I said. 'We saw it together, remember? I keep thinking about the terrible scene where the main character with Alzheimer's has written to herself that if she can't answer the questions on her computer she should go upstairs and in her bedroom drawer there is a pill. So, she has the brief moment of clarity that now is the time, and she goes up the stairs, and the whole movie theatre went still and intense.

It's terrible, but at some level you really want her to be successful. You want her to do what she wanted to do when she was more aware. But then the doorbell rings. She gets distracted, and...'

When I stopped talking and looked at him, his eyes were shining and he was blinking. 'Stop this,' he said. 'You probably don't even have it. Don't you get that?' He said he had to do something and got up, left the café, walked off down the road. I sat rigidly with the thought that he might not come back, but then there he was again, standing under a veranda opposite, ripping the seal off a packet of cigarettes. I watched him light up, take long hard draws, looking at the wet pavement, deep in thought. I hadn't seen him smoke like that since he had first moved into my place. He'd decided back then he would make me a new dining table and had laid out some recycled rimu planks in the backyard, and stood for days smoking, staring, solving. Planning how he would put it all together. When he had completed the whole thing, he gave up cigarettes entirely. And now he had started again because of me. Smoking, staring, solving. Was one of the options he was considering leaving me? I wanted it to be, because if he did not think seriously enough about leaving me, then he could not consciously choose not to leave me.

When he came back into the café he said, 'Shall we go to Serralves? At least it's out of the rain.'

We took a taxi, bought our tickets. The current exhibition happened to be works of Joan Miró. We followed crowds of people around the colourful, abstract, dreamy images. Sometimes we looked at the paintings together, other times we strayed off from one another. The images seemed at first to be bright and playful but after a while the squiggles and dots and linear faces began to seem to me like things you might see in a petri dish under a microscope – cells and proteins and rogue neurons. At the same time my mind was stuck on what Jay had said in the café. Live within your capacity. Maybe that's all you have to do in life. What had happened to that woman whose blog I'd followed for a while, eating her breakfast naked so as not to ruin her designer clothes? She'd written so lucidly about what she was going through, funny and insightful and self-aware, right up until her blog just stopped.

A message arrived from Mel, and I sat down on a bench to look at it. She'd sent a photograph of Christoph sitting at the table in her apartment, eating breakfast in his underwear. I stared at it for a long time, at every detail. He was mashing a boiled egg onto a piece of bread. The shell was heaped into a small pile beside his plate. Mel had stood in her kitchen boiling eggs in a pot? The photo was taken from the side, his boxers were striped, and his body language was so relaxed it made me think this might not be the only time he had sat there. And also he was looking at the camera, so he knew he was being documented doing this, and quite possibly that she would be sending it to me. When I looked up I couldn't see Jay anywhere. I searched for him in all the rooms, trying to keep a sense of panic submerged, hating all the people there, how popular this exhibition was. Had he done it? Pulled the ejector-seat option and disappeared on me?

I sent a message asking where he was. After an agonising few minutes he replied that he was outside.

He was standing smoking under a concrete overhang in the rear courtyard with a man who was wearing the shirt of museum docent. As I approached, the man put out his cigarette, muttering about getting back to work. He shook Jay's hand and nodded at me.

'He was just telling me about the controversy,' Jay said. 'The government got the Mirós when a bank here went bust. Some conservatives wanted to auction them off. They are worth a lot, millions, and there are many poor people in this country, he said. But that didn't happen and now they have a new home here. Not everybody is happy about it.'

Not abandoning me. Just out here talking to some random new friend, being Jay. My arms went around him and we hugged. Warm. Long. Relieved. When we came apart, I indicated the cigarette in his hand and said, 'Please don't start up again…'

'I know. But…'

'Yeah. This has been hard. At least give me one?'

We measured the next few days in small glasses of port. We hired a car and drove through villages of whitewashed houses with red-tiled roofs, winding along beside the Duoro River in a steep-sided verdant valley that was terraced with vineyards.

We stopped at wineries and did their tours and learned more than we wanted to know about the way the local schist reflected the sun, sweetening the grapes, and how the first preserved grape from the area pre-dated the first Roman grape by a thousand years, and how the Napoleonic Wars meant that the British came looking for new sources of wine, and while the shipments survived the gentle trip up the river to Porto the rough seas were another matter and so began the process of fortifying with brandy.

We looked more into the past than the future as we

became connoisseurs of Tawny and Ruby vintages, and also of the hard white cheeses that were put down in front of us at each tasting.

At night we fell into bed, at lodgings that had stone floors and four-posters, so drunk we could ignore the question hanging between us. We clung to each other and had hot, drenched, delirious dreams. Jay recounted feverish battles with ancient enemies in the morning, while I'd dreamed of Frankie galloping through the Australian desert, and Mel feeding a baby with a shiny bald head, and of having conversations with Felix von Luckner in the Adlon while he was holding Susie the dachshund on his lap and treating her like a young girl. I tried to hold on to whatever the Count had said as I was waking, as if it had real meaning, the sense that he knew the difference between his mythmaking and his reality, and some advice about not looking into dark mouseholes.

One morning we were sitting on a stone bench overlooking the river, still sluggish from yet another port hangover, when Jay cleared his throat. 'I've been wanting to ask you something,' he said. 'About what you were asking of me before, to help you to... I've been thinking about it and what I want to know... is it because of what your mother did? Does that make you think that it obliges you to take this as a way out?'

Bells on a church across the river were calling locals to prayer. Was it? Something deep down inside? It struck me that my mother must have had some of the same feelings, struggled with some of the same thoughts.

'And also,' he added, 'do you think that her leaving you so early like that is what makes you always think you're not worth it?'

'You don't know what it's like,' I said, standing up, ready

to go. 'Only people who are living with this themselves could know what it's like.'

Jay grabbed the back of my jacket and pulled me back down on the seat. 'What is it like?' he asked patiently. 'Try and tell me.'

'Like… like… well, like there's some mugger out there, biding its time, just waiting to leap out from behind a corner and begin…' Saying this out loud, it sounded not quite right, immature or too reductive. All along, I realised, I had been thinking of this thing as beyond me, outside of me, waiting to pounce and turn me into something unrecognisable, when really it wasn't that. It was inside me, part of me, whether I had the disease or not. It had happened at the very moment of conception, when my father's sperm met my mother's egg, and I had been carrying it around my whole life – either the clear gene or the faulty version. And if it did turn out to be the gene with the mutation, then maybe I just had to somehow accept that this is who I am, who I had been right from the beginning of existence.

It started raining heavily again that afternoon, so we drove slowly back to Porto, not saying much, and returned our hire car. We rebooked into the same apartment we had been in before and, as if coming home, got into bed in the pink room, made love with gentle relief and fell asleep.

When I opened my eyes in the morning, Jay was leaning on his elbow, looking at me.

'What?'

'Please just take the test,' he said. 'I've been lying here in agony. I can't stand this anymore. Let's just front up to it. Let's just know. Isn't it better? If you do happen to have it, we could try to get you whatever is available. Your life won't just stop if you get a diagnosis. We can do everything possible and, if nothing is possible, then that's just what it is.'

I nodded my head against the pillow. 'I'm not sure if I can just say yes that easily.' I didn't want to do this anymore either. I didn't want to keep resisting.

'You don't have it,' he said. 'I feel sure you don't have it. But, anyway, we can't keep doing this.'

'Really? You don't think how I have been behaving has been a bit… not normal?'

There was a brief pause before he said, 'You were never normal.'

'Can I say I definitely probably will?'

He looked resigned. 'Can I at least book us tickets home?'

'Home? But you've only just got here.'

'I only came here for you,' he said, before admitting that he'd taken on another building contract that started in a couple of weeks.

'Hang on. You took a few weeks off work and you flew to Europe, but not even to Berlin? What's with that?'

'Well, I've always wanted to see Porto,' he said, before adding more seriously, 'and I wasn't sure… you left me, remember.'

'I didn't really leave you. I left me.'

He rolled over on his back and stared up at the ceiling for a while. There was the sound of rainwater flooding down a broken drainpipe just outside the window, and a mouldy dankness was accumulating in the darkest corners of the apartment.

'And the Count?' he said. 'I've been meaning to ask.'

'Ah, the Count.' I searched for his warm hand under the sheet. 'I wonder if I'll have to give the grant money back.'

His fingers clasped around mine and I grazed my thumb over the familiar scar from the time he'd once accidentally shot himself with a nail gun. We lay like that for minutes before he said, 'So you're not going on with it?'

I didn't answer immediately. It was another betrayal. I'd appropriated a fond relic from his childhood and failed to make anything of it. 'Would you be able to forgive me if I said no?'

He let go of my hand and was up on his elbow again, looking down at me. 'Why not?'

I took a deep breath. 'Well, I suppose one version could be, and I don't want to think this, but it could be something is happening to my brain and I just don't have the focus for it anymore.'

'Nope. What's another version?'

All of the other reasons that ran through my mind felt less immediately accessible than that one. Jay deserved more, so I tried to articulate how the Count's character, his particular kind of untruthful, self-aggrandising had taken on an ugly contemporary semblance. 'I've been feeling like that sort of bombastic behaviour is both boringly redundant and also disturbingly perpetual… all those terrible men who have managed to acquire power these days… and maybe people in the world are so exhausted by bluster at this point that it's not even that amusing to be in the proximity anymore.'

When I raised my eyes to Jay's face, his expression was a little half-smile. 'I sort of get what you mean… but…'

I felt it too, in that moment. The loss. To let the project go was to register a failure of my own application, but also

I recognised that sitting just underneath was a small well of joy that I could free myself from having to spend any more time in the Count's company. It was like the mix of guilt and relief a person might feel after they've made the decision to rehouse a domineering and unbearably behaved pet. 'I guess I could try to work on some kind of deconstruction,' I offered. 'Or is it better to see that you've been pursuing the wrong thing, that it isn't the time for that story, and um... pivot?'

Jay did not disguise his pleasure in being able to be emphatic. 'Yes, it is,' he responded, as he reached over to the side table for his phone. 'Does that mean I can book you onto my return flight now?'

When I consented, he immediately took out his credit card as if he had to do this now before I changed my mind. His flight was leaving from Berlin, and as he booked my accompanying seat, the small bird that was my heart was already flapping its wings south towards our cat and the palm tree in the garden. 'Since we have a bit of time,' I suggested. 'I have an idea for a side-trip in Germany before we go. There's a castle near Füssen that I want to visit.'

'Okay, let's do that,' he replied. 'Anything you want.' We let ourselves feel the relief of having made a least one decisive move. Jay went to the window, looked out at the relentless rain, then turned and said, 'It's such a shame to waste this lovely weather. Shall we go out? I can show you the tiny house.'

We bought a golf-sized umbrella from a shop a few doors down, and Jay held it above us. I tucked my arm into his free one once more, and as we neared two side-by-side churches he said, 'I will do my best to explain it.' He pointed to one of the churches. 'So, this one was already there, then a priest came and said he wanted to build a hospital next door. He got permission from Rome to build it, but when it was done it was mostly church and the clinic was only a small section in the back.'

'When was this?'

'Oh, um, like 1700s, I guess. Maybe earlier. When was rococo? I don't really know. Quite a long time ago. Anyway, it was a law at the time that no two churches could share a wall. So in between they built a very small house, one-metre-forty in width. For a long time even the locals didn't know it was there. It had this mythic quality…'

'Oh, but like a mousehole.'

'A mousehole? What?'

'Sorry, just something the…'

A strong gust whipped up the street, tunnelled through the narrow lanes, snatching the umbrella out of Jay's hands. It tumbled, already broken and half folded in, like a capsized sail, out of control, over the cobbles, past the tiled houses, down, down toward the river. As we watched it go, I let a feeling creep over me that it all might be okay.

Acknowledgments

The author gratefully acknowledges the support of:

BOOK CLUB QUESTIONS

• What do you think of Zelda and her mother's decision to keep the truth of Ginny's mother's suicide from her? Was it fair to keep the Huntington's gene news from her all her life?

• *'For the first time in my life I believed I was really thinking about self-sacrifice. Wasn't the most noble act, the greater love, not to tell him, not to force his obligation?'*
Do you agree with this statement, where Ginny explains why she hasn't told Jay the news? Do you think Ginny really believes it herself?

• Through the lens of its secondary characters, how does *I Laugh Me Broken* address the themes of wanting to 'live life to the fullest'? What do you think of their lifestyles?

• *'...if I looked further back, then it was hard to see the courage gene in the previous generation, with a mother who couldn't summon up the will to live, and a father who would rather drink himself to death than talk about the past.'*
To what extent is Ginny's eventual decision to take (or almost definitely take) the genetic test an attempt to prove herself more courageous than her mother?

• *'I think my ambition might change,'* he said.
'How?'
'I'm trying to figure it out. Either I would start to think about legacy and become obsessed with my epic project, or—'
'Or?'
'I might start to not give a fuck.'
Which do you think Ginny chooses in the end?

• What did you think of Jay's reaction to Ginny's eventual confession?

• How does Ginny's initial fascination, and later disillusion with the Count reflect her own internal journey?